Bestseller

Other Books by Paul Levinson

Non-Fiction

Digital McLuhan: A Guide to the Information Millennium
(1999)

The Soft Edge: A Natural History and Future of the Information Revolution (1997)

Learning Cyberspace: Essays on the Evolution of Media and the New Education (1995)

Electronic Chronicles: Columns of the Changes in Our Time
(1992)

Mind at Large: Knowing in the Technological Age (1988)

In Pursuit of Truth: Essays on the Philosophy of Karl Popper
(1982) (editor)

Fiction

The Silk Code (to be published Fall 1999)

Paul Levinson's
Bestseller
wired, analog, and digital writings

PULPLESS.COM, INC.
775 East Blithedale Ave., Suite 508
Mill Valley, CA 94941, USA.
Voice & Fax: (500) 367-7353
Home Page: http://www.pulpless.com/
Business inquiries to info@pulpless.com
Editorial inquiries & submissions to
editors@pulpless.com

Copyright © 1999 by Paul Levinson
All rights reserved. Published by arrangement with the author. Printed in the United States of America. The rights to all previously published materials by Paul Levinson are owned by the author, and are claimed both under existing copyright laws and natural logorights. All other materials taken from published sources without specific permission are either in the public domain or are quoted and/or excerpted under the Fair Use Doctrine. Except for attributed quotations embedded in critical articles or reviews, no part of this book may be reproduced or utilized in any form or by any means, electronic or mechanical, including photocopying, recording, or by any information storage and retrieval system, without written permission from the publisher.

This collection contains fiction. Names, characters, places, and incidents either are products of the author's imagination or are used fictitiously. Any resemblance to actual events, locales, or persons, living or dead, is entirely coincidental.

First Pulpless.Com™, Inc. Edition June, 1999.
Library of Congress Catalog Card Number: 99-60335
ISBN: 1-58445-033-9

Book and Cover designed by CaliPer, Inc.
Cover Illustration by Billy Tackett, Arcadi Studios
© 1999 by Billy Tackett

Paperless Book™ digital editions of this and all other Pulpless.Com™ books are available worldwide for immediate download 24-hours-a-day every day from the Pulpless.Com, Inc., web site, either for a small charge, or *free* with commercial messages. Please visit our Catalog on the World Wide Web at
www.pulpless.com

To Tina, Simon, and Molly

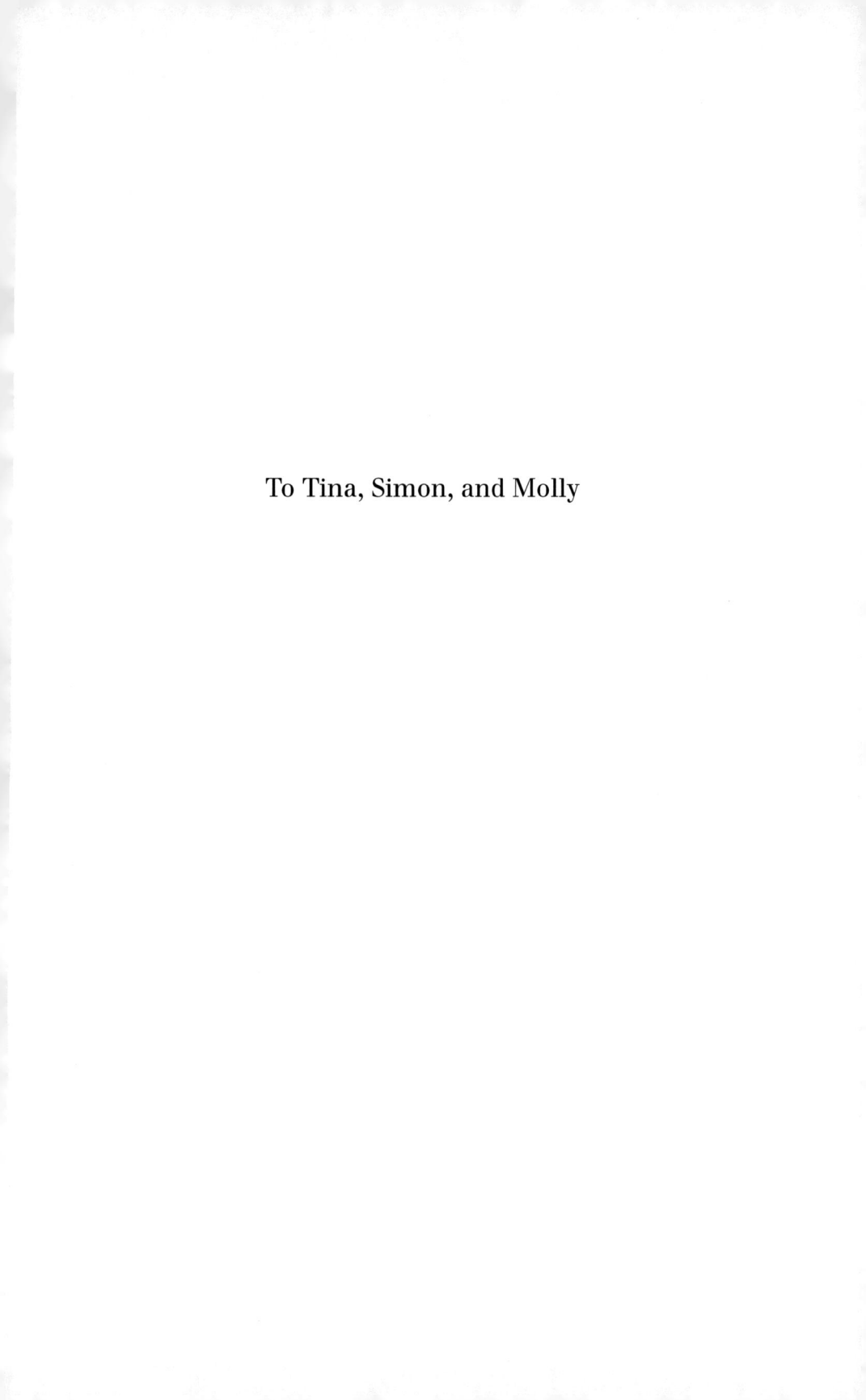

Table of Contents

CHAPTER	PAGE
Introduction	11

The Stories

"The 1st First Circuit Judge"	17
"Bestseller"	33
"Grace Under Pressure"	45
"Advantage, Bellarmine"	57
"The Copyright Notice Case"	69
"The Protected"	103
"Last Things First"	117
"Critical View"	133
"The Harmony"	151

The Essays

"On Behalf of Humanity: The Technological Edge"	165
"Innovation in Media and the Decentralization of Authority: The View from Here, There, and Everywhere"	181
"Entering Cyberspace: What to Watch, What to Watch Out For"	197
"Learning Unbound: OnLine Education and Mind's Academy"	207
"The Book on the Book: A Prognosis for the Page in the Digital Age"	221
"Author and Critic: Hazards and Consolations"	233
"Digital Amish"	243
"The Rights of Robots"	247
"The Extinction of Extinction"	253

Introduction

Bestseller: Wired, Analog, and Digital Writings is about our information age—its emergence, impact, and future—as seen through nine of my science fiction stories, and nine of my essays. That such themes can be treated alike in science fiction and scholarly writing is not the least bit surprising, at least to me. I have always found science fiction to be among the most vibrant modes of scientific and philosophic discourse—what are Isaac Asimov's robot stories, if not Socratic dialogues on the complexities of ethics and artificial intelligence? Similarly, the pathbreaking work of Marshall McLuhan in understanding media always read to me like science fiction in the best sense of the genre—experimenting with ideas, launching trial balloons and metaphors in ways seldom seen in the academic world.

Three of my stories appear here for the first time. The other stories, and all of the essays, were previously published in *Analog*, *Wired*, and a variety of other magazines and anthologies, in the past few years.

"The 1st Circuit Judge," never before published, leads off the science fiction first half of the volume. In New York City, where I lived most of my life and still teach (at Fordham University), there really are regulations about how far a car can be legally parked from the curb. When our hero gets a ticket for being a fraction of an inch over the limit, he must decide which kind of judge—human or computer—is likely to be most sympathetic to the circumstances of his case...

Next, "Bestseller," first published in the small, now-defunct *Fresh Ink* magazine, probes how a digital text could be literally universally appealing. I chose it as the title story for this volume because I hoped some of that appeal might enchant some of you.

"Grace Under Pressure," originally published in *Swashbuckling Editor Stories* (edited by John Betancourt for his Wildside Press), explores a different facet of a possible writer/computer symbiosis. What if there were an e-mail program that not only delivered a writer's work to an acquisitions editor, but did what it could to ensure that the work was accepted for publication?

We go back to a world of presumably earlier media, and Galileo, in "Advantage, Bellarmine"—first published in *Analog*, the world's leading science fiction magazine. Perhaps the Church's grasp of the scientific nature of the universe was more advanced than it seemed...

We go back further still in "The Copyright Notice Case," also first published in *Analog*, and winner of CompuServe's 1997 HOMer award for the best novelette in science fiction. Here Dr. Phil D'Amato—my New York City forensic detective who appears in two other novelettes published in *Analog*, and who will make his novel debut in *The Silk Code*, to be published by Tor Books in the Fall of 1999—looks into the propensities for murder in the oldest information "technology" of all: DNA, and its capacity to relay messages to us from the prehistoric past.

"The Protected," published here for the first time, pulls us well into the future, and a time when androids look and act so much like humans that they need protection from our worst instincts...

"Last Things First," originally published in Catherine Asaro's shortlived but influential *Mindsparks* magazine, is quite literally a media mystery. A linguistics professor who seeks to unravel the mystery of Basque—one of the few languages on Earth with no apparent connection to any other—disappears. His lover searches for him, and uncovers a series of letters, each written at a later time in his life, but each in a medium that existed successively earlier in time...

"Critical View," never published before, is my science-fictional contribution to film theory. We perceive motion pictures via our "persistence of vision," our tendency to hold one still image in our mind long enough so that it seems to flow into the next, so the scenes within appear to be moving. What would life be like for someone—a film critic, no less—who lacked this capacity?

"The Harmony," first published in Jane Yolen's *Xanadu 3* anthology, lends an ear to another mode of communication, one close to my heart: music, in particular rock 'n' roll, in further particular the "doo-wop" harmonies I sang with my friends on the streets of the Bronx back in the early 1960s. To be singing harmony is to be transported into another world, and our hero in "The Harmony" receives an even more explicit invitation than usual from this world.... If I tell you that this story is technically not science fiction, but urban fantasy, I know you'll forgive me for slipping it into this volume.

Next come the essays, which begin with "On Behalf of Humanity: The Technological Edge," first published in *The World and I*. As the title suggests, this article presents the case for technology in general: in spite of the unintended consequences it always gives rise to, it is under our rational control; it can do good and do evil in different hands, but on balance it helps us more than hurts; usually, when technology causes problems or does not work as well as we would like, this is because there is not enough of it (not because there is too much). I explore this last point especially, and how it relates to the so-called problem of "information overload"—which I unmask as really information underload, or problems caused not by too much information, but by not enough information at hand to guide us in how to make the most of other information.

"Innovation in Media and the Decentralization of Authority: The View from Here, There, and Everywhere"—first published in *Values and the Social Order,* Volume 3, edited by Gerard Radnitzky—looks at the historical tug of war between centralization and decentralization in society, and how different media aid and abet one or both of these tendencies. Today, the Internet is hurling us out of a world in which a small number of publishers, and even smaller number of broadcasters, controlled all the news and entertainment. Under the guise of curbing pornography, governments are seeking to re-assert some of that control. Thus far, the Internet has had the upper, centrifugal hand.

We therefore follow with "Entering Cyberspace: What to Watch, What to Watch Out For." This essay is a revision and compilation of articles which appeared in *WIRED*, *Omni*, and the *Journal of Social and Evolutionary Systems* (a scholarly journal, which I edit). It first considers what, metaphysically, cyberspace is—its connections with older kinds of "spaces" and systems ranging from DNA to religions—and then looks at some of its benefits and dangers. In a nutshell, its advantages work to best effect in those areas, such as education, in which information rather than physical presence is the paramount constituent. Similarly, its drawbacks are greatest when we seek to substitute information for situations in which tangible, flesh-and-blood experience is crucial—ranging from walking together hand-in-hand, to dining in a fine restaurant, to exploration of space, where even the best robots and images cannot convey the poetic nuance imparted by the direct vision of the human eye.

"Learning Unbound: OnLine Education and the Mind's Academy" and "The Book on the Book: A Prognosis for the Page in the Digital Age" are a pair of essays that explore areas in which digital media may well improve upon traditional human activities. The two first appeared in *Analog*, which publishes science fact and speculation as well as fiction, not unlike this book.

Although formal education may seem inextricably seated in the physical classroom, online communication for nearly two decades has been providing a magic carpet via which faculty and students can teach and learn from any place in the world, 24 hours a day. The organization that I founded with my wife, Tina Vozick—Connected Education—has indeed been offering online courses for graduate credit in cooperation with major universities since 1985. "Learning Unbound" discusses the major advantages of learning online—obstacles of place and time are nearly eliminated, and those of physical and economic disability—as well as the reasons for its slow acceptance in our society.

Books revolutionized education when they began pouring forth from the new presses of Europe in the Renaissance, and literacy has been a steadfast goal and amanuensis of education ever since. But are books the only or even best mode in which to read? "The Book on the Book" investigates to what extent our comfort with the book is nostalgia versus reflection of real advantages in comparison to online texts. No book with paper pages, however swiftly assembled and shipped, can provide hypertext links: clicking on a word in print leaves you in that exact same place. On the other hand, we may well derive an important sense of reliable location from the fixation of words in print, a sense that the very fluidity of words on the screen works against, and which therefore might keep books on our shelves for a long time to come.

"Author and Critic: Hazards and Consolations"—first published in *Tangent* magazine, in somewhat different form—shifts gears from media theory to literary criticism, or rather, analysis of why any author would also want to be a critic. Having done both, and experienced the aggravations and joys of this dual identity, I offer what advice I can—and the admission that the joy is more than enough for me to continue.

"Digital Amish," originally published in *WIRED* with a longer title and a shorter length, returns to the realm of technology and its general impact. We media theorists like to urge the world to take a closer look at new technology, rather than falling in love with it at first sight, or rejecting it out of hand as an incursion against nature. In several trips to Pennsylvania in the early 1990s, I discovered that the Amish, contrary to their image as abhorrers of modern technology, take just such a contemplative approach—rejecting not all technology, but mass media like television over whose content they have no control, and which run on electricity supplied by central power companies. Interestingly, the Internet, when accessed by palm-top computers and cellphones, suffers from neither of these shortcomings. (Look for the Amish to play a major role in *The Silk Code*.)

"The Rights of Robots," first published as a shorter piece in Canada in *Shift* magazine, examines our moral obligation to another community—the hypothetical future community of artificial intelligences, of our own creation. We presumably will try to invent machines that can truly think, the better to do our bidding. But if we succeed in the invention of autonomous thinkers, do we then have the right to rob them of their autonomy and treat them like slaves?

Bestseller concludes with another look at DNA, and the recipes for life it conveys, even after the carriers of those instructions are fossilized. To the charge that human wielders of technology have been destroying life on this planet, "The Extinction of Extinction" replies: true, and that should stop, but reclaimed DNA may soon give us the power to rekindle species long gone before humanity ever walked this Earth. The upshot of this essay—first published in *WIRED*—is of course familiar to science fiction, which in the case of *Jurassic Park* explored its capacity not only to yield beauty but horror.

But death was here long before we arrived. What makes humanity different, what distinguishes our technology from other known forces in the universe, is that we deliberately intercede with it on the side of imagination, dreams come true, and life. In that sense, we are all bestsellers.

—Paul Levinson
White Plains, NY
January 1999

The Stories

The 1st Circuit Judge

Tickets fall somewhere between a head cold and a paper cut on the grand scale of pain and injustice in this life. This one felt more like a head cold coming on—a nasty one.

"Can I help you, Officer?"

He was leaning over my car, poking his way through the handheld computer gadget that passed as a ticket pad these days. Had the advantage of uploading the ticket right to the court's central computer, a news report I'd seen just a few weeks ago had said.

The cop himself was completely the opposite of his digital ticket pad. Big, redfaced, beefy policeman, relic of an earlier generation. Probably on the beat for 30 years. Probably not bright enough to be promoted.

"Is there some kind of problem?" I asked again.

"See for yourself," he answered and slapped a thin yellow printout in my hand. I strained to read the faint writing as he strode away.

"Are you kidding?" I shouted after him. "You're giving me a ticket because I was parked 6 and 1/16 inches away from the curb in a 6 inch zone? What is this, a slow day for your ticket quotas?"

"Tell it to the judge," he grunted over his shoulder.

"I'm really furious," I said to Julia, my wife, after dinner. "I know I'll lose money in terms of my time even if I win, but I'm gonna fight this."

"Are you guilty?" She leaned over my shoulder and looked at

the ticket.

"I don't know," I said. "I measured it with my ruler and it said 6 inches. But my car obviously couldn't have been parked exactly parallel to the curb anyway. The whole damn law's ridiculous."

"His ticket machine may have generated a more accurate measurement," Julia said. She was a professor of communications and law at NYU, and knew a lot about what computers could do.

"I don't think so," I said. "See, it says here, 'based on officer's independent nondigital measurement.' That suggests he used an old-fashioned ruler even older than mine. I don't think they can lie about stuff like that on the ticket printout."

Julia agreed. "So it's your word against his. Every judge I've ever heard of sides with the cop in cases like this."

"What about innocent until proven guilty?"

"You're going make a Federal case out of this?" Julia asked.

I sighed and looked over the ticket. I noticed something I hadn't seen before at the bottom of the plea box.

"It says here I have the option of pleading not guilty, and having my case heard by an 'AI' judge. What have you heard about that?"

Julia made some calls the next couple of days. "The take is that if you're guilty but have an eloquent lawyer, don't go the AI route—the program will cut right through the eloquence and see your guilt. If you're innocent, it's anybody's guess. One thing everyone agrees on is it's ok if you come dressed like a slob without a tie to AI court."

"So what do you think?" I asked.

"I don't know," Julia said. "I suppose if you lose you'd have greater grounds for appeal—the AI judge is new, and its decisions likely haven't been tested out yet in many upper courts. The program's only in use in three states, and just traffic court at that. On the other hand, in a real sense you'd be beyond most attorneys' capacities to help you—no one I've spoken to has ever argued a case of any sort before this program. Mostly it's just a faster way of handling the rabble coming into court to protest their tickets."

"Suits me fine," I said. "I want to do this on my own anyway. What do you call that? Per se?"

"*Pro se*," Julia said. "In behalf of yourself. But you know what they say: the attorney who represents himself has a fool for a client."

"True," I said, "but then again, I'm not an attorney." I was just a professor of history, and still boiling about the historic injustice of this ticket.

I checked off the AI plea box, and put in the mail pile.

The Traffic Violations Court on 8th Street and Astor Place was much as it looked the last time I'd been there, and I imagined what it looked like for the last half century. Derelicts dozing in booze and drugs on the outside, smoke- and urine-tainted elevator on the inside, corridors in endless repair and construction. All crammed with all manner of poor saps, sullen and stupefied, waiting for their cases to be called. Most of these poor bastards had it far worse than I did, likely losing half a day's work and pay for the pleasure of proclaiming their innocence here. I took no comfort in that.

I was glad that the Traffic Court still conducted its business in public, though. Maybe I could sit in on a case and learn something about how keyboard justice operated.

Room 452—the room listed on my hearing notice—was at the end of a particularly stale corridor. The door had nothing on it but the number—no mention of this being an AI section, nothing. Typical of the city. I opened the door and walked in.

A girl sat with legs crossed-fishnet stockings—on the far side of the room. She had jet black hair and luminous brown eyes.

She looked a little scared.

I tried to smile at her in a gentle way. "Is this the room for the, ah, computer trial?"

She nodded. "I go next," she said. "The judge—the machine—called a 15 minute recess."

"I guess not because it had to go to the bathroom, right?"

That got her to smile. "No," she said. "The officer who gave me my ticket is late. The computer's giving him 15 minutes to show."

"Nice to see the computer has such compassion for the cops," I said, then realized I gained nothing by shooting my mouth off here. For all I knew, everything we were saying was being recorded.

"I'm innocent," she said.

"I don't doubt it for an instant," I said, sincerely. "What are they accusing you of?"

"Parking in a no parking zone," she said. "The sign said No Parking 9-5. I'm sure of it. I parked at 5:30. When I got back at 6, there was a ticket on my car. And the sign was changed to read No Parking, 9-6! They just changed the 5 to a 6 on the sign's little computer screen. Just like that! I didn't think they were allowed to do that!"

"I'm sure they're not." I shook my head in disgust.

She looked at the clock on the wall. "If the cop doesn't show in three minutes, I'm automatically not guilty—that's what the computer judge said. Dismissal for lack of accusing witness, or something."

"Fingers crossed," I said.

The door opened. A little weasel of a cop walked in, and rushed up to the judge's bench. There was no one there, but he spoke, his back to us, anyway. "Office Timothy Johnson here, Your Honor, with apologies for being late and appreciation for the urgent dispatch you sent to my radio. I'm ready to proceed in this case."

"Thank you, Officer Johnson," a voice boomed out from a speaker that I realized was mounted in some camouflaged way on the bench. I didn't know whether to laugh or what. This was the computer?

"Amelita Gonzalez," the basso voice intoned. "Are you ready to proceed?"

"Shit," she said under her breath. "Yes I am, Your Honor," she said loudly.

"Please approach the bench then," the voice said. "Officer Johnson, please begin by telling the court, briefly, why you issued a summons to Amelita Gonzalez on May 11 for parking in a No Parking zone."

"Good luck," I whispered at Amelita as she walked up to the bench.

Officer Johnson droned out his story much as Amelita had related it—"On May 11 at approximately 5:45 PM I approached a yellow Neon coup with New York license plate VBC 155 parked near 45 West 12th Street..."—with one howling exception. "The No Parking advisory sign read No Parking 9 AM to 6 PM," Johnson said.

Amelita kept her composure pretty well. I was impressed with her command of the situation—maybe she'd been through this before. When it was her turn to speak, she said simply, in a clear unwavering voice, "Officer Johnson's not right about the sign, Your Honor. It said No Parking 9 AM to 5 PM,' not 6 PM."

"Do you have any witnesses, Ms. Gonzalez?" the computer inquired.

"No, Your Honor."

"Anything more you wish to tell the Court?"

"Well, Your Honor," Amelita cleared her throat, "I saw on the news the other night that they're investigating a parking violations scam in the city—the parking-sign screens are being programmed to change after people have already parked there, so police can issue tickets and the city can make some money to reduce its deficit. I think that's what happened to me."

Johnson laughed derisively.

"Noted," the computer judge said. "Anything more you wish to tell the Court?"

"No," Amelita said.

"Please stand by, then, while I review the evidence and render a verdict," the computer said.

Amelita turned and looked at me. I raised my clenched fist in what I hoped still passed as a sign of solidarity.

Not more than 30 seconds passed. "Here are my findings," the judge's voice said. "Eight news reports in the past 60 days have discussed an investigation of the city's parking-sign screens. That investigation has as yet achieved no result, however; therefore I cannot allow it or a report of it to be entered here as evidence. Further, my scan of central parking systems reveals the parking-sign apparatus in the area of 45 West 12th Street to have been fully and correctly operational on the date May 11 of this year. My scan further reveals that the no-parking hours displayed on the sign's LCD were 9 AM in the morning through 6 PM in the afternoon. I therefore find the defendant guilty as charged, with no extenuating circumstances, and order that she pay the full stipulated fine of $150—"

"But Your Honor, I can't afford—" Amelita started.

"Please wait until I've finished rendering the verdict," the judge said. "I will repeat the last four sentences. I find the defendant guilty as charged, with no extenuating circumstances, and order that she pay the full stipulated fine of $150. She can appeal this verdict, but only after the fine is paid. She must pay the fine in full within seven days, either by electronic fund deduction from her accounts or by traditional means. She will be fined an additional 10 percent for each week the fine is late.' That is my verdict, Ms. Gonzalez. You may now ask me questions or say more, if you like. Officer Johnson, you are free to go, and the court thanks you for your time."

"Thank you, Your Honor," he nodded, absurdly, to the bench. To Amelita he gave a leering grin, and then walked out the door.

"I can't afford $150, Your Honor. I have three children, and the money I make doesn't stretch far enough as it is," Amelita pleaded.

"Shall I refer the situation of you and your children over to Surrogate's Court?" the computer inquired.

Careful, Amelita, I thought—don't let this hard-wired bastard get you even more tangled up in the system.

"No, please don't," Amelita said. She looked pale.

"Shall I officially enter your request for an Appeal Hearing and set a date?" the computer inquired.

Amelita shook her head. "No. I can't afford to lose any more time from work."

And what the hell was the point, I realized. The Appeals Judge whoever he or she was would likely act like a computer and say the same thing about this bucket of bits as it had said about the parking-sign computer system—"fully and correctly operational."

"You've been fined $150 for this offense," the computer judge said. "How do you wish to pay it?"

But Amelita was already out the door, struggling to keep her tears back. She looked back at me and I conveyed what reassurance I could.

"You've been fined $150 for this offense," the voice said again. "How do you wish to pay it?"

Then, "My scan of this courtroom reveals that the defendant in this case is no longer present. I therefore take her lack of response to my last question to be an assertion that she wishes to pay the $150 fine by traditional means, and am so noting in the records. Case number 1520947 closed."

I looked at the big clock on wall, an old-fashioned analog repro. Amelita's case had gone quickly, and I still had 25 minutes before mine was set to start. What had I learned from Amelita's case? Beating this damn circuitry judge wouldn't be easy. With any luck, Julia would be here soon, and we could talk about it.

Julia walked in the door five minutes later with coffee and bagels and open ears. "This place is enough to make you lose your appetite," she said, but we ate and sipped anyway, and I filled her in on Amelita's case in whispers in the back of the room.

"So it's unlikely that your cop will fail to show," she said.

"Right," I said. "The damn computer'll send some kind of a call through to him on his radio."

"Too bad," she said. "Complainant cop not showing up is one of the best ways of getting a dismissal." She sighed. "From what you've told me, Amelita lost because she had no witness. It was her word against the cop's, and she had no way of proving her contention that the parking sign was broken, let alone deliberately rigged. You seem in the same boat—"

The door opened. My beefy cop walked in. He was perspiring, and seemed more red-faced than I'd remembered him. He looked at Julia and me, gave no sign of recognition, then walked over to the other side of the room and sat down heavily. He pulled out his ticket pad, and started mumbling to himself.

"That's your guy?" Julia asked.

I nodded.

"Good," she said. "He looks more nervous than you—can't hurt."

"I look that nervous?" But I agreed with Julia's point. "Amelita's cop was so cool with the computer judge you'd think he slept with his dick up a comm port all night."

"You probably shouldn't offer that analogy to the judge," Julia said.

The voice boomed out from the bench, as if on cue. "Case 1520948 is next on my docket. If both parties are present in the courtroom and able to proceed, will each please so indicate by stating his name and willingness to proceed. Officer first, please."

I wondered for a second if the program were sophisticated enough to scan the ticket and discern the gender of the officer and defendant, or if the "his" was just some linguistic sexism yet lingering in the court systems.

"Officer John McClarity," my cop said. He stood up, pulled his belt up over his gut, and approached the bench. "I'm present and ready to proceed."

"Thank you, Officer," the computer said. "It was unnecessary for you to explicitly state that you are present here, however. Your very response already indicates that."

Jeez, was this judge program suddenly betraying a bit of humor?

McClarity grunted.

Julia nudged me to say something.

"Ah, I'm Jeffrey Siegel, Your Honor, and I'm ready to proceed."

"Thank you," the judge said. "Please approach the bench then. Officer McClarity, please begin by telling the court, briefly, why you issued a summons to Jeffrey Siegel on May 11 for parking 6.0625 inches from the curb."

McClarity sweated over his pad, eyes face down, shoulders hunched, feet set in stone, like he was praying in my grandfather's synagogue. "On May 11 at approximately 5:50 PM I approached a teal Toyota sedan with New York license plate TRS 096 parked in front of 17 Bleeker Street. I suspected it to be over the 6 inch parked-from-the-curb limit. I measured the distance with my ruler, and found it to be 6 and 1/16 inches from the curb at both front and rear axles."

The computer made no immediate response. "Anything more you wish to tell the court," the voice rang out after about 15 long seconds.

"Uh, no, Your Honor, that's it," McClarity said.

"May I then ask you to provide further details on your ruler's measurement," the voice asked. "I see that you elected not to use the automatic measurement function on your ticketing apparatus. This would have forwarded your measurement, with a photograph of the actual distance, to our central files. But I see no record of that here."

I turned to look at Julia. She looked thoughtful.

"That's right," McClarity said. "I used my own ruler."

"Why was that?" the judge asked.

I suspected the answer was that McClarity couldn't remember how to use the measurement function on his ticket pad.

He shrugged. "I always carry my old little ruler. It folds up easily. Works well."

"Can you state, for the record, the model number and exact make of your ruler," the judge asked.

"I, uh, it's a wooden ruler, Your Honor, an old wooden ruler. It has no model number."

"I show no record of the make wooden' in our files, Officer."

"Right," McClarity said.

"Anything more you wish to tell the court?" the judge asked.

"No, Your Honor," McClarity said, a reed of confusion sticking in his voice.

"Thank you, Officer. Mr. Siegel, you checked Not Guilty' in your box plea. Now is your opportunity to explain your plea to this court."

"Well, Your Honor," I tried not to sound too nervous, "my car was indeed parked in front of 17 Bleeker Street at the time the officer said, but it was not more than 6 inches from the curb in any place. I know this because I measured the distance with my own ruler after I received the ticket."

"Did you inform Officer McClarity of this discrepancy?"

"No, Your Honor, he'd already left," I said.

"Did you photograph the site, and upload this and your measurement to any central system for verification and storage?" the voice inquired.

The 1st Circuit Judge 27

"No, Your Honor. My ruler—a SONY hand-held 340—is an older model. It doesn't have any photo or telecom capacity."

"Confirmed," the judge said. "The SONY 340 lacks photo and telecom capacity."

"Yes," I said.

"Do you have any witnesses, Mr. Siegel?"

"No, Your Honor."

"Anything more you wish to tell the court?" the judge asked.

"Well, two other things, if I may, Your Honor. One, I frankly find it ridiculous that I be brought up on charges at all for such a—such a fractional infraction!—if you'll pardon the pun. And two, I object to the very 6-inch statute itself. I can't see who's being hurt when someone parks a bit more than 6 inches from the curb." I knew full well, based on what I'd seen with Amelita, that neither of these two points would get me very far with this literally hard-assed judge, but I couldn't help myself.

"Noted, and recorded as arguments one and two," the computer judge said. "Anything more you wish to tell the Court?"

I must've heard this at least 10 times now in the past hour.

"No, Your Honor."

"Please stand by, then, while I review—"

"Your Honor, excuse me," Julia had come up to the bench. "I'm sorry for interrupting, but may I make a point on the defendant's behalf?"

"Officer McClarity and Mr. Siegel, please excuse me while I address this intrusion. I will repeat what I was saying in its entirety after responding to the intrusion," the computer said. "To the person who interrupted me: Please be advised that although the court welcomes the presence of interested members of the public at these proceedings, the court does not allow haphazard testimony to be so entered."

"Thank you, Your Honor," Julia said. "I understand and apologize. I'm not just a member of the public, however. I'm Julia Goldsmith, the defendant's wife, and an attorney."

A few seconds of silence ensued. Apparently the word "wife" or "attorney" had some sort of clout with this program. I looked at Julia for a clue as to where she was heading, but she waved me off. OK, I guess I had confidence in her judgement.

"Confirmed," the judge now said. "I see the record of your marriage, as well as the date of your graduation from Fordham Law School and your entry of the bar. I see, however, that you are not a currently practicing attorney."

"That's right, Your Honor, I teach law at New York University."

"Confirmed," the judge said. "I also see that the accused, Jeffrey Siegel, declined to be represented by an attorney in his plea box."

"That's true, Your Honor," I piped up. "But could I now ask the court to allow my wife, as a very interested party as well as someone with great legal knowledge, to briefly address the court on my behalf?"

"And may I also mention to the court that this isn't a formal criminal or civil proceeding—it's a stationary traffic proceeding, and therefore less formal than the other kinds," Julia said.

"Does the Officer have any objection if I listen to what Julia Goldsmith has to say?" the AI judge asked.

McClarity looked at the bench and us as if we were all crazy. "No problem, Your Honor, only I have to be back at the precinct in 25 minutes."

"I promise to be brief," Julia said.

"Please briefly address the court, then," the program said.

Julia stepped back a bit, hands on her hips, and started to address the empty bench as if she were delivering a summation to the entire Supreme Court.

"I would ask Your Honor to consider this," she said. "This case involves a conflict of two testimonies—each supported by outmoded, offline technology. But I submit to you that these two outmoded technologies are not exactly the same. One is more outmoded than the other. Officer McClarity's device is an old wooden fold-up ruler. It's so old it can't even yield the 6.0625 measurement stipulated in Your Honor's presentation of the charges. It can yield only less precise analogic measurements—in sixteenths of an inch. Furthermore, wooden rulers can easily warp, expand and contract, in the sun and cold weather. Jeffrey Siegel's ruler, on the other hand, while old and unconnected and therefore not verifiable, is at least after all an electronic device. It provides standard digital measurements. It has a degree of reliability far in excess of a wooden ruler—a reliability shared by all electronics, including those of the most sophisticated legal AI programs such as Your Honor. I humbly ask Your Honor to take this into account when pondering a decision in this case."

"Ridiculous," McClarity grunted. "My ruler works fine. Who cares what name you give to the measurement? All that counts is it's more than 6 inches."

"Do you have something more you'd like to say to the court, Officer?" the judge inquired. "In response to Ms. Goldsmith's testimony?"

McClarity shrugged. "What's there to say? My ruler works fine. I've seen plenty of electronic equipment that doesn't—plenty of electronic junk in the scrapheap. At least my ruler never breaks down. Needs no batteries. Doesn't get upstaged by a new model every year. Sure, a lot of guys on the force like these electronic gizmos. But not me. I stick with my old ruler. It gives me the same measurements year after year. That's what *I* call reliability."

He was saying this more now to Julia and me than to the bench, as if he couldn't bear to address an empty bench any longer.

"Noted," the computer judge said. "Anything more you wish to tell the Court?"

"No," McClarity said, unable to conceal his disgust.

Julia was smiling.

"Anything more either the accused or his associate wish to tell the court?" the program said.

"No Your Honor, No Your Honor," Julia and I said, almost in unison.

"Please stand by, then, while I review the evidence and render a verdict," the computer said.

Maybe 10 seconds passed. "Here are my findings," the judge's voice said. "The Accused's argument that the fractional' nature of the alleged infraction makes it ridiculous' to prosecute has no basis in stationary-traffic jurisprudence, in which violations, regardless of how minor—be they parking meters that have only a few seconds earlier expired, or vehicles parked from the curb in any excess whatsoever of the six inch limit—are deemed punishable by fine or other measures as appropriate. As for Accused's contention that the curb statute itself is unfair, I suggest he bring that issue to the attention of his elected representatives; neither I nor any magistrate—digital or otherwise—has the power to repeal laws.

"Thus, the Accused's innocence or guilt in this case rests solely and entirely on the question of whether the Accused's vehicle was in fact parked 6.0625 inches from the curb, as the complaint alleges. On this crucial question, the Complaining Officer and the Accused make contradictory claims. Neither, however, is supported by any online evidence. The Officer did follow classical correct procedure. But, in my judgement, he failed to exercise the best discretionary procedure, in that he failed to use the best possible equipment available to him at the time he issued the summons. He elected to use a model ruler so old that it lacks a manufacturer name or model number in central files—a model so old that it provides measurements in non-digital fractions, measurements which therefore then must be translated into digital renderings. This in turn creates reasonable doubts that the Accused's vehicle was in fact exactly 6.0625 inches from the curb. Perhaps it was less than 6.0625 inches, and the Officer rounded that out to the nearest awkward fraction on his ruler. Perhaps it was so close to 6 inches that a proper digital measurement would have found it to be 6 inches from the curb. These are factors which the court cannot fail to take into account.

"As for the Accused, he supports his claim of innocence on the strength of a device, which, while similarly lamentably unconnected, at least has a recognizable manufacturing provenance and registration. The superiority of the Accused's equipment, along with the above-mentioned doubts about the accuracy of the Officer's equipment, supports a reasonable doubt as to the Accused's guilt in this matter. I thus find him Not Guilty. Case number 1520948 is closed."

"Fuckin' joke," McClarity muttered darkly. "City needs money, and they put in this goddamn computer-wire as judge," he pushed the door open and walked out. "You should short-circuit yourself and drop dead," I heard him mutter further in the hall.

"Thank you very much, Your Honor," Julia said and pulled me by the arm out the door. "No point hanging around here," she said. "We won!"

McClarity was still by the elevator—right outside the hearing room—angrily jabbing buttons. "Damn waste of time," he said, and walked cursing under his breath to the stairwell.

I pulled Julia in my arms, gave her a hug, and spoke to the elevator.

"Fourth floor, two to go down to the lobby."

We stepped into the nice new digital model.

"You did it!" I took her in my arms again. "You're brilliant!"

"Underlying strategy is the same," she said, "whatever the make of the judge. You appeal to their prejudices, if you possibly can. I realized we had shot as soon as McClarity began talking about his old wooden ruler. Your model was closer to the judge—given a conflict of evidence, it makes sense he would go with you. Silicon's thicker than water."

Bestseller

"The book's on the phone," Samantha's voice called up from from the velvet cushion, half a duplex below.

"Thanks," Morgan said to himself, switching from his write to terminal program in one swift keystroke. He had been waiting for this book for some time now—more than a week, at least, since he had read the literally glowing review in the *Lines*.

"Is it as good as you thought?" Samantha's voice called up again.

"Dunno..." Morgan mumbled. The lines on the screen flowed by like so many rapid snapshots of his eyes. Impossible to read at this speed, he knew the conventional wisdom, yet he also able to get a general something of what was flying by him anyway. He had heard and read so much about this book—the whole campus was talking about it. Doctoral dissertation into best seller in less than a month. And by an utterly unknown writer from Techoslovakia.

He leaned back in the chair and closed his eyes to a squint. God, it was good indeed. "... daisies shimmering whitely in the field," the last lines said, "pure play of light—no colorful illusion here." He sighed. He was always a sucker for Impressionism.

"So?" Samantha walked over and kissed him softly on the ear, massaging the top of his back with her fingers. "I got tired of waiting for you downstairs."

"Mmmm, feels good," Morgan said. "And the book does too. "I'm gonna love it..."

"I don't know." Jeanne was carrying on in the Cafe the next afternoon when Morgan pulled up a cola stained chair. "I like my books to seduce me. I want to be not too sure at first, maybe even dislike the book, but something about it won't let me let it go, and so I keep reading, almost against my will, and then I give in totally, adoring it."

"Lucky book," Mark O'Brien said with real longing.

"So you're saying you have a problem with the Havcek book?" Morgan well appreciated Mark's point of view about Jeanne, but today he was more interested in the conversation.

"Right." Jeanne focused on Morgan. "I haven't received my copy yet, but I'm suspicious of love at first sight for books."

"You sound like my Librarian in Junior High School—Mrs. Dayson." This was from Karen, of the Psych Department. "She used to drive me crazy because all I cared for was science fiction. She used to tell me that reading the same fare over and over again was as dangerous to your mental health as eating a one-course diet was to your regular health."

"But that was a genre," Jeanne said, "which really does give you a lot of room to grow in, and this is about a single book."

"What's it about, by the way?" Mark asked.

Glances ricochetted quickly around the table, and stopped at Morgan.

He smiled deeply. "It has a softness, a real beauty—"

"No kidding?" Karen broke in. "One of my students told me it has an incredible ugly edge of reality quality..." She stopped. "Sorry for interrupting." She gestured to Morgan. "Please continue. I don't think I've ever seen you so positive."

He smiled and shrugged slightly. "Well, I haven't read the whole book yet, but—"

"Has all the makings of a classic." Now Jeanne interrupted. "Something in it for everybody."

Jeanne and Mark strolled along the campus walk to the Bookstore. The April humidity was sweet and unassuming, and gave a freshness to the air that was rare in the city.

The Bookstore, true to its college heritage, made a point of displaying many soft- and even hard-cover editions. But most of its trade had for several years been via CDs. Now actual Web transfers of entire books were beginning to compete with those. People of course could order them via their home and office computers, but some still enjoyed coming into the Bookstore and placing their Web orders there, for old-time's sake.

"I still haven't received mine." Jeanne pointed to the smiling holo of Vlad Havcek next to the snake plant.

"What can I tell you?" The clerk held up his hands. He looks like some weird sort of permutation of Woody Allen, Mark thought, as he did every time he saw him. "It's not up to us when the publisher sends you the book by phone," Woody continued, "and the book isn't available on disk for this one..."

Jeanne waved her hand in disgust and walked away.

"I'm going to order mine now anyway," Mark said.

"Glutton for punishment," Jeanne muttered.

Mark sat down at a terminal, and keyed in the start-up code. He placed his Amex Card in the slot next to the disk drive, entered the title and author of the book, and drummed his fingers as the machine played its staccato terminal music.

"Phone delivery ok?" the screen finally prompted.

Mark touched the icon for phone.

"Advisory that phone delivery delayed at present at least 10 days from today's date. Do you wish to proceed?"

"Yes," Mark clicked, and proceeded to enter the requested transmission speed and other data necessary for electronic delivery of the book.

Jeanne was grumbling. "Amazing that these devices are supposed to save time, and yet I can get any of those paper books on the shelves far more easily."

"*If* they're on the shelf," Mark replied. "Reminds me when Citibank first introduced automatic bank machines in NYC in the 1970s. Customers complained that they got quicker service from human tellers. But in the long run the ATMs did much better, cause let's face it, people don't like seeing their money touched by the same grubby hands that crumple dirty little tissues and who knows what else."

Jeanne smiled. She was beginning to like this, what was he, professor of technology studies. "I've always placed literature in a realm higher than money."

Mark laughed, and typed something else into the terminal. "Havcek, V.," the screen began, and quickly coalesced into a digital portrait of the author. He was young and weaselly looking, Jeanne thought, more so than in his holos. "Caltech doctoral student," the display continued, "native, Technological Republic of Czechoslovakia. Prior publication: Cross the Cartesian Rainbow: Thoughts on Intelligent Personal Systems, and their Fulfillment of Human Needs,' *Journal of Social and Evolutionary Systems*, June..."

Mark looked away from the screen and up into Jeanne's soft green eyes. "He does have a poetic touch about him, you've got to give him that."

Jeanne shook her head slowly. "Hard to believe in a computer programmer."

"So McLuhan's point," Mark told his weekly Seminar on the Millennium the next day, "was that cool media always provoke much more involvement from the consumer than hot media. A piece of poetry usually gives us less information up front than a piece of prose of the same length, and therefore requires much more work of the reader to understand. Understand?" He chuckled. "Good. We'll continue this discussion online."

The class broke into a happy babble, and began dispersing through the doors. "Do you have a second, Professor?"

Mark looked at the longlegged redhead, one of his best students in years. Her pants were a tight terrycloth yellow, and she held two purplish disks in her hand.

"Sure, Carol. I see you've got the hypertext version."

"This?" She held up one of the disks. "It's marvelous. Connections radiating out from all of his thoughts. As the Preface says, it's the way McLuhan was intended to be read in the first place."

"I knew you'd like it. And what's that?"

Carol stroked the other disk, and slightly blushed. "I ... I've never read anything like it. The ending was so sad, so deeply piercing, but so *satisfying*, I've never felt this way about a book."

Mark suddenly had a bright idea. "How would you like to do a McLuhanesque analysis of the Havcek book?"

"My assignment?" Carol was surprised. "That's what I wanted to ask you about. But I don't think I could do it about this book—it's too personal. Too true to be explicable." She smiled, aware that she had managed to produce a nice phrase for the Professor.

Mark grinned back, and realized that there was an emotion going on here that hadn't been between the two of them before. She had always been very attractive, yes, but in a lean and edgy way—she always seemed to have a keen hunger for knowledge that tempered her sexuality, at least for him, because it kept him on his toes as her guide in the world of ideas. But now she seemed different, more at peace, softer, more inviting, and he felt drawn into her... "Well, you could write about precisely why you find the book so moving yet undiscussible," he brought himself back, "but I won't puncture the enthusiasm you feel for this book with an assignment if you don't want me to. So what did you want to ask me about McLuhan?"

The shower felt good on Mark's head and body. It was just the right mixture of water and liquisoap, and its heat modulated in response to the temperature on Mark's skin.

He ran his hand through his wet hair, and thought. Something about this book was disturbing—too perfect, like the shower—yet unlike the shower it wasn't the least bit soothing to him.

This was likely because he hadn't yet read it.

Hamlet suddenly popped into his mind. Something about Hamlet had relevance here. He remembered a teacher of his, years ago, commenting about the last line of Hamlet. What was it? ... "And the rest is silence ..."

This was a great ending, his teacher had told him, because it had more than one meaning—"a delicious ambiguity," the old guy had said. It means different things to different people, or even to the same person in a different mood—or better yet, at at the same time. Could mean, and sleep is silence, or, the remainder is silence, or...

Ambiguity—this was substance of all great art and popular culture. It made "Ode to Billy Joe" a rock hit decades ago, as kids endlessly discussed what it was that Billy Joe was dropping off the Tallahatchee Bridge. Had the same effect on Don McLean's "American Pie," as stanza upon stanza was pondered and tweezed for meaning.

Mark frowned, and the temperature of the shower cooled just a bit to counteract the slight increase in body heat that his annoyance generated. Ambiguity had something to do with this book, but that wasn't quite the answer either. People who read the book said nothing about ambiguous passages, only about how fundamentally satisfying it was.

But how could a Caltech programmer create a book that was satisfying to everyone who read it? Techoslovakia was in many ways the most technically advanced country in the world—surpassing the US and Japan in microchip accessories—but what did this have to do with a best-selling book?

Damnit, if he could only get his hands on one, he could figure this out.

He stepped out of the shower and pulled a big towel around him.

"Hey, it's cold!" His wife Teri yelped as she stepped into the shower behind him. He was so focused on this book he hadn't even seen her. "Don't worry, it'll adjust to you in a second. Your blood temperature is obviously different from mine." He leaned into the shower and kissed her on the neck.

"Mmm, and mine's going up if you keep doing that." She licked his lip and pushed him out of the shower.

He rubbed the towel against his chest, and walked slowly into their bedroom. Something about McLuhan, Hamlet, and the shower all had relevance to this book phenomenon. But what? He shook his head in frustration and sat down on the bed. And then he had it! He reached over to the phone and pressed in a number. "Hi Jeanne?—Mark here. I know it's late. But can I come over and see you for a minute?"

Mark walked up the cobblestone path that led to Jeanne's fine old red brick home on the north end of the campus. "It's open," Jeanne called out, as he reached for the glowing yellow chime.

"Uh, hi," Mark said, and walked into her parquet living room, shoes clacking more loudly on the polished floor than he wanted, and suddenly feeling a bit embarrassed that he had rushed over here. Jeanne's back was to him—she was at the terminal on the far side of the room—and then she suddenly turned around.

Mark flinched. Something about her didn't seem right. Her smile—it looked like something out of "Invasion of the Body Snatchers." Much too happy and content for a critic like Jeanne. He suppressed some combination of shudder and laugh.

"It turns out it's great after all." Jeanne pointed at the screen and beamed. "Well, well, *well* worth the wait."

"The goddamn book!" Mark said. "I should've known." He rushed over to the console, nearly shoving Jeanne out of the way. "Here, let me have a look at it."

"Sure...," Jeanne said, shocked at the rudeness but too pleased by the book to mind.

Mark looked at the screen. He pressed the page-up and then the page-down keys, again and again. "There's nothing here," he practically screamed. "Absolutely nothing!"

Jeanne looked mildly bewildered, then snapped her fingers. "Of course—I saw the notice at the beginning of the text. It's specially encoded so that it's viewable only by eyes with my unique retinal shadow. Sort of an anti-piracy procedure to make sure that only the person who purchases the text can read it."

"Right." Mark nodded. "They've had retinal shadow parameters keyed to credit card purchases for nearly a year now. But tell me, what do *you* of all people now find so wonderful about this book?"

"Its sophistication is marvelous," Jeanne exulted. "The conflict within conflict. Nothing too quickly or easily resolved here. And the ending—a field of flowers whose undulations in the wind produce every conceivable color of human emotion. Breathtaking." She saw the expression on Mark's face. "But you really have to read it."

"I'm sure I do," Mark said sarcastically. "But look, doesn't what you just said bother you at all?"

Jeanne's brows furrowed. "No... Why should it?"

"Well, Morgan's a nice enough guy, but don't you find it strange that he and you both find in this book some ultimate experience? And last week, that redhead in my class—extremely bright, no doubt about it, but 20 years younger than us—was having orgasms about this book too. Is it possible that you and Morgan and she all have the same tastes?"

"No, I guess that's not likely. But the hallmark of great art has always been that different people see different but equally valid and profound things in it. That's the secret of the Bible, right?"

"Yes, but the Bible is the same Bible—or pretty much the same—for most people. If anything, it's been too institutionalized—frozen in time. The Havcek book is quite the opposite."

"What do you mean?"

"Havcek's book is an intelligent, manipulated text—quite literally." Mark's voice was getting loud again. "Do you understand what that means? There is no book.' This programmer has somehow produced a program that produces many books—a different book for each person who reads it, a book perfectly suited to his or her tastes."

"That's impossible. No way it could be done."

"You're wrong," Mark said. "I can think of several ways, and I'm not even a programmer. Why do you think the electronic delivery of everyone's book is delayed? Our purchase histories—titles and subjects of the books we've bought for at least the last ten years—are in publicly accessible data bases. Havcek's program simply accesses these, creates a reader profile, and then produces a version of his book appropriate to our inclinations."

Jeanne shook her head and laughed. "And what about purchase of pre-programmed disks?"

"They're not available, remember?"

Jeanne stopped laughing, but still shook her head. "You have to read the book. Its use of language and subtlety is far too good to have been designed for me on the basis of a general profile of my reading tastes. I mean, the book gets better and better as I read it—the words are more and more on target, perfectly chosen. I just don't see how that could have been put in the book beforehand in response to my general reader profile."

"You may be right," Mark said, looking carefully at Jeanne's eyes. They were dilated, likely from the pleasure of reading Havcek, but were constricting now as a result of this discussion. "I bet the reader profile is just the first step. My guess is that the hypertext on your screen is interactive—it scans your eye dilations as you read, keeps track of what words and phrases generate the widest dilations, and then proceeds to insert an increasing amount of this language in the text as the book proceeds. What's just happened to you is not the experience of great literature, but the massaging of your emotions by a clever programmer!"

"That's ridiculous," Jeanne laughed again. "I can tell when I'm being manipulated, and—"

"The illusion of every person who's ever been manipulated, Jeanne. You think because you're so intelligent that you're immune to this sort of thing? Wrong. This program probably has a field day with your imagination and your capacity to see multiple meanings."

"The hallmark of all great art is multiple—"

"You already said that," Mark said, "in fact, you also said that last week, but when you said it then, it was with the proper derision. Another consequence of this book' is that it seems to disarm the critical faculty of its readers."

"Mark, you're overreacting." Jeanne put a soothing arm on his shoulder.

"No I'm not." He pulled the arm off of him. It felt cloying and dead-fishlike—and he suddenly caught himself and hoped that Jeanne didn't realize what he was feeling. He looked at her and that smile, that so-satisfied smile, that still sat in the middle of her face like she'd passed out drunk-ass-happy at a party somewhere. She was beyond realizing anything except her own loop of pleasure at the moment. He looked at her with concern, and spoke quietly. "Jeanne, you should be the first to agree with me. There's something essential about the objective existence of a book or a work of art—that which endures and shines through regardless of who sees it. That's what makes art worthwhile—the way we all have to teethe on its edges as we attempt to make sense of it. But when we get something on a silver platter-something that has no objective reality at all—something that effortlessly makes us happy—then we might as well be swallowing some drug. I'm sorry, but I—"

The phone rang. Jeanne picked it up. "It's for you," she said, still happier than Mark had ever seen her.

"Hi honey." It was Teri on the phone. "Just wanted you to know that your book is coming in on the computer!" Her voice was manic with delight—like a housewife wild with joy about the laserclean in a videtergent commercial. "And guess what? Mom sent me a copy too. An early birthday present—"

"Baby don't read it," Mark shouted. "It's—"

"—wonderful, absolutely wonderful," Teri said, dreamily, barely hearing Mark as she focused on her copy of the book that scrolled in slowmode read on her screen. "I've never read anything like this—"

Mark hung up. "It's in my house now."

"Go home and give it a chance," Jeanne said. "I know you'll really love it."

He walked out of her house, and back along the cobblestone path. The shadows on the street seemed to curl up and sneer at him. What would it do to you to give you everything you ever wanted in a book? What would be left when every last itch in your soul was scratched and satisfied? Omniscient imbecility with a blissed-out smile? Embalmment of the mind in a shimmering bottle screen?

He wasn't sure where he was going, but home was the last place for him now.

Grace Under Pressure

"Can you take this author's call?" Cindy Jeffries stuck her head in from the next room, waving the phone in her hand. "I'm late for lunch, already."

"Sure." I smiled and went for my own phone console. I enjoyed talking with authors directly once in a while. "Ray Walters," I said in my deepest voice. "What can I do for you?"

"Are you Mr. Walters, Editor of *Strange Sorties*?" The voice was young, quavering, incredulous.

"That's what I said."

"Mr. Walters, I can't believe they connected me directly to you."

"Happens sometimes. How can I help you?"

"Well, I've got a story I wanted to submit to your magazine and—"

"Send it in to the address on our masthead, along with an SASE." Jeez, Cindy couldn't handle this herself?

"—I wanted to send it to your Web page," the high pitched voice continued. "But I keep getting gibberish on my screen every time I try to connect to your address."

Our Web submission line was supposed to simplify things. If authors had to call for instructions, maybe *Strange Sorties* should go back to insisting on paper. "Our address is http/www—"

"You're still using http?" the voice blurted out. Then, embarrassed and stammering a bit, he added, "I mean, I didn't mean to imply that, I mean, that your system was outdated or—"

"No problem," I said, wanting to get this over with. "So can you send us your story electronically?"

"Oh, of course I can. I can plug in a downward chip. And I also developed a special new program that automatically—"

"Good." I looked at my watch and realized that I too was now almost five minutes late for my lunch appointment. "Thanks for calling, ah...?"

"Hadden, James Abbott Hadden."

"....James, and we'll look forward to seeing your story. Goodbye now." I pressed the End button on the console, and reached for my jacket. You could tell these first time authors a mile away. Still, you had to keep lines open to them, because you never knew where your next Hugo-winner might come from.

The story was waiting for me in e-mail when I got back from lunch with an acid stomach. Damned miso soup tasted like they made it with kerosene. I'd try not to hold it against the story. It sat there at the end of the queue—"Grace Under Pressure by James Abbott Hadden."

I chuckled. I liked the title. Somehow, I wasn't surprised that the kid had sent in his story so fast. And I also knew I wouldn't be able to resist reading it.

"The UE Seal slipped smoothly under the teal waves," the story began, "like a lasered needle in a pale blue arm. Inside, Grace McBride prepared herself for her first submersion in an United European subranger. The goal was a cavernous drop not far from the coast of Norway..."

I read the story quickly. At 3300 words, a plus. And the story wasn't bad. But it lacked that certain emotional sophistication I liked to see in *Strange Sorties*, and didn't merit publication. It certainly warranted a personal rejection note, though. Who knows, the kid might come up with something better the next time around.

I typed in a reply with the three to four fingers I used to milk the keyboard...

"...Grace is a strong character, but you weaken her by changing too often from active to passive. She's unconscious when the captain kisses her on the neck, yet she feels very close to the captain later after she's awake. On what basis would she feel closer to the captain? How could she know that the bruise on her lower back was turning reddish-purple?"

The intercom buzzed. "Call from Bill Jameison on 607," Cindy said.

I picked up the phone. "Bill..." I sent my reply along with Hadden's story back to his e-mail address.

Bill and I talked about a great new Stokes story. After that, I had an hour-long meeting with my ad manager, then came another hour of calls to distributors. Finally, I had to run to make another meeting across town.

"See you manyana," I told Cindy with a smile as I left. The piece of Jarlsburg cheese on her desk—"Norway's finest," the wrapper said—caught my eye and made him think again about Hadden's story. Not a bad first story at all, I thought—it'll probably turn up somewhere in a semi-pro magazine.

I saw it the next morning, revised to a tee, with my first batch of new e-mail. At first I thought the posted time was a mistake—the story looked like it had been resubmitted ten minutes after I had sent my response to Hadden yesterday—but several other stories had come in after, and the general time sequence looked right. The kid's a fast writer, I thought, and brought "Grace Under Pressure" up on my screen.

The story was pretty much the same as yesterday, but with each of my suggestions astutely worked in. Grace now had an active posture throughout. The captain was written as kissing Grace just as she awoke, so her good feeling towards him was motivated. And the bruise on her back felt merely sore, not purplish.

Still, the story lacked something, some sort of depth, some sort of subtlety. I wasn't quite sure what, but knew it still wasn't right for *Sorties*. I wrote James a short, conclusive e-mail indicating, as gently as possible, the story's lack of depth even with the revisions, and suggesting that Hadden send it to one of the young adult SF magazines.

I went to the john, and was shocked to see a new revision by Hadden on the computer when I returned. Christ, this kid's ridiculous, I grunted to himself, and proceeded to type in a command—one I had never used before—that would return the story to the author unread.

I then read the story that Bill had talked about yesterday. "Lobachevki's Revenge" by Chavez Stokes—fine little time travel tale about some guy from the future who burns the papers of the 19th century mathematician who thought he had proved Euclid's parallel postulate, leaving the field open for Lobachevki's geometry, Einstein's relativity, and the bomb. Just right for *Strange Sorties*—real science fiction, not mushy mystical realism!

"Could you print out the Stokes story for me?" I called out to Cindy on the intercom. My legal people still wanted paper manuscripts for all purchases.

Cindy walked into my office a few minutes later, looking a little confused. "Uhm, Ray, I've got two stories for you. I don't know why this happened."

I took the printouts. There were two stories here alright—the Stokes that I had requested, and that damned Hadden story. Second revision, it said at the top, so this would be the one that I had returned unread a few minutes ago. What the hell was going on? I was starting to get angry.

"Cindy," I said, "please get me Hadden on the phone. His number should be in our directory."

A few moments later Cindy said, "James Hadden on line 605."

"Mr. Hadden." I had calmed down a bit. "Ray Walters here."

"Mr. Walters!" James said with joy in his voice. "You liked my story?"

This kid thinks the only reason an editor would call would be to buy a story, I realized. I suddenly felt bad about what I had called to tell him. But I had no choice. "No, I'm afraid not. Quite the opposite."

Silence on the other end.

"In fact," I continued, "I'm calling to ask you to please stop sending us these revisions. It's not for us. Try it someplace else."

"Revisions?" the kid sounded surprised. "I don't understand."

"Come on James, don't make it worse by pretending you don't know what's going on. I was hungry once, too. I know what's it like to be knocking on doors. But you've got to lay off on this Grace' story with us now, ok?"

"Believe me, Mr. Walters, the last thing I want is to offend you. But I really only sent you my story once and —"

"I'm gonna say goodbye now, James." I was starting to get angry again. "Please think about what I said."

I hung up and sighed. Sometimes this job was more science fiction than the stories I published. I didn't know what to make of this kid—something about his tone seemed sincere. I picked up the paper printout of Grace, second revision, and started reading, despite myself. It looked like more or less the same story again, but this time with some nonsense about Kierkegaard and angst under water thrown in. I shook his head as if trying to shake off a bee or a bad dream, and crumpled the story into a messy ball. I threw it towards a nearby waste basket, missed, and turned to the contracts on my desk.

Then I remembered something about my e-mail options. I entered a lockout command that automatically returned any e-mail by specified individuals, in this case Hadden. That should end the problem.

The day was autumn beautiful, and it was Friday, so I left before lunch to pick up Barbara and the kids and get a jump on the weekend traffic out of town. As I drove up the FDR Drive, I thought again about Hadden's story, and was glad that I wouldn't have to see it again.

The Cape was especially spectacular this breezy October Saturday. The water still had a bit of summer warmth, and Barb looked great in her new Prague bikini that nearly exposed one sweet cheek. Even after ten years of marriage, I still couldn't wait till the kids were asleep and I was in bed with her...

Later, she lay sleeping on my chest, her mouth open. The keen white moonlight played upon her skin, and for some reason I thought of the captain in that stupid story, kissing Grace as she lay senseless and soft and vulnerable from that sea urchin's sting. I kissed Barb gently and slipped out from under her. I knew I wouldn't be falling back asleep for a while.

Rising, I walked quietly into the next room. The moonlight glimmered off my laptop screen. I wandered over, sat down, turned it on—might as well as put the time to some use. Let's see. Contents, Strange Sorties, volume 8, number 3 ... volume 8, number 4 ...

I finished looking at number 3, was about to call up number 4, when I noticed something at the bottom of the list. God damn it—"Grace Under Pressure, 2nd revision."

I jabbed the delete key in a spasm of rage. Few things bothered me more than being hounded by authors. Only distributors who tried to beat *Strange Sorties* on payments were worse.

How the hell could Hadden know I'd be here? I scratched my head and shivered. How could he get my private unlisted number on the Cape, and e-mail his story to me in the few minutes I had the computer turned on? Well, I guess it was a pretty short story... Too upset to work, I turned the computer off and shuffled back to bed. I didn't sleep well at all.

Still, the next morning was nice. The air was warm again, and the kids were having a great time feeding the seagulls.

A small plane appeared overhead from the direction of Wellfleet. Long tufts of white that clung to the sky came from the plane's rear. "It's skywriting, Dad," Mark, my oldest son, said. "What do you think it's gonna say?"

"For cryin' out fuckin' loud, I don't believe this!" I shouted and kicked the sand a minute later. "That skywriting plane must have a program that is connected to a computer that the kid somehow hacked into!"

The letters in the sky were G R A C E U N D E R P R E S S U R E. I explained about the problems I'd been having with the author.

"Is it a good story, honey?" Barb asked as the kids squealed with pleasure.

"See for yourself," I said, sourly. "I'm sure I'll have another copy waiting for me next time I turn on my computer." The plane flew away, leaving only a trail of puffy ellipses behind.

"Do you intend to press charges against this kid or what?" FBI agent Robert Henley leaned over my big office desk and asked. He was clean cut and good looking, but something was missing from his clear blue eyes. He seemed very well educated, in a technician sort of way. Killer with a masters degree, I thought.

"I don't know," I replied. "I don't think we want that kind of publicity. And the kid isn't so much a criminal as a pest." But an incredible pest, I thought. That story has been chasing me *everywhere* since I got back from the Cape. I didn't like the authorities, but I guess I had no choice but to call them in on this.

Henley laughed. "Let me tell you something, Mr. Walters. These kids are just as bad as criminals. They break into computers, steal people's information and property, do all sorts of damage. Now from what you tell me we're dealing with much more than some over-anxious writer on the Web here. This bozo has a program that somehow has a beat on everything you have access to—your computers, cape skywriting, video screens in department stores where you shop. To be honest with you, we weren't sure until this case that such a program was possible, though it's a logical outgrowth of stuff that's been around for years."

"Hard to believe," I said quietly.

"Believe it," Henley pressed on. "You're the one whose life's been invaded by this bugger. You're disturbed by it—that's why you called us. And believe me, if our scenario people are right about what a program like this can do, it won't let you go until you agree to publish the story. It'll haunt you for life. But we can't do anything unless you're willing to take the next step."

"But how could a computer program do that?"

"Hard to say. But our guys figure that each time the story is submitted, it scans the files around it for any relevant information. It learns from its surroundings and adjusts its behavior accordingly. It's what you might call an intelligent' program. You know, like intelligent buildings and smart cars? Probably makes some twisted use of the Leipzig algorithm. You're smiling, but I assure you, the joke is on you. First, the story seems able to incorporate any suggestions for revision that are made about it via e-mail. But if this directive is frustrated—if for some reason it cannot locate any suggested revisions—then it scans any computer files it has access to for details on where to locate the source of new revisions. In other words, you, Mr. Walters."

I stood up and shook the FBI man's hand. "I understand and want to thank you, Mr., ah ..."

"Henley. Agent Robert C. Henley."

"... Mr. Heinlein, for the valuable information you've given me. But my decision is final—at least for now. I'll somehow handle this in my own way." I wasn't sure that I really understood what this guy was telling me, but I knew enough that I didn't want the FBI and its machinations involved, and was sorry I had called them.

"Ok," Henley said, "but I think you're letting yourself in for some trouble." He walked out the door.

The phone rang. I picked it up, listened for a long minute, then hung up, livid. "Get me that FBI man," I screamed to Cindy, too furious for the intercom. "We're gonna press charges."

"Was that Hadden on the phone?" Cindy turned from the plants she had been watering and moved towards the door.

"Worse," I stood up, shaking. "That was Barbara. We're supposed to have lunch at Kyoto's. I have a meeting across the street from there in five minutes, right?" I looked at my watch. "This goddamn idiocy has made me late again, damn it!"

"Right, but what did Barbara tell you?"

"Kyoto's is near Times Square. She told me that big electronic sign over the square is now spelling out, G R A C E U N D E R ...'"

Cindy suppressed a laugh, and ran out to get Henley.

"Good to see you've come to your senses," Henley said as Cindy returned with him a minute later. "Now are you gonna give me that kid's number?"

"Grace Under Pressure," Ted Koppel's voice intoned, as the Times Square scene with Grace Under Pressure filled the TV screen. "One of the strangest cases of computer hacking in the new millennium. An unknown author, an 18-year old from Wilkesbarre, Pennsylvania, submits his story via computer transmission to a New York publisher. An editor turns it down. Then the story appears everywhere the editor goes. The FBI is called in, but they can't find the author. He's gone into hiding. And now the story may creep into our nation's top security computers. Grace Under Pressure.' Our guests will be Ray Walters, Editor of *Strange Sorties*, and John Finkelman, well-known hunter of computer hackers." The opening strains of the classic Nightline aria blared forth.

"Daddy looks great on television, doesn't he?" Mark said and beamed from ear to ear as the camera focused briefly on his father.

"Lucky boy that I'm letting you stay up so late tonight," Barb kissed him on the forehead and gave him a piece of bagel.

Koppel was talking: "Now as I understand it, the full text of this story has appeared only on your computer screen, is that right Mr. Walters? So the public has no idea what this story is really about."

"That's right," I answered, feeling stiff and monosyllabic on my first national TV appearance.

"Ted, if I could jump in here," Finkelman asked, a pro on this medium.

"Go right ahead, Dr. Finkelman."

"I'm concerned that thwarting the program's design to get the story published is keeping this thing going," Finkelman said, "and who knows what the ultimate consequences will be. If I understand this program correctly, it will penetrate any space, private or public, that could logically bring the story to Mr. Walter's attention. He'll likely see the story on the screen the next time he goes to the bank, but of more concern to the public is this program's manipulation of all mass-media potentially viewable by Mr. Walters. Ted, our discussion of this story on this very television show may be part of Hadden's plan. Publication of the story may be the only way to stop the program."

"Just a minute!" I said, suddenly finding my voice. "Are you saying that I should publish this story in *Strange Sorties*? No way—we've got standards! I'm not going to be badgered into publishing this!"

"Why not?" Finkelman continued. "The story has already achieved enormous publicity. Your magazine would probably sell millions of copies to new readers. That's what you want, isn't it?"

"Well, sure, but not like that.... Let me ask you a question, Doctor. Have you ever read any science fiction?"

"We've watched every episode of Star Trek ever made, all generations. Why?"

"Gentlemen, I'll ask the questions here," Koppel said. "Dr. Finkelman, you raise some interesting issues, and when we come back, I'd like you to address the question of whether you see any cosmic significance in all of this. Whether —"

"You're kidding," I said. "You think Grace Under Pressure' is some sort of religious message to the world at large? Some sort of divine signal written all over, like everyone please be cool in these rough times?" I laughed sarcastically.

Grace Under Pressure 55

"Easy baby," Barb said to the TV, "don't antagonize Ted. You'd like to get invited back sometime."

"Tell you what, Mr. Walters," Koppel said. "I know you're upset, and you'll get your chance to respond when we return."

The screen faded to a Honda commercial.

"Dad's right to be angry about that dumb story," Mark said with a nine-year old's righteousness and loyalty.

"Not so dumb," Barbara said. "It's made James Abbott Hadden a household name."

I sat in my office and pondered my options. In the past two days, newsstands had been selling out their copies of *Strange Sorties* like it had pictures of everyone nude, and the issue had been rushed back to press twice already to meet the demand. And all this was happening without publication of Hadden's story. I knew we'd break all records if we did publish it.

I shook my head. I was tired of being on the spot, certainly could use the money, and a tiny part of me was saying, what would be the big crime if I did publish this story?

The crime would be to the public. They bought *Sorties* expecting to read what I liked, not what I was pressured into publishing. But the question of public benefit was complicated. Which was worse: giving the public a lousy story that they wanted—for reasons extraneous to the story—or a story I liked that they might not care to read?

Hadden's story wasn't great, but a lot of people were urging me to publish it. I suddenly wondered if the program was designed to set up the people around me to get me to publish the story...

No, that was paranoia. A program couldn't do that. But—

"Guess who I have on 605?" Cindy's voice sang in on the intercom. "James Abbott Had —"

"James!" I grabbed the phone before Cindy finished.

"Mr. Walters? I hope this is okay with you. I mean, you were the editor I first submitted the story to, and I never officially withdrew it. And now that *Far Rim* wants it ..."

I was momentarily speechless, choking on shock, relief, and maybe one percent perverse regret. "Yes, of course we understand, and wish you well," I finally said. "I'm pleased you found another publication for it. But the important thing is that computer program of yours. Can you do anything to shut it off?"

"Oh, no problem," James said. "As soon as I got the signed contract from *Far Rim*, I scanned it into my computer, and this automatically deactivated my program. You see, all it really wanted was for someone—anyone—to keep reading my story until it was accepted for publication."

"Good. So the program's not on the loose any more. You wouldn't believe the tension it's caused, and —"

"I hope so, Mr. Walters."

"Hope so'?"

"Well, about the program not being on the loose. I deleted my copy of the program, cause I don't really need it anymore. But—"

"I don't think I like the implications of the word *copy*, James."

"Well, I was very proud of the program. You know, before it went berserk? So I put a copy on several Web sites—you know, not my story, but my underlying program, so that new writers all over the world could use it? Then when I realized all the trouble it was causing, I logged back on and removed my program. But, ah ..." Hadden's voice trailed off.

"Yes?" I prompted.

"Well, you know, when I logged back on to the Web sites again, after I deleted my program? I found my program had reappeared! So I removed it again, and it came back again. Every time I erase it, it reappears. And more and more writers are downloading it. It's like it has a life of its own now."

I just screamed.

Advantage, Bellarmine

Roberto Francesco Romolo Bellarmine—*consultor* of the Holy Office, head of the Roman College, Cardinal, former Archbishop of Capua—turned to his guest with a weary smile. "So, Maffeo, any words of wisdom about Galileo? He'll be in Rome next week, and we have arranged a visit."

Maffeo Barberini, scion of one of the wealthiest, most powerful families in Italy, a Cardinal too—one day to be Pope, Bellarmine was sure—removed a grape pit from his tongue. "Only what you already know—he is right."

"Pity more of our people cannot grasp that," Bellarmine said. "The nonsense that has been produced in our own College—that the moon is really pure, perfect, sublimely spherical as Aristotle held, and the mountains and craters seen through Galileo's telescope are but imperfections far below that heavenly invisible surface—you would think it was 615 not 1615, and Rome had just been sacked of all common sense, all reason!"

"Ah, yes." Barberini chuckled. "And, as I recall, Galileo had a good answer to that one: if we accept that heavenly surfaces are invisible, then we could just as easily agree that the real surface of the moon, constructed of that same magical substance, actually rises in towering mountains ten times *higher* than his telescope has seen."

"He is clever," Bellarmine said, unsmiling. "And that is what makes him dangerous. I have tried to convey to him the thought, the path, that his mathematics, his observations, may be right—that we may welcome them, rejoice in them, as an improvement over Ptolemy's epicycles—but that the underlying, everlasting truth is just as it ever was."

"And what truth is that?" Barberini asked.

"That is no doubt the question that troubles Galileo,"

Bellarmine replied, "and why he sometimes gives the appearance of accepting our arguments, yet in his truest soul rejects them. It is because we ourselves are unsure of just what the underlying, everlasting truth really is."

"As we have good reason to be," Barberini said. "But that is our burden—not the world's. And part of our burden is to keep the world—not only the physical world, but the souls of its people-stable."

"Which brings us back to the problem of Galileo," Bellarmine said, sadly. "His theories, his publications, presented to the world without our mediation, cannot help but sow confusion in the common soul."

"Have you implied to him anything at all of the Instruments?" Barberini asked, as delicately as he could manage.

"No! I have not! Therein lies the road that was taken with Giordano Bruno. And it did no good—it did worse than no good. In the end ..." Bellarmine could not bring himself to finish.

"In the end, our Holy Church had to kill him," Barberini said. "Still, the result need not be the same with Galileo. He is a different kind of man—more practical, more of a scientist than a mystic like Bruno. He may see a different kind of lesson in the Instruments."

"No," Bellarmine insisted. "I will not have it."

Barberini permitted himself the slightest of smiles.

"You are a stubborn man," Bellarmine said to Galileo.

"Stubbornness has nothing to do with this, Your Eminence," Galileo replied. "Truth is what this is about. I can say 'the Earth does not move,' as easily as the next man. But if, in truth, the Earth does move, then it matters not what I say. For in time others will make the same observations as I, and they will say that the Earth does move. And where will our Holy Church be then?"

"You are stubborn because you assume that future telescopes, perhaps with power far greater than yours, will see the same things in the heavens as your device," Bellarmine answered. "How can you be sure of that?"

"I am not sure of that," Galileo said. "Devices change, and so then does the knowledge they produce."

"Precisely," Bellarmine said. "The only thing constant in this world is the Lord's word, and the only constant path towards that is the Church's teaching."

"Yes, but if device A contradicts the Church's teaching, then even though it may be improved upon at some future time by device B, then ought we not at least consider the evidence of device A at this time?"

Bellarmine looked away. "Devices," he said at last. "Believe me, there are more devices in this Universe than you with or without your telescope have ever dreamed of."

Galileo squirmed. "Are you referring to the Instruments? Do you seek to intimidate me by intimations of your Instruments of Torture?"

Bellarmine said nothing.

"I am a weak vessel," Galileo continued. "I might well sooner lie about what I know to be true than be subjected to your torture. But what would that gain you in the end? Do you suppose you can torture the whole world—impose your will on every human eye that looks at the heavens through a lens?"

"I was hoping you might be persuaded—not by torture, but by reason itself—to see the dangers in the way you proselytize your theories," Bellarmine replied. "I was hoping that once so convinced, we might even enlist you to help in our cause—explain to the world that, although science always progresses, always changes, the soul and its place in the Universe remains constant, remains forever, and our Holy Church is only reliable guide to that."

"Forgive me, Eminence—but I fear it's the Church that is treading on the domain of science here, not vice versa, in your insistence that the Earth is the unmoving center of the Universe. And you have no evidence that the Copernican theory, which my telescopic observations support, is wrong."

Bellarmine sighed. "Suppose I showed you evidence."

Galileo scoffed. "What, in the Holy Bible?"

"No," Bellarmine said very quietly. "In Instruments perhaps not ultimately unlike your telescope—Instruments of vision. Dangerous Instruments—far more dangerous than your telescopes." He wrung his hands. "I had hoped not to have to speak to you of this. But I see there is no other way."

Galileo shuddered. "You are speaking to me again of torture? Of burning out my eyes?"

"No, not of torture—at least, not of physical torture, I assure you," Bellarmine replied. "Please, come with me."

"We think they are a kind of illuminated manuscript," Bellarmine said. "Except, the words can be changed upon them."

Galileo stared at one of the devices, in rapt attention. "The writing appears to be Italian."

"Latin editions are also available," Bellarmine advised. "Many in vulgate as well. A few are familiar to us, most not."

"Each of these—manuscript Instruments—contains a different edition?" Galileo asked. They were three in the room.

"No," Bellarmine said. "Each Instrument contains many different editions—just as each tree contains many different leaves. But each of these Instruments appears to contain the *same* different editions."

"Ah," Galileo mused. "Such as three libraries, perhaps, each of which contains the same editions?"

Bellarmine nodded. "Yes. Perhaps."

Galileo studied the words on the screen—they were a treatise, of some sort, about Copernican theory.

"This essay talks of planets," he said. "Do these manuscripts have pictures, engravings lit from within, like the enlumined Books of Hours?"

Advantage, Bellarmine   61

"Yes," Bellarmine replied. "Except these Instruments truly display a passage of time—they show pictures of things I think no man, truly, has ever seen."

Galileo's eyes lit up brighter than the manuscript. "Prester John's Speculum, come to life!"

Bellarmine made a sarcastic sound. "Prester John is an old wives' tale, designed to give hope to children. These Instruments, as you can see, are plainly real."

"Yes, yes, I see that," Galileo said, growing more and more excited as he read the text. "And this treatise has some connection to my work..."

"More than you realize," Bellarmine said. "Touch that emblem." He gestured to one of many little multi—colored ovals that occupied the margins of the text. This one contained a tiny, stylized arrow that pointed up. "It will cause the manuscript to scroll backward, to the beginning."

Galileo did as told. The text slowly scrolled, until it came to what was clearly a title page.

Galileo gasped.

The title read, *Dialogo sopra i due massimi systemi del mondo*. It was indicated as published by the presses of Landini, in Florence, in the year 1632.

Its author was Galileo Galilei.

"Clever forgery!" Galileo exclaimed, half in anger, half in admiration. "So your scribes at the College seek to publish some confusing document under my name, and therein mislead the world about my real contentions!"

"I think it is not a forgery," Bellarmine said, "or, at least, something not as simple as a forgery. I think you will agree, if you read on."

But Galileo turned away from the text, and focused instead on Bellarmine. "It is a Dialog about the Two Chief World Systems, purportedly written by me, except I did not write it. Therefore, it must be a forgery."

Bellarmine shook his head no. "I think you would do better to say, not that you did not write it, but you did not write it yet."

"Preposterous," Galileo said. "How could you possibly know that?"

"Would it surprise you to know that I read your *Sidereus Nuncius*, on that very Instrument at which you have just been staring, in 1599, the year Clement VIII made me a Cardinal—a good decade before you would even make the observations with your telescope that would form the basis of that essay you published in 1610?"

"Forgive me, Eminence—that cannot be true!" But Galileo's mouth hung open.

"I assure you it is," Bellarmine said. "You see, I have been an admirer of yours—albeit secret—for quite some time. Perhaps even longer than you."

Galileo harrumphed, and looked back at the text on the Instrument.

"I grant you, of course, that there is no way I can conclusively prove what I have just told you," Bellarmine allowed, "not about seeing *Sidereus Nuncius* in 1599, eleven years before you wrote it, nor about the legitimacy of your authorship of the *Dialogo* that you see before you now, which apparently has seventeen more years before it comes into being in … in the outside world."

"The outside world in contrast to what other world?" Galileo asked. "In contrast to this illuminated world—this, moving manuscript lit from within? What is this, then, a portal on to the Platonic world of eternal truth and verity? That world is a figment of imagination far greater than Prester's Speculum!"

Bellarmine ventured a small truth in jest. "Oh, I would say there is little chance of the information contained in the Instrument being eternally true, my friend, if you or any mortal wrote it."

Galileo looked fitfully at the text. "What other manuscripts does this Instrument contain?" He jabbed another emblem.

The text disappeared. "Oh no!"

"Do not be alarmed," Bellarmine said, and leaned over Galileo's shoulder. "At least, there is no need to be concerned about the words disappearing." He touched a third emblem. The words returned. "You see, they are easily recalled. Here," he said, gesturing to another oval. "That one makes the text proceed forward. The one underneath speeds it to the very end. You will find at the end of your text a listing of other authors whose works are within the Instrument."

Galileo touched the speed-to-the-end symbol—a miniature of Mercury, god of thievery as well as speed. Words flew upward on the screen, like souls freed from hell. Finally, a profusion of proper names settled into stability at the end of the document.

Galileo looked, muttered. "Most of these are not known to me," he said.

"Try that one," Bellarmine offered.

And his finger pointed to: Einstein

Galileo stayed in the room with the Instruments, poring over their contents, for nine days and nights.

Bellarmine brought him food and drink and consolation.

"I think I have read enough," Galileo said at last.

"Good," Bellarmine replied. "The word outside is that we are torturing you, or have killed you, or are threatening to do one or both. It would be helpful if you could show your face and assure everyone that you are unharmed."

"But I am not unharmed," Galileo said. "My soul has been fed to the breaking point. I will never be the same."

"Ah, yes, well, this is the price we pay for knowledge, is it not? This is the price you want the whole world to pay—a world of people with intellect far feebler than yours—when you feed them your theories, your theories which you are so sure are true, about the Earth and the heavens. Except, you are not so sure any more, are you."

"No, I am not," Galileo said, with profound fatigue.

"You need not worry for your physical being—nor even for the survival of your soul," Bellarmine said softly. "Others before you have seen these Instruments—not many, but others—and most have survived."

"Others? Who?" Galileo asked.

"Well, I told you that I first saw this sixteen years ago, and I am still here, and alive."

"Yes, but I meant—"

"I know what you meant," Bellarmine said. He pondered for a moment. "Leonardo da Vinci saw these Instruments—he studied them for years—I suppose there is no harm in telling you that."

"Yes, that would make sense," Galileo said. "He is rumored to have made sketches, extraordinary, of flying devices, of machines that could live under the sea..."

"The rumors are true," Bellarmine said.

"But where did you get these Instruments? How long have they been here?"

"That I am unable to tell you, not because I do not want to, but because we honestly do not know," Bellarmine said. "Some say Marco Polo brought them back from Cathay. But there is no real evidence of that. The first definite record we have of them here is in 1357. The three of them. Why three? Maybe as protection in case one or two of them were lost. Who knows. The first people who read the words within could barely understand what they meant. Oh, they understood some of the Ancients. But when they came upon you—Galileo Galilei—they had as much comprehension of you as you do of Albert Einstein."

Galileo trembled. "I understood not much of Einstein—most of his mathematics is beyond me. But I grasped some of Isaac Newton, and from that vantage point, and what little of Einstein

I could comprehend, I can see that my work is ..."

Bellarmine shook his head sympathetically.

"I can see that the notion that the sun is the center of our system is ... is a *relative* thing, not as absolute as first I thought. We must take care not to make the same mistake with Copernicus as the world has been making for lo these fourteen centuries with Ptolemy."

"Good," Bellarmine said. "My faith in your judgement has not been misplaced."

"So much knowledge to be had here," Galileo said, rubbing his eyes and looking again at the Instrument. "Will I be permitted to return?"

"Perhaps," Bellarmine said. "We shall see."

"But our problem remains," Galileo said. "Even if I renounce what I have said, even if I publish not another word about my telescopic observations and their support of Copernicus, that will not stop others from following in the path I have started."

"We do not want you to renounce anything—not now," Bellarmine said. "Word of course eventually will indeed spread about your discoveries and your theories. We of course know that from the Instruments. We cannot stop that. Nor do we want to. What we want is to make sure, as much as possible, that word reaches the people at the right time, in the right way—when their souls are ready to accept it."

"But how?" Galileo asked.

Bellarmine put his hand on Galileo's shoulder. "Leave the details to us. You can continue writing and publishing as you have been doing—but try to take care to make sure you distinguish between science and its explanation of appearances, and faith and its explanation of the way things truly are. In time, you will write your *Dialogo*—you have already read it, so you will have an advantage." Bellarmine smiled a beatific smile. "Who knows, perhaps some of our very discussions in the past few days will find their way into that fine book."

Galileo nodded. "Yes."

"Do not worry," Bellarmine said. "We will provide you with instructions—detailing just when you should write your treatises, just when you should appear obstinate, just when you should give in. Leave it all to us."

"Yes," Galileo said.

"A fine wine," Bellarmine said, and offered a glass to Barberini.

"And a fine day too, judging by your countenance," Barberini replied. "I take it all went well with Galileo. I told you the Instruments were the best way to proceed."

"Well, we must be ware of the deceptively easy wisdom of hindsight," Bellarmine said. "Our brethren showed Bruno the Instruments too, and his reaction was very different from Galileo's. He was uncontrollable. He had to be burned, as you know. Just a year after I had become a Cardinal. That was terrible. It should never have happened. It must never happen again."

"But you seem sure that Galileo is on the right path," Barberini said.

"Oh, I am very sure of that," Bellarmine replied.

Barberini looked at him with just the slightest quizzical expression.

"You know," Bellarmine explained, "our people are constantly studying the Instruments—our small, select group—trying to understand how they work, the limits of what they convey, where they might have come from. We have learned some things. The texts sometimes change—very slightly, but we have made records of originals, of some of the listings, and, once in a while, we notice something new, something that was not there before."

"Yes, I believe I heard of that fluctuation," Barberini said. "Almost as if events we have influence over here have some effect on the texts in the Instruments. Well, that makes sense, does it not, because we in the past are of course creating our future."

Advantage, Bellarmine 67

Bellarmine smiled. Barberini definitely had not only the family and the wealth but the intellect to be Pope.

"That is so," Bellarmine said.

"So, something in the Instruments, some change in the text, perhaps, tells you that we are on the right path with Galileo?" Barberini pressed.

"Yes," Bellarmine replied. "I checked all of the listings under my name just this morning—I do that from time to time. And I found a new one—one I am sure had not been there before."

"Yes?"

"It seems to have been authored almost 400 years from now," Bellarmine said.

"Yes?"

"It is a brief piece, in fictional form—like many of our contemporary dialogues—entitled, Advantage, Bellarmine.'"

The Copyright Notice Case

The gust caught my umbrella the second I got out of my car, before I'd even had a chance to fully open the thing. I struggled for a bit, then gave in to the inevitable. Another insideout dripping mess to deposit in the trashcan. The wild force of nature wins again.

I turned my collar to the cold rain and hustled up the brownstone stairs. I pulled out my ID and showed it to the uniform.

"Down the hall, one flight up, second door on the right. They're waiting for you, Dr. D'Amato."

"Right," I said. I hated these long brownstone stairs—rushing up them always made me breathless these days. I guess I could've walked up slowly, but that wasn't my way.

"Phil," that was Dave Spencer, even less hair and more belly than I, bent over a body, male, looked to be in his late 20s. "Come take a look at this." Dave was the coroner. He often called me in for special consultations—came with my forensic territory.

I looked. The corpse had his eyes wide open, like he'd been shocked to death. But there were no electricity burns on the body that I could see, and in fact the nearest electrical outlet was some 15 feet away next to a computer on the other side of the room.

"Chemical, food allergy, lethal injection?" I rattled off the usual suspects in cases like this. And of course there was the unstated omnipresent social tetrad of choices: death by natural causes, accident, suicide, or murder.

"Not likely," Dave shook his head. "No obvious puncture marks. No discoloration of the lips. We'll know more after the full test course."

"So what's your best guess?" I asked.

"I have none," Dave said. "That's why I asked you in. It's like something reached in and turned up the juice in this guy's nervous system. Turned up the volume to lethal levels. Looks like heart attack and ten other things gone wrong here—never seen anything like it."

"All right," I said. "I'll have a look around." For some reason, I had a reputation in the Department as the forensic scientist to call in when something inexplicable seemed to have happened. Well, I knew the reason—I'd been involved in my fair share of weirdo cases in my time, some of them public. And my popular writings in fields ranging from physics to genetics were pretty well known. "This guy have a name?"

"Glen Chaleff," Dave replied. "Some kind of computer programmer."

Chaleff's apartment was nothing out of the ordinary. Bland furniture arranged unsurprisingly around off-white painted walls. The computer was the only thing that caught my eye. It was a sophisticated machine, lean and very powerful, it seemed to me, something well beyond the latest commercial chip. The screen had two words on it.

"Copyright Notice"

I put on my gloves before touching the keyboard—never mind the standard precaution of not doing anything to disturb possible fingerprints and evidence, I was thinking more about not getting electrocuted on the outside chance that's what had happened to Chaleff. I pressed the up and down arrow keys to see if there was any other text above or below on the screen.

Nada. Just a bunch of hash above, three quarters faded to nothing, like I had come in on the end game of some kind of program that self-destructed after use. I arrowed back to "Copyright Notice."

It was fading away now too.

Jenna Katen was the girlfriend. There's almost always a girlfriend in these sorts of cases. Lieutenant in charge asked me if I wanted to come in and interview her. She was the reason Chaleff was considered a possible homicide.

"She discovered the body, she says he was working on some kind of genetic project that seems on cloud nine to me, I thought you might have a better chance of understanding what she's talking about, you're a real hound for that stuff, right?" That was the Lieutenant's briefing.

"Right." I said.

Jenna was really striking. Looked a lot better than girlfriends of the deceased usually do, except on television. Soft green eyes and soft brown hair falling around her shoulders just the way I like it. Keep your mind on business, D'Amato.

I could see she'd been crying. "You look too smart for me to offer you a smoke," I said. "How about some caffeine?"

"Sure," she looked up.

"Hot or cold?"

"Diet soda would be nice."

I went outside and coaxed a can from the machine.

"Why don't you tell me your story from the beginning," I said, trying to pour the soda into a cup so that it didn't fizz over the top. Never worked. "Pretend I'm an ignoramus about the science—but tell me everything, and spell it out as much as you can."

She sipped the soda and squeezed the cup. "Glen was working on a special facet of the human genome project."

I nodded. "The one that hopes to eventually identify and map the function of every gene—and every protein compound—on human chromosomes."

"That's right," she said. "Except there are actually a whole bunch of interrelated human genome projects. And this is a special section of a special project. Early on—about two years ago—the main team discovered some odd material at the far edge on some X chromosomes."

"On all female chromosomes?" I asked.

"No, the material has so far been seen on only about eight

percent of the X chromosomes studied."

"Ok," I said. "And what do the researchers think this odd gene is responsible for?" I knew that that area of the X chromosome was home to at least one interesting human gene—the so-called gay gene, still under intense investigation.

"Well, that's part of what makes this so unusual," Jenna said. "The material's not really a gene, and doesn't seem responsible for any behavioral or expressive trait."

"I'm not following you," I said. This is likely where the Lieutenant had lost comprehension.

"Well, the material's chromosomal—it's some sort of protein code—but it's not really a gene. Only five percent of the DNA in our genome actually goes into genes. The rest is sometimes called junk DNA,' and I guess you could say our little corner of the genome project has been prospecting for an unlikely fortune of information in that junkpile. You know, more clues as to how the human genome works as a whole—how proteins outside of the genes themselves prime them for operation, act as regulating enzymes, that sort of thing."

"Ok," I said. "And how did Glen fit in?"

"Well, we've—Glen's—been trying to, well, read the code on that odd genetic material."

"Come again?"

"The code seems amenable to some sort of binary transformation—you know, a mapping that would translate the connections inside the protein complex into a series of yes and nos, or ons and offs. Genes themselves operate on a four-part code-adenine binding to thymine, cytosine to guanine. They're nucleotide bases, you know—A and C on one side of the helix zipper connecting to T and G on the other. I'm sorry, I'm getting too technical for you—"

"Not at all," I said, though I could've lived without her reciting the specific names of the nucleotide bases. This was basic textbook stuff for DNA fingerprinting. "Please continue."

"Well, like I was saying, the special material that Glen was working on actually has slightly different forms of the nucleotides that make them more like a binary than a four-part system."

"And —," I prompted.

"And, well, the hope, the goal, was that if we could get a reliable transformation of that genetic code, whatever it was, into binary, then we could take that binary rendering and in turn convert it into words on a screen."

"Read the genetic code, literally?" I asked.

"Well, again, yes and no. Not really the genetic code in our genes proper, but this code in a tiny part of the other 95 percent of our DNA on the X chromosome," Jenna said.

"I see," I said, though I didn't yet, at least not fully. "And Glen's death?"

"He phoned to tell me he had completed the final translation of the code, had words up on his screen ... and when I came over, he was dead," she started sobbing. "I think those words killed him."

"Ok," I poured more soda in her cup. So now I knew something: either she had killed her boyfriend, and cooked up this story to throw us off track, or there was something genuinely strange going on here. The coroner's extensive autopsy had already found no demonstrable cause for the sudden massive failure of all of Chaleff's systems that had killed him—"looks like everything just blew at once for no apparent reason," Dave told me—so we knew Chaleff hadn't just died of your common heart attack or stroke while he was doing his research. It was something more. Like something had reached in and turned off—or on—some master switch, as Dave had said yesterday. The question was who—and what. And the what was not only what reached in, but what was the switch?

I could see why the Lieutenant was thinking homicide. In cases like this—cases involving dead young bodies—the cause of death was all too often murder. Barring tragedies like AIDS, young bodies don't very often expire on their own.

Now it might shock the public to hear this, but in many ways murder is the forensic scientist's best friend. Once the cops get a confession of murder, however inarticulate, it points to the facts, and we can use it, working backward, to piece together a detailed description of the death and its circumstances. Reverse engineering is always easier than working from the ground up.

But truthfully, I hated confessed murder as the cause of death, always resisted it as the explanation until impossible to do so. Not only for the obvious moral reasons—I'm as glad as the next guy to find a bit less depravity in the human species wherever I can—but because, well, I savor the thrill of an investigation in which I don't know the final conclusion beforehand, in which science leads to the cause of death rather than vice versa.

And I'd learned the hard way that some kind of nefarious intervention, something worse than mere murder, always loomed as a possibility when research scientists were involved. I'm not talking about dressing up a lover's quarrel or cutthroat professional competition with a fatal malfunction in a laboratory like they do in the movies. I've had experience with things much worse. The public had no idea.

But what was the agent of death here?

Words on a screen?

They made sense neither as a weapon nor a lethally malfunctioning piece of equipment.

"You have any idea what those words were?" I asked.

She looked up at me and her eyes re-focused, as if my voice had pulled her away from some contemplation deep and distant. "No," she said. "The screen was blank when I arrived."

So now I knew she was probably lying about at least one thing.

Some of her facts were easy to verify. Jenna had been telling the truth about Chaleff's last call to her apartment. And there was no sign of anyone entering Chaleff's apartment between the time of that call, and the time Jenna arrived, about 45 minutes later, when she said she'd found Chaleff dead.

Her story about the special section of the human genome project took more work to confirm. She'd told me the MIT Media Lab had a piece of the research action. Nic Negroponte, head of the Lab, was an old friend of mine. He didn't know much about that part of the project, but put me in touch with an associate who did.

"Ralph Hertzberg here," the voice on the phone said. "Nic told me to expect your call."

"Great," I said. "Ok. Let me start by trying to explain to you what I think you're working on—what I understand and what I don't—and you tell me where I'm wrong."

"Shoot."

"Ok," I said. "DNA is commonly said to be a genetic language, but that's not quite right. It's really a recipe for the construction of other proteins into cells that have specific properties—heart cells, brain cells, and so forth in humans—cells and organs and systems that come into being during gestation."

"That's right," Hertzberg said.

"Ok," I said. "So in fact, DNA isn't really a language at all—it's really an arrangement of proteins that causes other proteins to develop in a certain way, into heart cells, etc. So really DNA is a catalyst for the development of living organisms. But we say as a shorthand that it's a code or a set of instructions. Am I on the right track here?"

"Very much so."

"Good," I said. "All right, then. So tell me this: How do we get from DNA, which isn't really a language—or is only a language in a metaphoric sense—how do we get from that to this chromosomal material which Jenna Katen says Glen Chaleff was able to read on his screen?"

Hertzberg sighed. "Not very easily, but I'll try to explain. First, you have to understand that there's lots of protein material associated with chromosomes that we have no idea what the function is. Not everything there is just genes. In fact, most isn't. Some material we've identified as seeming to have a catalyst function for the genes themselves—sort of meta-catalysts—some seem to control timing of genetic instruction of other proteins in ways we're just beginning to fathom. But most of this extra genetic material is still a mystery to us."

Right, the so-called junk DNA, I thought. "And the, uh, the linguistic material on the eight percent of X chromosomes is, was, in the mystery area?"

"Yes."

"Has this material been found only on human chromosomes?"

"So far, yes," Hertzberg said. "Primate chromosomes were the first other place we looked—chimp and ape DNA is 99 percent the same as human—and we found nothing like it."

"Nothing that could generate words on a screen?"

"Look, let me be honest with you," Hertzberg said. "I know what Jenna told you, but we don't even know for sure that this binary chromosomal material can be converted into readable words. It seems transformable into a binary code, yes, but we have no way of really testing the accuracy of that transformation, since we have nothing precisely of this kind to measure it against. And we certainly don't know for sure if that code can support actual words. What we get from that code at first is some sort of general proto-language, strongly resembling Indo-European in its subject-predicate structure, and therefore recognizable as a real language to some researchers, I guess. And assuming that to be Indo-European, or proto-Indo-European, we can make rough translations into English, Sanskrit, what have you. But the results are extraordinarily speculative to say the least—I'd say the noise to signal ratio must be well over 40 percent in the final translation. Though that's conjecture too—the actual distortion could be far more, or less, for that matter. Bottom line: We're dealing with a hell of a lot of conjecture here. That's why we haven't published anything about this yet. It's still in the very early stages of research. Most of our work is."

"All right," I said. "Let's back up a little—I'm very much a layman when it comes to linguistics. What made you think in the first place that the binary transformation of chromosomal code yielded patterns that looked like Indo-European?"

"Ah," Hertzberg said. "That was the relatively easy part. We already have ASCII table renderings of most known human languages, including many long extinct. ASCII and binary configurations are readily transformable into one another. So when we converted the binary chromosomal code to ASCII, its similarity to primal Indo-European in ASCII was noticed right away."

"Yet you don't sound very optimistic." I appreciated the value of a research leader willing to pull in the reins on the wildest fantasies of the team, though personally I preferred someone who jumped on the lead horse and urged it to fly even further.

Hertzberg grunted. "It's the monkeys on a typewriter typing Shakespeare problem. Or maybe sticking a duck's feet in a can of wet red paint, and having it walk across an empty canvas, is a better example. Is that art? It looks like art. But we can't accept it as art, because we know its resemblance to art is just a coincidence. Same with the chromosome code—the fact that it looks like an Indo-European language doesn't mean it is. Sometimes the reason that two words in very distant languages look like each other is just coincidence. If I were pushed for an assessment at this point, I'd have to say that that's what we're dealing with here."

I on the other hand was never a big fan of coincidence. It often was a shorthand gloss, a convenient cover, for significant connections we didn't yet understand. "But if it isn't?"

"Look," Hertzberg sounded like his patience was beginning to wear. "Mapping the genome is much more drudgery than the public imagines it to be. We make a connection here, trace a sequence there, but discovering what each of 300 billion nucleotides can do is a massive undertaking. So we look for relationships, for patterns of expression in the proteins. But even that is slow, slow work. Most of the breaks come from the other direction—not in studying how genes express themselves, but in anchoring an already-known expression, like an illness or a maybe a behavioral pattern, to a genetic combination. Like cystic fibrosis, or depression among some of the Amish. And the DNA outside of the genes is doubly harder to understand, because *its* connection to the phenotype is even more removed—we've got no known illnesses to tag them to."

"Right, no confessed murders to work backwards from," I said.

"What?"

"Just thinking out loud," I said, "Tell me more about the words on the screen. What'd they say?"

"Well, so far, Klein's the only one who's claimed to have actually produced them on the screen. Chaleff was a good worker, but no genius, and if you want my appraisal I'd say he was exaggerating when he told Jenna—"

"Klein? Who's Klein?" I asked.

"Manny Klein—Emmanuel Klein," Hertzberg replied. "He's the one who started this special part of the genome project rolling. He discovered the odd chromosomal material two years ago, made the first transformations into binary, and said he eventually got some text up on his screen."

"You don't believe him?"

"Well—"

"Never mind," I said. No point in going over that ground again. "What did the text actually say?"

"Some kind of history lesson," Hertzberg said. "It wasn't gibberish, but it didn't make much sense. Even had a copyright notice at the end," Hertzberg laughed. "That's why, to be thoroughly frank with you, I keep emphasizing that I have serious doubts that this project will ever pan out. Seems to me a much more likely explanation for what Manny saw on his screen is that his computer somehow dumped some text from another file into what he was working on. It's happened to me from time to time—I once found part of a very personal letter I had written months earlier right in the middle of a grant proposal I was about to print out and FedEx. Damn good thing I caught it in time—"

"I can imagine," I said. "Where can I get in touch with Klein?"

"You can't," Hertzberg said. He paused for a long second, then spoke in a much lower tone of voice. "Look, I know what you'll be thinking when I tell you this. But believe me, the stroke was entirely natural—Manny had a long history of them. And the one he got after discovering this chromosome material was, well, very big. He was out like a light. Seventy-one is too young to die these days, but at least he had a satisfying life."

Hertzberg was right about what I was thinking. A death of one young scientist and I guess I had to go with the Lieutenant: it was most likely murder. The death of two scientists, both working on the same project: jeez, I'd been down twisted paths like that before.

Prospects for Jenna Katen suddenly were looking up.

I couldn't say the same for the rest of the world.

"All right. Who can I speak to for more information about Klein?"

"Jenna's your best bet," Hertzberg answered. "She was Manny's research assistant."

Short-lived reprieve for Jenna. The fickle scales of probability were tipping against her again.

I've always found Neapolitan food to be good accompaniment to the resolution of crises. But I wasn't there yet, not by a long shot. I didn't know enough. I invited Jenna to lunch at Taste of Tokyo in the Village.

I noticed more of her eyes this time. They were an absolutely alluring species of green with flecks of violet. Lucky would be the guy who saw to it that the DNA for those eyes made it into the next generation. But I had more important things to think about right now.

"Glen didn't die of old-fashioned natural causes," Jenna said.

"We agree," I said. "Death by natural causes is a process—like Michael Baden says—you see a history, however subtle, of body breakdown that leads to the circumstances of death. Even in heart attacks and strokes. We found no history like that in Glen. Something else was at work there."

"Who's Michael Baden?" Jenna asked.

"Used to be Chief Medical Examiner in New York City. Testified in the O.J. trial."

"But I didn't kill Glen," Jenna said.

"Well, that's the part that, to be straight with you, we're not as convinced about. If Glen didn't die of natural causes—if the breakdown of just about every major system in his body was triggered by something *un*natural, as it almost certainly had to have been—then the cause of death was accident, suicide, homicide. There are no other choices. We have no evidence, really, that any one of those three more likely happened than the others. But the guy is dead. You were in the room with him. That moves the needle just a bit into the murder part of the meter, with your shade of lipstick, as they say."

Jenna sipped her green tea. I could see her lips quivering around the edges of the hot cup. They had no lipstick on them. Just soft and pink. "I didn't say Glen didn't die of natural causes," she said.

"But—"

"I said he didn't die of *old-fashioned* natural causes," she said.

"Meaning?" I asked.

"I tried to tell you in your office on Tuesday," she said. "Somehow the words on the screen killed him. The words that came from the chromosomal material. I'm not sure how—but that's about as natural a cause of death as you can get—death by DNA, or more accurately, by transformed DNA—algorithms on a screen."

"Is that what killed Emmanuel Klein?"

She blanched. "He wasn't a young man. Everyone says he died of a stroke."

"What do you say?"

She took another sip of the tea, sucked down a gulp. "He died of the same thing as Glen," she said very quietly.

"And you were there both times—or at least working, or involved, with both of them, right?"

She didn't answer.

"Look, you seem like an intelligent, sensitive person. I want to help you—I want to believe you. But you've got to be more open with me. On the face of it, you're in a bad position here. You have a connection with two people who died—one mysteriously, maybe the other mysteriously too. Cops don't like coincidences—they're like red flags to us. There's a common denominator here. And I think you know it."

She got up as if to leave.

"Not a smart move," I took her hand. "Believe me, things can get much worse for you, in a hurry." I sighed. I didn't like badgering her, frightening her, but I had to get through to her. "Ok, let's try a different tack. Why'd you lie to me about not seeing anything on Glen's computer screen?"

"You saw them?" Her eyes were wide.

"Just a fading sliver. Why didn't you tell me?"

She sat down heavily, shaken. "It's personal," she said.

"Obviously—this whole thing is personal. But—"

"No, I mean the words were personal," she said. "I should have told you. I'm sorry. But it was too painful. To think that I— I just couldn't deal with it anymore on Tuesday. I just wanted to leave. I should have told you."

What was she talking about? A Dear John letter on the screen? That's what she thinks killed Glen Chaleff?

"The chromosomal material that Manny and Glen were working on came from me, from my body. My words killed them. My body's the goddamned murder weapon."

The sushi and tempura arrived. I looked at Jenna a long time. "So you're saying you're a—what?—a carrier of some type of genetic code that when transformed into words kills anyone who happens to read it?"

She nodded. "So far I'm the only one—as far as I know. The strange DNA material has been found on eight percent of the X chromosomes we've examined. I told you that. But so far mine's the only one that's been translated all the way into English words."

"How'd you get involved in this to begin with?"

"Manny—Professor Klein—first came across the special DNA in a graduate student at MIT. Standard procedure—lots of students give DNA samples for this kind of research. I'd already given some of mine out at CalTech. Manny put out a request on the Internet—hundreds of scientists around the world were on his list, each already had DNA samples from hundreds of students and locals. Mine came up positive—the special DNA is easy to spot once you know what you're looking for. I wanted an excuse to come back East. I got in touch with Manny and asked if I could join his team. He said sure. He was that kind of man. If I'd known that my DNA would kill him I'd have taken every bit of it back and grabbed the next plane to Antarctica. But even after he died I wasn't sure. I mean, people get strokes. But now it's happened again. This—this *insanity* in my DNA has killed two fine people!" She slammed her fist on the table. The tea in the cups shimmered, along with the tears brimming over her eyes.

I put what I hoped would be a consoling hand on hers. "Have you spelled this out in detail to Hertzberg? Why hasn't he stopped the project?"

"You've talked to him, right? You know what he's like," Jenna said. "He's an Occam's Razor man—he goes for the simplest explanation. He's comfortable with thinking Manny died of a stroke. He'd probably rather believe that I killed Glen with a chemical that left no trace than Glen was somehow killed by the words on the screen. He'll always pick the mundane rather than the exotic. He's a classic example of Kuhn's workaday scientist—don't rock the current paradigm, milk it for all it's worth."

Yeah, that jibed with the impression I already had of the man. Would take a few more bodies in his face before he'd take notice—and by then who knows what kind of genetic demons would be let out of the bag.

"Look, we're really talking in the dark here," I said. "Any chance you made a copy of the, uh, offending words, so I could see what they looked like?"

"No," she said. "They're too dangerous—they already killed two people, for God's sake. I don't want to take the chance—"

"All right," I said. "I understand. But can't you at least summarize the gist of what they say, so I can get some idea of what it is you're talking about?"

She considered, then nodded. "First you scan the exact chemical composition of the chromosomal material. We use a new kind of polyacrylamide to do the electrophoresis, the imaging, if you need to know. Gives an extremely clear image, especially good for small nucleic molecules. And the results, as you know, fall into a clear binary series. Then you transform that series to an ASCII table—and in Manny's case, in Glen's too, they got words..."

"Right. First the Indo-European proto-language, Hertzberg told me, then the tenuous English translation."

Jenna nodded.

"And the translation said?" I asked.

"It comes out to about three paragraphs—"

"Paragraphs?"

"Yeah," she said. "Paragraphs. There was a small amount of null material between sentences, and larger amounts after three groups of sentences. So we called them paragraphs."

"Ok," I said. "Sorry for interrupting. Please go on."

"Well, the sentences talk about how intelligent species can leave their marks in history. How some, like the human species, have left some of their marks in stone, and these have survived. And how these could be easily recognized by other intelligent people—or species.

"We're not really clear whether the word in that paragraph is species or people.

"Then the text continues with what looks like a question:

"But what of species who lack the capacity to work in stone, to leave their records in unchanging media? How might they tell the future about their existence? They might try to leave a marker, a message, in a different kind of stone, a living stone, a medium—a medium over which they had power.

"And the notation of life—as the text seems to put it—was their medium. They must've had the capacity to penetrate our DNA, maybe re-arrange it, and leave this message.

"And the message says it will be passed on from generation to generation, without knowledge of the bearers, and it will therefore last longer than any message carved in non-living stone."

I whistled.

"Wild, I know," Jenna said. "I mean, there are lots of individual words in there that we're not completely sure what the meaning is, but that's our best estimate as to the general sense of it."

"So what are we talking about here? Intelligent pieces of viruses that can penetrate our chromosomes, our DNA, and leave messages for us? Intelligent aliens who were able to perform genetic engineering on our ancestors, and leave their calling card in case we had further business?"

Jenna made a helpless gesture. "That, and every possibility in between," she said. "I don't know. I didn't say they were viruses. I just said that was the thrust of the message they left—in me. I saw it. Twice." Her lips were quivering again.

"All right," I said, and tried to give her a reassuring smile. Though I didn't particularly feel that way. "And was that all there was? That was the entire text on the screen?"

"That's the substance of the message," Jenna said. "There was something more at the end—a sort of notice I guess."

"Tell it to me," I prompted.

She closed her eyes, as if trying to get these words exactly. Apparently she felt they in themselves posed no threat. "Anyone who reads these words, who possesses our codes, is free to use them. As allowed under our Copyright Notice."

"Copyright Notice?" So there it was. I was glad Jenna was at least being honest with me.

She shrugged. "That's what the ASCII translation table printed out in English. The newer approaches try to go for figurative rather than literal translations where possible—they convey the culture with more flair, though increase the likelihood of error. The proto-Indo-European was closer to Proclamation of Possession, or maybe Announcement of Ownership Privileges—I've become an expert on that damn language, already, believe me. Truthfully, we didn't pay all that much attention to that last part. The stuff in the body of the message seemed much more important."

"Hard to believe that some non-human intelligence would share our notion of copyright," I said.

"Harder to believe they could create a code that could be rendered into something that looks anything like Indo-European, and store it in some of our chromosomes," Jenna said. "But there it is. And the sense of property, possession, is very old, biologically."

"You mean like mice pissing—urinating, sorry—to mark their territory?"

"Right," Jenna may have smiled, first time. "And hamsters mark stones near their dens with secretions—ethologists say scent marks are chemical property signs. It's all over the natural world.

Birds, fish, even insects mark and defend their property. And the closer we come to human beings, the more abstract the notion of property becomes. Monkeys, baboons, chimps have all kinds of very complex expressions of property, aggressively excluding this or that member of the troop, family, whatever from the privileged circle of users."

"So maybe the authors of your text were human," I said.

"Well, could be," Jenna said, "And who really knows what people—any species—were really capable of seven or eight thousand years ago."

"That's the first sign of Indo-European in human history?" I asked.

Jenna nodded. "Nostratic supposedly goes back even further—more than 12,000 years—and has some resemblance to Indo-European, but its existence is still hotly contested. Anyway," she took another sip of tea, with steadier hands this time, "the chromosomal algorithms print out like Indo-European, or something very close to it."

"How do we know the linguistic DNA wasn't inserted into the genome more recently?" I asked.

"We don't—not for sure," Jenna said. "But the eight percent of X chromosomes with the odd material comes from people all over the world, many way off the track of usual scientific research. Doubtful that an insertion of recent vintage could have that kind of in-depth dispersion. No, I think we're on reasonable ground assuming that the authors of the text, whoever or whatever they were, were contemporaries of early Indo-European. Our problem then becomes how to account for such early people—if they were people—having any sort of gene-insertion technology. But like I was saying—like the message itself says—all we really know of the distant past is what has come down to us in obvious long-lasting media like stone, bone, petrified wood. People in Asia probably did things that would surprise us in bamboo, but all that's disintegrated now. I don't find it impossible to consider that some early human group, speakers and writers of an Indo-European root language, found a way to manipulate DNA. Even non-literate groups show enormous sophistication in deliberate breeding of animals and plants. And if our Indo-European gene-authors could do that, inserting a message that could play out on today's computers doesn't seem impossible either—DNA and computer codes operate in similar ways, both prescribe patterns of organization. Adleman's already demonstrated that DNA in a test-tube can be used to compute solutions for mathematical problems. And they just had to do it once—encode their message into DNA and attach it to the X chromosome just once—all it required was one fluorescence of their culture. The knowledge to do this could have come and gone all in one or two hundred years. And after that the natural process of DNA replication would see that the message would live on and on. That's the beauty—and the horror—of it. We have in DNA the most effective of all known replicative devices."

"Your perception is impressive, for someone—"

"For someone just a few years out of grad school? For someone so young? Not really. This is my *life*. I guess in more ways than one."

"I know," I said. "That's the problem with most of these quests to understand who we are, where we were, where we're going, isn't it? Sooner or later all the fine science boils down to lives at stake." I closed my eyes, opened them, focused entirely on Jenna's face. "Until we can relate what that prehistoric Stephen Jay Gould or whoever wrote, connect that to Glen Chaleff's body falling apart, maybe Manny Klein's too, your life is the one at stake here in the short run. Doesn't matter how appealing your DNA-to-Indo-European-ASCII hypothesis is, the cops won't care. They'll come after you for Chaleff's death. And in the long run...," I shuddered, "well, if something in those words killed Chaleff and Klein, then who knows how many others are at risk."

"You believe in my work, then?" Jenna asked, for an instant

more pleased to have an ally in her adventures in knowledge than frightened about where that knowledge might be taking her.

"Let's just say I have a very open mind." But the truth was my mind was set—on finding a way out for her.

"Two people are dead," Jenna said. "There has to be a connection."

The Lieutenant informed me the next morning about a connection that didn't work to Jenna's benefit at all. "Chaleff was dipping the wick with a blonde. Going on for at least a few weeks. Three witnesses saw Katen throw a glass of wine in his face and scream at him about it at a party week before last. There's the motive."

"Yeah? And how exactly did she do it? With a magic wand?"

"That's for you to find out, Doc."

I called Jenna and asked if I could come over. She lived in a new highrise in the West Village. She obviously had money.

Her face flushed when I told her about the witnesses at the party. "So what?" she said. "Lots of people fool around, lots of people scream and yell at each other. Doesn't mean I killed him, for crissakes."

"I'm more concerned that you didn't tell me," I said.

"What? You want a complete exposition of my life? You want a calendar of every fight I had with Glen?"

"No," I said. "Look, this isn't going well for you. I tried to tell you that yesterday. Cops are like hounds moving in concentric circles—once they get a sniff of the quarry, they go round and around, tighter and tighter, until they close in totally and arrest you. And don't believe the movies and TV shows—once they arrest you your chances are not very good. You're near the pit now. You've got momentum against you. We've got to come up with some sort of evidence of what you're talking about, soon, or the situation may be out of my control."

"What kind of evidence?" Jenna asked. "I've already told you what I know."

"Real evidence," I said. "Not just your rendition of the words on the screen. I'm talking about firing up your computer, putting a disk with a binary map of the chromosome stuff in the drive, running the ASCII/Indo-European transformation, and videotaping that whole process including everything on the screen."

"And then what? Running it on HBO as America Under Cover and killing the millions of people who watch it?"

"Well, if it came to that, I could probably get some prisoners on some death row to volunteer to read it, but I don't think reading it can kill anybody."

"Why not?" Jenna asked.

"Well, for starters, you obviously looked at it and you're still alive. And I saw the words 'Copyright Notice' and I'm still in peak condition."

"That was just one phrase," Jenna said.

"Of course," I said. "But your survival and my survival certainly suggest that whatever's going on with the text, just reading it isn't ipso facto lethal."

"So where are you headed then? Back to proving by process of elimination that *I* killed Glen?"

"No, I don't think that either. All I'm saying is that something more than just looking at a screen is the culprit here."

"What, then?" Jenna asked.

"I have an idea," I said. "But first things first. Can your computer handle the ASCII transformation?"

Jenna nodded.

"I assume you have some of the binary codes from your, ah, biological system available on disk?"

She nodded again. "I already have the Indo-European proto-language rendition of my DNA message on disk. Part of this phase of the research was to see if more than one programmer could come up with the same English words independently."

"Ok. Then all that needs to be done is the final translation into English. I brought this new little camcorder along with me from my office—I can set it up right there in the corner." I slipped the three-pound wafer out of my briefcase. "How long would it take you to get the words on the screen?"

Jenna was hunched over her computer, totally enmeshed in her work. She jabbed a key and leaned back, hands clasped around the back of her neck. "About 7/8ths complete at this point," she said. She had that look of total satisfied absorption I'd seen many times in faces of researchers.

"Good. The camcorder's all set to record, the printer looks good too." I fiddled with the paper tray one more unnecessary time. Paper—marvelous invention. I didn't like the tendency of those words on the screen to fade, and I never put one hundred percent trust in any camera. A paper printout was just the ticket to give me a reliable permanent record of those words.

"You're sure you want to go through with this?" Jenna asked, her expression suddenly changed. The larger realities apparently were still very understandably pressing her.

"I'm sure," I said.

"You know it's possible that the reason that I read it, and haven't been harmed, is that the DNA source code is mine..."

"Possible, yes. Lots of things are possible. But I think the key point here is that Manny and Glen did something more than read it. I can't imagine that just *reading* some words on a screen could kill—"

She shook her head. "I really don't think we should go on with this."

I could see she was working herself up—

"I mean," she continued, "even from my selfish point of view, if you die here, with me right next to you, there'll be no way the police won't believe that I killed you. And even if that wasn't the case, I don't want you to die—"

"I've already taken care of that," I said. "I left an outline of my theories about this case in my desk before I came here today. If something should happen to me, the Lieutenant will read that and you'll be in the clear. You've got to trust me on this."

"I *do* trust you," Jenna said. "I like you—that's why I don't want you to die. I mean—"

"No one's going to die," I said. "I'm not going to be sitting there staring at the screen like a wide-eyed lamb when the words come up. We'll be in the other room. The video recorder will start automatically. The words will print out on the laserjet. Whatever killed Glen and Manny, it surely wasn't the meaning of the words—you've already recited that to me—it had to have been some kind of energy that was generated from the computer, released somehow along with the words. I've been saying that I don't think that just reading the words released that energy—I don't see how it could. But even if it did, there's no way that energy could be carried along to a simple printout on paper."

Jenna still looked doubtful. "What about the video tape?"

"We won't look at it directly—I'll use the digital scan to confirm that something was in fact recorded, then get it over to the lab for further testing."

"I don't know," she said.

"Jenna, I'm appealing to you not only as a woman who may need this evidence to save her own freedom, maybe even her life, but as someone who cherishes the pursuit of knowledge. You and your colleagues started this. Who knows what lessons this DNA message may ultimately hold for the human species? We've got to see this through."

She sighed, shaking her head, but she swayed back to the computer. I could see her body, first limp and sagging, now energized and vibrant as she returned her full attention to the work on the screen. "We should have the text up here any minute now," she said. "The program will beep 30 seconds before the words all become clear on the screen, so that'll give you enough time to get into the next room. Don't be like Lot's damn wife—make sure you don't turn around and peek at the screen."

The camcorder clicked and whirred into action.

The phone rang. "Should I get it?" I asked.

Jenna motioned yes.

"Hello? D'Amato. Phil. Fine, thanks. Uh huh. I see. Jeez—How? Ok. I understand. Of course I will. I'll be back to you."

The computer beeped. "Words are on the screen in 30 seconds," Jenna turned and announced with a mixture of triumph and trembling.

"That was Hertzberg on the phone," I said.

"What's he found? Anything of interest?" Jenna rose from her chair.

"Someone else on the project died—of 'natural' causes. Denise Richter. You know her?"

"Of course I know her," Jenna sobbed like someone stuck by a knife. "Of course I do. I didn't know her well but—for God's sake, how'd it happen this time?"

"Same as the last two," I said. "At least you're off the hook now on the murder charge."

"Oh God. I just thought of something."

"What?" I said.

"Denise was using my genetic material. Glen told me the batch she'd been working on had been accidentally ruined—the stain was too strong—so he sent her some of his stock, which was mine... Oh god." Now not only her lips but her entire body was quivering.

"It's ok," I said, and I put my hand on her shoulder to calm her. "Hertzberg's putting a halt on the project. That's why he was calling you. I guess he has the requisite number of bodies now—"

"And I'm gonna put an end to *this*," Jenna cried out, and I saw her hand reach down to the keyboard.

My hand shot out in reflex, faster than Jenna's. I caught her wrist in midair, jerked it away from the keyboard. "Don't," I said. "We've got to go through with this."

"Are you crazy?" she screamed. "How many more dead do you want?" And her fists were pummeling my chest, unclenching into hands that were frantically trying to push me away, break free so she could get to the keyboard and prevent the words from getting on the screen, maybe erase all the crucial preparatory work on her hard disk as well.

But I set my arms firmly around her body and moved her out of the way. And I had a clear view of the screen.

And God help me, I couldn't stop myself.

I looked and read.

Jenna's voice came to me and said, "Are you ok?"

The words on the screen were as Jenna had described them in the restaurant. Down to that peculiar copyright notice that I had seen a fragment of in Glen Chaleff's apartment, and Jenna had quoted verbatim to me in the restaurant.

"Anyone who reads these words, who possesses our codes, is free to use them. As allowed under our Copyright Notice."

"Are you ok?" Jenna asked again. "How do you feel?" And I could see she was staring at me intently.

"So far, so good," I said. "Just the usual hunger rumblings in my stomach."

Jenna continued to stare at me, as if keeping me in the crystal clear focus of her green violet eyes would prevent me from dying.

"I'm ok, really," I said. "I'm sorry I had to shove you out of the way." Actually, my body wasn't—she'd felt very good with my arms around her. But that was hardly the point.

"Oh God," she put her arms around me and pulled herself close. Professional, think professional, I thought. She's still officially a subject in a murder investigation, though I knew she wasn't guilty. I controlled myself to the point of allowing myself just one or two strokes of her soft brown hair. "I'm so glad you're ok," she said, crying. "What am I? Some sort of goddamn Typhoid Mary of an ancient genetically engineered curse?"

"No," I said. "This isn't a disease—even though I said virus the other day. I mean, it could be a virus, it could be some early advanced variant of the human species, hell, it could be aliens from outerspace like I said. The point is that whatever, whoever rigged this booby trap, was an intelligence. And disease isn't intelligent. Deadly sometimes, yes. But not intelligent. And this isn't a curse either. We're dealing with fact here, hard science, not magic—something in your DNA. And that's about as real a reality of life as you can get. You know that."

"But what's the booby trap?" Jenna asked, pulling herself away and drying her eyes. "You're still alive. Even though Manny and Glen and now Denise..." She shook her head.

"The answer has to be in the words on the screen—the last two sentences if I'm right. The words of course are not exact—how could they be? Hertzberg says you have no way of confirming the accuracy of the transformation. He's right in terms of the usual modes of linguistic confirmation. They can confirm the accuracy of the Indo-European to English part, but not the initial chromosome—ASCII to Indo-European part. How could they? It's never been done before. We're in a technological variant of Plato's Meno paradox here—you have to already have knowledge to recognize, to validate, potential knowledge, so where does the first knowledge come from? But the chromosome ASCII looks like Indo-European—not like Chinese or Korean. So, ok, it may just coincidence, like Hertzberg thought, but let's assume it *is* Indo-European, or related to it, and proceed from there. Where does that lead us? Hertzberg says there's a high noise component. But no reason to think it's evenly distributed throughout every word in the message. Some of the text on the screen may be way off from its original meaning, some may be right on the money. How do we tell which is which? What does the evidence suggest?"

Jenna held her hands up in an I-don't-know gesture.

"Well," I continued, "we've got three fatalities now as evidence. What part of the text could they possibly relate to? I don't see anything in the history lesson, fascinating as it is, that could be the culprit. But I do see a possible suspect at the end—in the copyright notice. As allowed under our Copyright Notice.' Let's assume the noise in that section of the text is low. Let's assume that Copyright Notice, or something close to it, is an accurate rendition. Now: Seen in that light, maybe the deaths make sense as punishment for what's *not* allowed under their notions of property."

"What's not allowed under copyright?" Jenna asked. She cast a sideways look at the screen. I followed her gaze. The words were mostly gone now.

"Let's think about what *is* allowed, first," I said. "The text says it's all right to use' the words, or maybe to use the codes'. What does that mean? How do we use printed words?"

"We read them?" Jenna asked.

"Yes," I said. "And that seems to be ok—at least for me. I read the words and I'm ok. And I have no special connection to these words. They didn't come from my chromosomes."

Jenna nodded and looked at me, still not completely convinced that I would *be* ok.

"All right," I said. "So let's get to the codes'. How would we use' genetic codes?"

"Well, the most common way is we have sex, reproduce, and the codes create new versions of us. And the codes within our cells create new cells, as long as we're alive."

"Right," I said. "And that seems ok too. I mean, people reproduce all the time, right, and few seem to die of mysterious natural causes. Most people's cells reproduce ok too, for at least most of their lives. For that matter, Adleman used real DNA codes for his computations—I pulled some summaries of his work off the Net last night— and he's all right. Though presumably he didn't use yours."

"True," Jenna said, not in any mood for my humor. "So where does that leave us?"

"Where it leaves us is at a clearer answer to the question you just asked: What do those words on the screen forbid? Not reading the instructions. Not implementing the instructions—not implementing the genetic codes. Those things are ok. We're free' to do them. We can use the words and the codes. But what is that Notice saying, in some sort of implicit way, that we *can't* do? What does a copyright notice seek to protect against?"

"Plagiarism? Theft of intellectual property?" Jenna asked.

"Yes," I said, "but those wrongs seem too subtle for what's going on here. The proscription has to be against something much more basic—more common. Something that Klein and Chaleff and Richter all did, no doubt in all innocence. Something that people do almost without thinking with computers all the time."

Jenna held her hands up in frustration. "What?"

"Do you have a way of automatically making a copy of a file on your computer? You know, giving the command to copy in some sort of delayed way that would allow us to walk out of the room while the copying was taking place—rather than staring at the screen, or being anywhere near it?"

"Well sure," Jenna said. "I can put the copy command at the end of a command chain—a long chain—that would definitely give us time to get out of the room. But—"

"OK, well could you do that right now then—for the chromosome text on the screen and its underlying program?"

"You think that making a *copy* of this triggered everything off?" Jenna asked, disbelievingly. "Making a copy killed Glen and Manny—and Denise?"

"Well, it's a copyright notice, isn't it? And making copies is precisely what DNA is all about."

She entered the delayed command string in the computer, and we walked quickly into the next room. I told her not to look anywhere near the computer screen. We looked at the opposite wall—at the hand-me-down shadows of Plato's cave, like dogs baying at the moon—and saw nothing. No effect at all. A brief play of light on the blue wall, like heartbeat of a photocopy, maybe, and that was it. The paint didn't even so much as peel.

But the camcorder, which presumably had been recording all this time, made a sharp whining noise and flashed an erratic red light. I turned it off manually, and did a digital scan of the tape. "Goddamnit. That pulse or whatever it was must've erased the whole tape. We've got nothing here."

"What now?" Jenna asked, very tiredly.

"We call in the mice," I said.

A half hour later, my friend Johnny Novino from the Berg Institute at the NYU Medical Center—an animal research lab—arrived with a cartload of white mice.

"What are they for?" he asked.

"You wouldn't believe me if I told you, so I won't," I answered. "And I'd rather you didn't know anything beforehand, so you can conduct a completely unbiased examination if need be."

"Figures," he said, gave Jenna a wink, and he left.

We set up a pair of mice in a cage in front of the screen, and Jenna entered the delayed copy command. We hurried out of the room, and saw the same light kiss on the wall.

But for the mice, it was the kiss of death.

We repeated the act ten times, and produced twenty dead rodents.

"Was that really necessary?" Jenna asked.

"Yeah," I said. "I don't like this anymore than you, but we've got to have redundancy to really pinpoint the exact cause of death here. Better them than us."

"Poor little things couldn't even read the damn text," Jenna said, then rushed into the bathroom and threw up.

The lab report came back five days later.

"Phil, you know about circadian rhythms?" Johnny returned my call about the report.

"Well, as much as the next guy," I said. "They control our waking and sleeping patterns, and are governed in some way by light. They seem to affect the brain's sleep center through the optic nerve."

"That's right," Johnny said. "So what seems to have happened to your little mice is some stimulus, likely some kind of light, switched their circadian rhythm to infinite awake—as in impossibly high blood pressure, instant heart failure, instant everything failure, adios muchachos."

"And your evidence for that?"

"Like the report says," Johnny replied. "Incredibly high residues of serotonin—natural chemical found in the brain, contributes to the sense of wide awakeness, well-being, also raises the blood pressure."

"So at least the mice died with a smile in their hearts," I said, and filled him in on all the details.

"Jeez," Johnny said. "Likely Glen Chaleff died of that too, then. But your guys must've missed it because serotonin's a natural compound, on no one's list as an abused drug. We missed it too on the first six mice. But there's no doubt about it now. So my best guess for the full trajectory—assuming you didn't administer serotonin to the mice yourself—is light provokes extreme circadian reaction, causing huge overdose of serotonin, causing lethally high blood pressure, causing heart attack and general system failure across the board. The only real mystery here is what the hell kind of light could do that?"

"We're working on it," I said.

"But how could a people eight thousand years ago know how

The Copyright Notice Case 99

to make our current computers emit a fatal light?" Jenna asked over dinner at my favorite Italian restaurant the next evening.

"I don't know," I said. "But that's no more a puzzle than that they could insert a special binary code in some of our chromosomes that could read out ASCII Indo-European—and you've been willing to believe that. We don't understand the relationship of electricity to light in anything like its entirety even now. Maybe they did—or at least knew something we don't yet. Maybe they had some kind of organic computers—that ran on DNA algorithms like Adleman's math calculator—except rather than solving equations they caused electrons to form light patterns that in turn controlled circadian rhythms."

"Lots of primitive people understand circadian rhythms," Jenna said. "I can believe that. And the DNA computers—"

"Rotted away," I said. "Or maybe they're in us. Who knows."

"Their media were life and light," Jenna said, "more ephemeral, but also much more lasting, than just plain stone."

And the red wine came and we both got good and drunk...

Some things are too bizarre for me ever to put in a public record—not if I want to keep my job.

Hertzberg called an end to that small project within a project, but Jenna's going on. She and I contacted all of the original researchers, explaining our theories to them. Most thought we were nuts, a few believed us. Doesn't matter if they believe us or not—the important thing is that those who pursue this aren't likely to risk making a copy of the text any time soon. We can't do anything more than alert them—to the enormous possibilities of this research as well as its dangers. The rest is up to them.

The problem is we don't have any evidence. Videotapes, motion photography—all equipment seems to be blind to that deadly little light, able neither to transmit nor record it. We can make no record of what happens when Jenna's chromosome text is copied, no record of that thin bright thread that's emitted. Puts a crimp in any research program.

And we of course have no copies of the text. Videotapes, photographs of the screen, endless printouts—they all come out blank too, as innocent of DNA and Indo-European as the driven snow. The lethal light hadn't erased the video-recording that first time; the recording hadn't occurred to begin with.

"What kind of words can appear on a computer screen and defy recording, printing, on any other piece of equipment?" Jenna had asked.

"Maybe the kind that kills you if you try to copy them," I'd replied. "Maybe the words don't really exist on the screen at all. Maybe the program somehow projects them right onto our optic nerve."

But the corpses existed all right. Three good people, and a pile of who knows how many rodents now. They, ironically, were the sole proof that the ASCII derived from the DNA not only looked like Indo-European, but was Indo-European or something much like it—stark confirmation that at least some of those words meant what they said. Jenna thinks that might be enough to give us a shot of getting something published, maybe in one of the fringier scientific journals.

We—Jenna—stumbled upon something, yes. A primordial copy protection scheme. A copy protection technique from Hell. DNA as ultimate shareware: *use* this little program to your heart's content, enjoy it, be fruitful and multiply with it, implement it—let it implement you—but don't copy the words without authorization. Not unlike many of our own computer programs—and books—really. Except authorization to copy the Indo-European DNA text has likely been quite impossible to get for something going on eight thousand years or more.

I guess I was able to see this when Jenna didn't because, well, my job is always at the intersection of science and the law, of life and property and the canons for its protection. And this canon was effective, I'll give at least that to its authors.

Who were they? They apparently left their message in in the far reaches of some eight percent of human X chromosomes, their precious copyright notice in who knows what fraction of those. Maybe they were in some way responsible for setting the human species on the course it took.

Why would they attach such a deadly penalty to a violation of their notice? In that they were no different than organisms throughout the animal kingdom ready to protect their turf by deadly force. Jeez, didn't I read just last week that even some trees emit a resin that kills any insects that trod too heavily on their bark.

Only further research will tell. And that, obviously, Jenna and her colleagues will have to be do exceedingly carefully. Like they were researching a deadly new virus.

In the meantime, we'll just have to take what pleasures with our DNA we more or less safely can. Those we are "free" to enjoy...

I ran my hand against the skin of Jenna's back. She lay sleeping on my chest. She'd been cleared of all charges—Denise's death had seen to that—she was no longer a suspect in any way.

I often wondered if somehow hers was the only one of the eight percent of the X chromosomes that not only had the binary DNA material, but the DNA that yielded that brief meditation on modes of preservation, along with the copyright notice. Not likely, I guess. Further research would answer that question too.

But in the meantime, the sensible course would be to assume that Jenna was the only one. She was the only one we knew about. And if that was so, then my responsibility to the human genome, the human species, was to see that Jenna's special DNA survived. Not only in frozen storage, which Jenna had already taken care of, but in actual in situ living usage—the far more reliable and time-honored way of getting DNA into the future.

I of course knew, in spite of what I had told her that day in her apartment when we'd first glimpsed the light, that what she carried in her DNA was indeed both a blessing and a curse—a blessing in terms of the knowledge about our very origins that it could hold, a curse in terms of the price that three unknowing people had already paid in quest for that wisdom. A mechanism of beauty and horror, as Jenna had said herself. But to the degree that it was a blessing, I had to help it survive.

Yes, until further research could sort all of this out, I was willing to do my part to insure that the text she carried was passed on to future generations in its original form, where minds wiser than ours might come to better understand it, plumb it for its secrets, and neutralize its deadly penalties.

After all, the lethal qualities of the DNA she carried didn't extend to reproduction. That, the copyright notice said, she was free to do.

I was prepared to help her do just that.

I moved my head over and kissed her face.

After all, I was a forensic scientist, but a scientist first, and though I'd pretty much reached the limits of my capacity to contribute to the ongoing research here, that didn't mean that I'd shirk my responsibility to help the subject of the research live on.

That, and I so enjoyed looking into Jenna's green violet eyes when they were happy...

The Protected

She didn't *look* like an android. That's what made it so damn hard.

Most androids—however totally their expression, their behavior, simulates a human's—have something that gives them away. Some micron of a difference in the angle of their eyes as they squint past the sun, in the flare of their nostrils when you make a bad joke, shows you immediately that you're dealing with something not human.

But not Shara. Maybe that's why they wanted so badly to kill her. Maybe that's why I felt about her things that could get in the way of my job to protect her—could addle my reason with a spike of emotion at the wrong time...

"You see, it's something I call the paradox of the android in our popular culture," Mark Wolfson, the best of my advisors, was speaking. "If you go back to the beginning, to the *Star Trek* and *Twilight Zone* videos a hundred years ago, you find that the androids are of course played by human actors—because of course there were no androids then. And this warped everyone's expectations about androids from the start—when people envision androids, even now, they see the human actors who portray them, and this obviously is quite a different thing from real androids, whatever they are. And that's one of the reasons that real androids make everyone so uncomfortable."

"Makes the Blood Party want to kill them," I added.

Wolfson nodded. "They're religious fanatics, of course. But they express a deep-rooted public opinion, and they're highly intelligent, as you know from your briefings. They'll watch her constantly, like they did with the others, and at the first moment of vulnerability, the first time you relax, they'll come at you."

"You still sure that it doesn't make sense to get her to some more remote place—Antarctica, or off-planet all together—where she'll be harder to reach?"

Wolfson shook his head. "I'm not sure of anything. The President's sure. The Committee's sure. They think Shara would only be more conspicuous in an uncrowded place. And they want to smoke out the BPs in a place where they can be traced back to their leaders. So we make our stand now here, in the heart of New York City, a half a mile from the Tappan Zee, with you and Shara trying to live like two normal people, going about your business like everyone else." I thought I saw a tear glisten in the corner of Wolfson's reconstructed eye. "Shara's the last—at least from me," he said. "I can't build any more. And no one else has my touch..." He turned away, regarded some far wall of the office. "They blinded me, my eyes have been regrown, I'm told I should have 100-percent good vision, maybe I do, I don't know, maybe it's psychological, but I just don't see the same. It's different. I can't build anymore."

"You're lucky you're still alive," I said.

"Luck? No—human life is sacred to the BP. That's what they're all about. They'd never deliberately kill a human being, even me... Yeah, maybe I am lucky at that—a human being lucky enough to know that he'll never be able to create anything as beautiful as his last creation. All I can do now is talk."

I put my hand on his shoulder. "You love her too," I said.

"I'm her father," he said.

She taught a course in American history at the Tarrytown-borough campus of Polytechnic University. The course and the campus weren't much—"live theater of education" was the sign on the lone building—with more than 95 percent of higher education conducted through sundry online networks. But even such low-profile professoring was dangerous, by my lights. Her name was in some catalog somewhere as teacher of this course. Why couldn't she have taken a totally anonymous job someplace, as a waitress or a gardener?

"They want to smoke out the BPs," I heard Wolfson's voice say to me again. Yeah—and that requires something a little more out there than totally anonymous.

I eyed the class as I walked in. Shara was finishing up for the evening. They seemed innocent enough, stroking their screens with one last note, joking and laughing at someone's expense, usually some long-dead American President in a course like this.

Any one of these people could be a fanatic bent on killing Shara.

"Hi baby." Shara reached up on her toes to kiss me. I'm tall—a plus in my profession, so you can see over the crowds. But my clients don't often call me "baby"—usually "Jack," sometimes "Mr. B.," for Bellman, like ringing a bell...

"Hi," I said, and permitted myself one quick stroke of her soft brown hair.

The sound of someone's throat clearing interrupted whatever I was about to say next. "Uhm, Shara," a blond guy, maybe 25, said. "Can I ask you a question about the report?"

"Of course," Shara replied.

I stepped back—to get a better view of the guy, as well as give them some space. The rest of the class was at or out the door already. This would be a prime opportunity for a quick slash.

"... so the problem I have is when Gore...," the guy was talking. His hands were in his pockets, screen closed and pressed against his side—not much he could do except with his mouth, and Shara was immune to every known projectile poison.

He finished explaining his problem. Shara gave him some bearings. He thanked her, looked apologetically at me, and left.

"I'm starving," she said and smiled at me. "How about some Station?"

"Sure," I said. Station food—supposedly an outgrowth of cuisine recently concocted on Mars Station—was all the rage these days.

I looked at Shara as she sipped her wine and talked at me. I was still amazed at how human she looked when she ate, drank, did anything we associate with the biological part of our being.

Oh, I knew the science behind it, of course. Every part of her body, except her brain, was grown from recombinant DNA. That meant her circulation, her respiration, digestion—and, yes, the physical part of her sexuality—was no different from that of a human being who had come to be via the old-fashioned way.

So why bother about androids at all, if they're not really any different from people? Why bother to make them? Why try to kill them?

All because of that one big exception—the brain. It defied being grown from recombinant DNA. Or rather, it could be grown all right, but it functioned nothing like a brain, except on the most primitive levels. Little more than a glorified spine, really.

And necessity was in this case truly the mother of invention. What couldn't be grown biologically could be constructed siliconically—well, more than silicon, but silicon was still the guts of it. The stuff of which circuits are made. Circuits which could be programmed to do much more than human brains—

"Hey, are you listening to anything I've been saying?" Shara asked, as a servomech interrupted her train of talk with our food.

"Sure, you were, ah..."

"Yes?" she pressed.

"Ok," I admitted. "I wasn't thoroughly paying attention."

"You never do," Shara said angrily, shovelling the food in her mouth. "I was saying something important—"

"Look, I'm sorry," I said. "But I've got your safety to think about."

"You're *choking* me with your concern for my safety. That ever occur to you?" She was getting angrier, and looked like she might choke on her food.

"Take it easy. I said I was sorry," I said.

"You're concerned about my safety?" she said, loudly. "Then

why don't you listen to what I say when I talk to you? I was telling you that I've decided to go to that conference next week."

"What? I don't think that's a good idea at all—way too much exposure."

She laid her fork deliberately down, so it rang on the table, and got up to leave. "I just spent the last 10 minutes explaining to you why it would be ok. Enjoy your dinner." She stalked away with a flourish.

"Wait!" I called after her, but she walked out the door. This wasn't the first time I had seen it demonstrated that she was all too capable of anger. I turned quickly to the table mike, pressed it into activation. "Ok on all the charges, 40 percent tip, please wrap our food and I'll be back to pick it up in five minutes." And I rushed out the door—

Just in time to see another vehicle smash into mine, and its driver emerge to confront Shara.

"Back off, buddy," I said as calmly as I could. "It was an accident, we're sorry for any way in which my vehicle may have contributed, we'll reimburse you fully for any damages." How my vehicle could have contributed in any way, being fully stationary, was beyond me, but that was hardly the point. I wanted Shara safely in the car, and this guy out of our faces as soon as possible.

It wasn't to be.

He wheeled around, obviously drunk, from Shara to me. Another bozo who'd managed to outprogram the drunk restraint on the manual override. Crystal clear now, how he'd come to smash into my vehicle. Though there was always the possibility that the drunk was an act, that he hadn't managed to override anything after all...

"—Oh yeah?" he was saying. "You gonna compensate me? How are you gonna compensate me for my *time*, the *aggravation*? Your car's ass stuck out so far I'd have to be on the moon to avoid it." He looked back at Shara. "Speaking of asses...," he made a wide groping swing in her direction—his hand no more than a foot or two away from her.

Shara was frozen. She had no physical aggression in her. Wolfson said it wasn't her programming explicitly, it was just the way the anger mechanism in her brain somehow didn't interface with her body.

"Look, just step back, we'll compensate you for your time and aggravation." I moved closer, as casually as possible. My hand was on my weapon.

"Aw, what's the matter, you don't like me looking at your little princess in this way," he said with thick, mock solicitude. "Here princess, I got just the thing for you—"

He reached into his pocket.

I had time for just one move. No mistakes. Had to be right the first time. I blew his whole arm off with one blast.

He staggered backward, bottle of booze that he held in the hand of his severed arm now smashing on the street.

Shara cried out.

He fell, smashing his head on the newly cobblestoned curb.

My arms were around Shara. I ushered her into the car.

I called the local police, and knelt down to check his condition. I sighed. His brain was shattered, blood oozing like the booze from the bottle. Brains were the one thing they couldn't reconstruct. I'd killed him—when goddamn rudeness was likely his only crime.

I had the *authority* to kill him, no doubt about that—the Committee's damn writ, available to any cop on any screen, clearly stated that I was empowered and urged to err on the side of using any force necessary to stop a potential assassin. But that didn't make me feel any better inside for taking this slob's life.

I got into the vehicle and looked at Shara. "The cops'll be here any minute," I said. "Now you see why I don't want you to go to that conference."

"It was Mark's idea," Shara said, and burst out crying. "That's what I was trying to tell you."

"You want to tell me how going to a conference on Cape Cod, exposing Shara to a whole new cast of characters, makes any sense at all here?" I demanded of Wolfson the very next day.

"The idea is she lives her life like a normal person."

"Bullshit," I said. "What the hell happened to making our stand right here in New York? Normal people live quite normal lives without going to conferences on the bay at Cape Cod."

"Was I the one who programmed the Society of Historians of the Americas to hold their annual conference there this year?" Wolfson retorted.

I glared at him. That didn't answer my question about why Shara had to go, and he knew it.

He returned my glare, then looked away. "They want to bring this to a head," he finally said, very quietly.

"What?"

"You heard me," he answered.

"They want to do what? Set Shara up to be killed?" I rasped.

"They want to draw the BP out," Wolfson said. "Justice apparently has the whole kit and kaboodle of them ready to fall, if only they can be tied to an actual attempt at killing Shara."

"And I'm supposed to be the difference between the mere attempt to kill Shara, and their actually killing her?"

Wolfson smiled, without joy. "Apparently. We all have faith in you."

"You said you love her, for crissakes. And you're just willing to go along with this?"

"I'm not a factor," Wolfson said. "It'll happen whether I want it to or not. Anyway, Shara understands the risks, and wants to go. She says she doesn't want to live the rest of her life, whatever that may be, with this group of nutcases after her. She wants this to end, one way or another."

"She's not competent to make a decision like that," I said. "Jeez, she's just—"

"An android?" Wolfson said. "So you're saying that as an android, she's not entitled to exercise her free will?"

I shook my head. "Don't try to tie me up with your philosophy. I'll tell you one thing. *I* have free will, and no one can force *me* to go. Who's gonna protect Shara then?"

"I'm glad to hear it—that you have free will," Wolfson said. "But I think that, when you exercise it, you will indeed go."

"How's that?" I said.

"Because Shara's going whether you and I like it or not."

"We'll see," I said, and turned to walk out.

"And if Shara goes, you'll be there all right," Wolfson said. "I have complete confidence in that."

"That's so?" I turned around. "What makes you so sure?"

"You love her," Wolfson said.

Shara snuggled up to me, her body naked and still vibrant in the afterglow. To say Shara was better than any human women was an understatement—truth is, I couldn't even remember what it felt like to be with another woman since I'd been making love to Shara.

"You still awake, baby?" she asked.

"Yeah." I smiled, and stroked her head.

"You thinking about tomorrow?" she asked.

"Can't help it," I said. "I just can't understand why, with all the other androids killed, they'd want to risk you like this. Doesn't make sense to me."

Shara kissed the soft underside of my chin, grazed her fingers along my breast. "I think the other androids all being killed is why they want to risk this," she said softly. "They felt they had to try something different—to break out of the cycle—so androids were not just sitting ducks anymore."

She had a wonderful way of distancing herself from these very events that were life-and-death to her—talking about androids as if she wasn't one of them, just as vulnerable. I wished I had that ability.

"I can't be sure I'll able to protect you," I finally said, and immediately regretted it. No point in burdening her further with my fears—we were here, and there was no backing out now. Maybe she'd already fallen asleep.

"Mmm...," she murmured. "You'll be fine..."

An in-person academic conference has to be one of the biggest security nightmares imaginable. An endless procession of "I read your text online," "Didn't I see you at the holo-meeting last year," and the like from people jostling elbow to elbow, drinks and who knew what else in hand, each with a long boring story to tell, more than enough time to get in a kill. Any one or more of them could be BP—the fact that Shara and even I were familiar with a few of them was no help—you can't know for sure that someone is Blood Party until actual blood has been spilled, as the saying goes. All I had going on our side were my instincts and reflexes.

The two days passed pretty much without incident—the closest call was some professor from Kansas who'd had too much port, and was making a pest of himself with Shara. She'd handled that fine—my fingers only touched my weapon once.

"Can we go for a little walk on the beach?" Shara asked me at the end of the second day. "They say it's spectacular on the bayside at sunset—not many places on the East Coast you can look out over the water and see the sun go down."

A perfect place for a killing, I thought. "We're still not out of the woods yet," I said. "We can see sunsets other times."

Her face darkened. "So the kind of life I have to lead deprives me of the simple pleasure of seeing the sun set in the flesh on Cape Cod Bay. I bet you've seen it lots of times already."

"I haven't." I looked at her rich brown eyes. God, if that wasn't a soul shining through them, every bit as real as mine, whatever that was, longing for experience, longing for life, looking for sunsets, then nothing else in this universe was real. "Ok," I said. "But just a short walk. And we leave as soon as the sun goes down. I don't want you out there in the dark—my infra-reds give me only 92 percent of my day-vision, and I don't want anything less than one hundred percent."

She squeezed my hand.

The beach off Ellis Landing Road in Brewster-on-the-Bay was beautiful indeed.

Seagulls soaring above, sandpipers and plovers doing their little skate dances on the sand, boats bounding on the water, almost indistinguishable from the white-caps, and the sun a deepening shade of indescribable red as it made its way like an antique hour-hand from five to six on the water.

No one had followed us, I was sure. No one was close to us on the beach. I could breathe in deeply and take in the scene...

We squinted at the setting sun...

"Those boats on the water are the perfect touch," Shara said, softly.

"Yeah..." I buried my nose in her soft hair, worked my lips to her neck, keeping at least one eye on the beach and the water...

"Jesus! Get behind me!" I shoved in front of Shara, pulling my weapon.

"What's the matter?" she shouted, startled.

"Those goddamn boats are much closer than they were a few seconds ago. No way their all coming in at the same time could be a coincidence."

I took a quick glance behind me—we didn't have time get back to our vehicle. There was a small outcropping of rocks, though, at the edge of the sand. I looked back at the water—there must've been at least six or seven boats, holding 2-3 killers each, coming towards us. I fired a wide pulse in the water—maybe it would capsize a few of the boats.

"Let's go!" I said, and directed Shara towards the rocks.

We crouched behind them, and I managed to get in a call to the local police. I looked back at the boats. I'd disabled two of them—but four were still coming on strong, across an horizon too wide for a direct shot on any but one of them at a time. I took aim and fired.

"You sure they're not just ... tourists?" Shara asked, voice quavering.

"Yeah, I'm sure." Because now the passengers were disembarking from the three remaining boats, scattering on the shore, pulling out their weapons. I got off a couple of more shots, knocking down a few of them, and pulled the security-blanket out of my pocket. It took but a second to raise a protective shield around Shara and me—but it had the drawback of not allowing me to fire out. The bastards fired at least a dozen rounds at us, from as many different directions. Thank goodness, the shield held. I knew its resistance was severely finite, as the specs said, though—a temporary last-ditch measure whose staying power was dependent on the number and intensity of the hits it took. That's why I'd waited until the last minute to put it up.

"What do we do now?" Shara said.

I put my arm around her. "We wait for the cavalry—the local cops—to come rescue us."

I knew the local cops were of course robotic, and utterly reliable in terms of their punctual response. They arrived about 3 long minutes later in force, first stunning most of the BPs on the shore, then taking them all into custody.

One of them approached our shield. "Sorry for the problem, folks. I think we have it all in hand. We'll be glad to escort you back to your vehicle now, if you like."

In the state I was in, I don't know if I would've let the shield down for another human being—who, for all I knew, could have been BP him or herself. But for a gleaming robot... I asked it for the SRCC—the special robotic cop code.

It displayed a sequence of 16 numbers, all correct, on its small shoulder screen.

I let the shield down. "You did a fine job—"

And the air crackled with some sort of bolt, lots of bolts, and Shara and I went down, and the last thing I saw before I blacked out was robots with weapons pointed at us, and a big gaping hole in Shara's head...

I awoke in a hospital room, with a sickening smell of medication in my face.

Wolfson was at my bed, crying.

"I'm not gonna lie to you," he said, looking me in the eye. "Shara's gone."

"No!" I tried to sit up, but tubes and God knows what other tethers kept me down. Every muscle in my body ached.

Wolfson's hand was on me, half in restraint, half in comfort.

"I *told* you it was a goddamn crazy idea to go to that convention," I rasped. "I hope the President and his asshole Committee are happy now."

"No one's happy," Wolfson said, tears still in his eyes. "But we rooted out the conspiracy—it was much deeper than anyone had expected. Even to the point of robotic hacking. They had the police frequencies monitored, they'd broken the robotic police code, as you probably saw on the beach." He hesitated. "Our own robots got there, the real cops, a few seconds too late. I don't know how much you saw..."

"Enough," I said. And I saw Shara's sweet head, open, bleeding, pooling with the colors of the setting sun...

"We won," Wolfson said, the word coming broken out of his throat, like a piece of jagged glass.

"Won? You and I lost someone we dearly loved, the world lost what may be its last android, and you think we won?"

Wolfson's lips were quivering. "You're right about the first, wrong about the second."

"What?" And I saw Shara's head again, ruined ...

"It was a brilliant plan," Wolfson said. "And it worked. We couldn't risk making the last android a target—you were right about that. Yet we had to draw the conspirators out. So we made him a protector. Presumably a human, someone the BP might wound, but never try to kill."

Protector... I hadn't protected Shara's head from bleeding ... wide open ... There were no circuits inside!

"You're the android," Wolfson said. "Shara was just acting the part of an android—a human playing an android—like the old videos. She'd been off-planet for the past six years, she grew up in Sidney with her mother, so hardly any one knew her here..."

"*I'm* the android? You're insane."

"No," he said. "You'll come to realize who you are, when this phase of your programming runs its course. You're a protector android—that's why the government invested so much in this—and you performed wonderfully, better than any human could have, under the worst possible conditions. You felt all the right things, made all the right decisions, given the circumstances. You passed the test, perverse as that sounds. I can take some solace in that. Even pride, bitter as it may be. You should too."

I hissed, and turned my face away.

"Listen to me," Wolfson continued. "No one—no android or human—could have have prevented what happened. The conspiracy was too wide spread. It couldn't be stopped—not this time. The best we could do was draw them out—the way we did—so there wouldn't be a next time..."

"You so sure you rooted them all out—that one of their little cancerous cells isn't still out there, waiting to strike?"

"They have no reason to strike anymore," Wolfson replied. "They think they killed the last android. Our robots got there before the other ones had a chance to see that Shara ..." He broke down, crying again.

"To see that Shara's wide open head had no silicon inside, that she was human?"

Wolfson nodded, unable to speak.

"But why would Shara risk her life like that? Let herself be set up as the target?"

"She was incredibly devoted," Wolfson managed to say. "More than even I."

I shook my head in disbelief. "How could anyone be that devoted?"

"This project—my work—meant everything to her," he said. "She volunteered. I begged her not to. I resigned a dozen times. But she insisted that she was the only one who understood android psychology well enough to work with you on this project—that she was the one to right the wrong for what the BP did to my eyes. And when she came to know, and love, you, that gave her more incentive. She didn't want you to die. She didn't want to die either, but she was willing to take the risk."

And I began to understand, because I remembered what Wolfson had told me about Shara, except it was not in the way I had understood it at first, not in the way he had intended me to understand it…

I reached out my hand to comfort him.

"She was your daughter," I said.

Wolfson nodded. "I didn't make her, not that way, like an android." He paused. "But she was my little girl."

Last Things First

II. New York City

Crowley was droning on about shortfalls in the travel budget. To Mariposa Lopez his voice was a fingernail on the blackboard, and she did what she usually did at these departmental meetings. She looked at John Romano, the only kindred spirit in this Sociology Department of tenured hacks, the only professor who shared her zest for adventures of ideas and her aversion for academic infighting.

John knew how worried she was about Winston. It's the oldest story in the book, John had said. I'm surprised at you. A professor burns out in the middle of a term, picks up and disappears for a few weeks, comes back at the end of the term with a sheepish grin and some story about a sick aunt in Florida.

That's not Winston, Mariposa thought. I know about the aunts in Florida, the kids in California, the unexpected conferences in London—I've heard it all, and from the best of them—but that's just not Winston. He wouldn't leave his beloved Intro to Linguistics course up at City College in mid session, wouldn't leave without a word or an assignment. He wouldn't do that to his students. He wouldn't do that to *me*.

"—Mariposa, we still have $275 in funds from your Petrie grant unused this year. Could we apply it to Martha's project?" Great, now Crowley was talking right at her. Martha's project was some business about the number of times the word "ass" was said on network television.

"Sure," Mariposa said. Give them what they want. The money was small change anyway. "Best of luck with it," she said to Martha and stood up. "And I've got to get out of here now—late for an appointment."

"Of course," Crowley said. He and the rest of the table smiled at her. And why not—they'd gotten her travel money. Her purpose at the meeting had been fulfilled.

"Ok, then, see you next week," Mariposa said, strode to the door. She heard John excuse himself from the meeting also. Crowley began—what was it?—his fourth review of the curriculum in the past year. She felt billiards in her stomach, but realized that the departmental meeting was not entirely to blame. Part of it was due to Winston. Most of it, in fact.

John caught up with her. "Where are you headed?"

"I'm going to his apartment."

"You think that's wise? You have a key?" John asked.

"He has a new computer pad lock." Mariposa answered only the second question. "I know the code."

"He'll be angry if you just go into his apartment and he's not there."

Mariposa shrugged. "If he's dead he can't be angry."

"Oh come on," John said, and laughed. "Now you're going too far."

Mariposa ignored the laugh, and pushed through the big building door to the street. Washington Square Park was soaked to the benches with cold April rain.

John caught up with her a second time, and winced as a sloppy thick raindrop fell on his eye. "I'm coming with you," he said louder than he needed to, as if the two of them were on a pier somewhere in the middle of a hurricane.

Mariposa squeezed his arm and nodded agreement. She was glad for the support.

The brownstone on the corner of 80th Street and Columbus looked chilled in the wetness. So too were Mariposa and John.

"I'll never get used to this damn New York weather," Mariposa shook her long hair and entered the building. The old brass doorknob felt like ice in her hand, fit accompaniment to the cool high-tech medley of light and chrome inside.

"You've lived here all your life," John said, pulling his dripping umbrella in after him.

"Yeah, but my blood is still Iberian—hot and Basque," Mariposa said.

"Not like this cold fish of a linguist of yours." John frowned, running his finger over the sleek tenant directory that glittered in the vestibule. "Here he is—3B." John pressed the button and looked at the screen on the wall.

"Please enter your first code," the screen said.

"That means he's not home." Mariposa sighed. "Nothing I didn't know before." She leaned over the console at the base of the directory and entered a code. The vestibule door buzzed and swung open.

"Looks like you know that code pretty well," John said.

"Let's go." Mariposa gestured towards the stairwell. They trudged up three polished ebony flights. "You know, he's not cold at all when you get to know him," she said. John just grunted.

3-B was at the end of a long freshly painted hall. Mariposa pressed the buzzer three times, and looked at the keypad.

"You sure you want to do this," John said. "Waltzing into someone's apartment is a lot more outrageous than walking into an inner lobby."

"Shush," Mariposa said, "this code is a little different from the one downstairs." But her fingers played the right tune on the keypad and the door bolt slid open.

The single room within was crowded but empty. Books and tapes and papers in various states of undress poked out of walls and chairs. The double bed on the far side of the room had a slightly rumpled but unslept—in look.

The screen of a nearby computer stared out bluely with shimmering letters. Mariposa walked over and began to read.

April 2,
Dear Mariposa,

I can't recall the first time I heard about the Basque language—but I remember clear as this morning the first time it grabbed my attention. It was in Keller's class in linguistics, one of the last I took at City College back in the 60s. Keller was yammering away about Indo-European and mentioned something about Basque, just a throwaway line, but something that stuck in my mind. And it's been there like a half-buried splinter ever since.

Basque is a language with no known origins, he had said. But how could that be? How on Earth could a language currently spoken have no known antecedents? I don't know why, but at that instant my mind locked on to that puzzle like an antibody onto an antigen. That's a good word for it—antigen—because my obsession with the Basque language has been like a low-level, ever-present allergy, a mental itch beyond my ability to scratch. How many times has my mind taken flight to the northern part of Spain, to that place near the Pyrenees, some twenty-thousand years ago, only to come back more frustrated than when I'd left?

You know what kind of guy I am. I always give my best performances in private, where no one sees them. I get into a tight parking spot on Park Avenue, with maybe inches in the front and back, and in two or three swift moves, but who sees that? No one that I care about. Not you. I come home after faculty meetings, after dinners with friends, after conferences with colleagues, and I make the cool repartee in my mind, the witty rejoinder in my head, that I should have made at those meetings in the first place. My scholarly papers are always a pale reflection of what I really have to say. I'm my own best audience—because I'm the only one who ever sees the best that I can do.

But I'm going to change my mode on this Basque puzzle. I know the answer, and this time I'm going to trumpet it loud and clear, so the whole world will know who I am.

"Interesting," John said, squinting over Mariposa's shoulder at the screen. "Ok with you if I read it?"

"Sure," Mariposa said, and stepped aside.

John contemplated the letter and rubbed his chin. "I didn't think he had such passion in him. What do you make of it? You think he went off to Spain to do some Basque research?"

Mariposa shook her head. "Not without letting me know. Certainly not without letting his classes know." He had a passion indeed, and that love of new knowledge had somehow really taken her over too. In the past year she had come to feel like a real scholar for the first time in her life. She enjoyed the sense that there was more to her work than tired stories told to half-asleep students.

"Well maybe he expected to be gone for just a short time," John said, "but got more involved in the project, and ... but no, he still would have at least called his school." John scratched his scalp. "Can you confirm the date on that note?"

Mariposa saved Winston's file to disk, and called up a date directory. "Fourteen days ago," she said. "Just like it says at the top. Precisely the number of days that he's been gone."

John whistled. "You know Winston DeVries pretty well, I'll say that for you. So what now?"

Mariposa thought for a moment. "He has no family that I know of. His teaching is his whole life. Doesn't make sense to me that he would just leave with no word."

"Well, not with no word." John pointed to the computer. "He left that."

"There's got to be more." Mariposa looked again at the computer file directory. "No, nothing here—just a bunch of program utilities." She looked around the room again. She stopped at the bed, replaying the last time Winston and she had been in it. He was gentle in a way no one else had ever been for her. He had a hurt in his eyes that she could never touch, but a hurt that somehow saw the inner core of her, that understood how hard she had strived for her accomplishments, how much of her life she had put on hold to get this far, how she still felt that there was something far more important that she had yet to do, but she didn't know what that was...

"Hey, Mariposa, take a look at this." John was on the other side of the room, near the rain-streaked window, hunching over a small end table with a typewriter on it. He pulled a sheet of paper from the machine with a flourish, and handed it to Mariposa. She read aloud.

Dear Mariposa,

Further to my last —

My first hunch was that Basque was a remnant of the Cro-Magnon language—the culture that put symbols on the caves in nearby Altamira. Actually, this hunch wasn't mine. Ever since they discovered that Cro-Magnon skull in Basque—dating from 9,000 BC—scholars have been jabbering that current Basque may be a survivor from Cro-Magnon times. But that's all it was—jabbering—because one skull, after all, does not a conclusive theory make.

My contribution came in recognizing the importance of the cave paintings. Illuminated by our bright lights of science, these paintings told us nothing. But imagine the paintings bathed in the on-again-off-again flickering of firelight. Imagine lying on your back, and looking at the markings on the ceiling above in Altamira—the cave goes dim and sharp, the animals in the carvings pop in and out in different places struck by the trembling light, and suddenly you realize they're in motion. And you realize you're seeing a primeval motion picture—the Loews Paradise in prehistoric stone.

And the sequence of these moving pictures—the relationship of one picture to another—is precisely the same as the refinement of meaning by suffix-adding in the language of Basque. Just as a deer followed by a spear means a successful hunt, so "hunt-success" is the Basque phrase for a successful hunt.

But that's not all I found.

"He's got an eye for imagery, I'll give him that," John said.

Mariposa held the typewritten paper up to the light—it was a semilucent onion skin, and the black letters upon it were smudged. "Somehow this paper looks a lot older than two weeks," she said.

John laughed, nervously. "If it comes after the computer text, it's gotta be less than two weeks old, right?"

Mariposa ran her finger over the typed letters, then put the paper to her nose. "This certainly wasn't typed last week, or even last month—feels pretty old to me. But how could that be?"

"Why would he start this letter to you on a computer and then switch to a typewriter?" John plopped down in a dusty chair and coughed. "You sure the second note was really typed after the first?"

"I can't see anything otherwise, can you?" Mariposa turned up her palms. "The first talks about how he got hooked on Basque, the second about his subsequent reasoning and research. It's like he's playing a game—leaving a trail for me."

"So where's the next piece?"

Mariposa walked over to the window and looked out. The rain had just stopped, and the new sunshine spread like butter on the graffiti in the street below. "That may not be the right question. What we need to know is *what* the next piece will be on."

"Not a computer or a typewriter page," John said.

"Exactly," Mariposa said.

She found it about half an hour later—a yellowed piece of blue lined paper, clipped under an old calendar on the side of the refrigerator. The Frigidaire was yellowing too—she had told Winston a dozen times to get a new one—and flickered like a light show on the inside. The light, or maybe the stale smell, made Mariposa nauseous. She rubbed her eyes and read the uneven handwritten scrawl to John...

Dear Mariposa,
    Further to my last —
    I think Plato understood it—all that talk about the images on the cave wall, and the ultimate unknowable reality behind it. All that talk about past and future being the same, but quite beyond any ordinary human ability to perceive without error. Except that Plato maybe had an inkling of what it was, and I've got much more than an inkling.
    Plato feared the power of the image—the artist was banned from his ideal *Republic*—just as he feared the poet. Plato knew that the images of the past—the ceiling in Altamira, the hieroglyphs in Egypt—preceded his Greek alphabet, and they had emotional strength that could undermine his temple of rationality. He knew that a picture was worth a thousand words, and the streams of pictures run deep within us.
    How right he was about the frailty of the written word and its sway. Did he foresee the onset of photographic and electronic media, and their capture of the human mind in the 20th century? Did he foresee the rise of the icon, the triumph of the window, on the computer screen whose first love had been the alphabet?
    Did he know that not only the past but the future belonged to the image?

John cleared his throat. "Philosophy was never my specialty."

Mariposa smiled. "Well, what the hell *is* your specialty?"

"Sociology of criminality-crime." John grinned. "I should've been a detective."

"So what does your detective bent tell you about our missing Dr. Devries?" Mariposa asked.

"Well, we've got three clues here. A few paragraphs on a computer screen, a typewritten page, and this." He touched the oxidized piece of paper.

"No way that paper is less than ten years old," Mariposa muttered. "I know, because—"

"Don't tell me—you're an expert on paper aging too?"

"Ha ha," Mariposa said. "No, I know because your desk must be filled with paper that looks like that. Your notes are always on the verge of decomposition."

"Security precaution." John smiled. "No, I'm a deconstructionist." He paused. "But look, if the computer text is two weeks old, and this handwritten paper is ten years old, chances are the typewritten page is somewhere in between?"

"Right."

"Right. And that means we have a three part story here, but each later part was written earlier in time—the second part a few years before the first part, and the third part a few years before the second. So what's going on? You're Basque—does that have something to do with this?"

Mariposa sat on the floor and leaned back against the wall. She still felt a bit nauseated, and now a deep exhaustion which seemed to drain strength from every part of her body. What indeed was going on? "There's got to be more—more writing from Winston—that will tie this all together. We're still missing a piece of the picture." She fought off an urge to sleep.

"What'll that be written on—stone?" John asked.

"Computer, typewriter, handwriting, stone." Mariposa considered. "Has a logic to it."

"Jeez," John said.

Mariposa closed her eyes and absently ran her hand against the grainy wallpaper. Of course her being Basque had something to do with this—that was undoubtedly why Winston had been so interested in her. She replayed the first time they extensively talked—at that endless series of lectures in Florida. He looked the epitome of the disheveled professor, trousers so old that they shined in the knees, but the urgent gleam in his eyes, and the dreaming brain behind it, was what so attracted her to Winston.

He told her over dinner by the quiet water how struck he was by her black hair, her dark eyes, her classic Spanish features, how they spoke to him of a mind that had a reach of the ages. She was flattered, and told Winston that she was actually Basque. His eyes had widened for an instant in delight—and in that instant she thought she saw things, an affinity for her people rare in outsiders—and maybe an appreciation of her, and what she could do. And this too had been so rare in her life. To most of the world, she was an attractive footnote—a blacklaced daydream for men on the plane back home after scholarly conferences, a handy opportunity for scholarly sisters to demonstrate their solidarity with an Hispanic academic. Few people wanted to understand the depth of her thirst for truth—just as few understood the wisdom of her people. But Winston did, or she thought he did, in that dilated instant...

Then the window closed—maybe not completely—and he went on to other things, and other windows opened, and they talked only once in a while about her Basque heritage, and his fascination with the language. But she had no idea about his obsession. He did say odd things now and then. "I love watching you sleep," he once said, "and stroking you slowly awake. It's like I'm making part of history come awake to me." She had not really understood that, but took it as a deep compliment anyway, and felt both strange and good about it. That was right before he had put in this new wallpaper. The old had too many scribblings on it, he had said, too many writings on the wall...

"John, help me peel off some of this wallpaper." She jumped up suddenly, and pointed to behind the desk. "Here, you do that part, and I'll do this."

"Wonderful," John mumbled. "Now we take apart his walls..."

They went through three lower layers before they found it. First the old pale green that Mariposa remembered. Then an older off-pink stucco that she had never seen. Then a paisley print that looked like it came straight from the 1960s.

Mariposa carefully peeled back the last of the paisley like a sleeping eyelid, and read what was underneath.

Dear Mariposa,
   Further to my last—
   So much in life—and therefore in theories about life, and reality around us—depends upon perspective. I've come to realize the truth of this more and more in the past few years.
   Basque is said to have no known connections to any languages. But this of course is said from the perspective of languages that we know—languages of the past and the present. What about languages of the future—languages that haven't been developed yet?
   Basque may have connections to Cro-Magnon culture, to the cave paintings in Altamira. But since Cro-Magnon culture is long gone, other than its possible survival in Basque, we have no way to judge the accuracy of the Cro-Magnon hypothesis. No way, that is, on the evidence of the past.
   But what of the future? If the icons on our screens, and the logic they employ, light the path to our future, then perhaps we'll find on that path the missing foundation of Basque. The ideographic quality of its grammar reflects not pre-alphabetic but post-alphabetic culture. All this time, linguists had been looking at Basque through the wrong end of the telescope. This was my great insight: Basque comes not from the past, but from the future.
   But that leaves me with a problem, doesn't it. If Basque comes from the future, what's it doing here in the present—and for that matter, for the past few thousand years—even longer, if we accept the Cro-Magnon connection?
   Somehow, the future speakers of Basque travelled to the past—maybe to the very origins of our species. And my task is to prove that, or at least demonstrate it to enough people's reasonable satisfaction, so my

place in history will be assured. Well, no one ever said the scholarly life is easy.

"The man's totally insane," John said.

"The classic compliment from those first exposed to unexpected originality," Mariposa replied.

"Oh? And what would you make of this?"

"How many years would you say this part of his confession has been here?" Mariposa answered with a question.

"Mmm, forty-five, fifty years at least, maybe longer," John said. "My ex's first apartment had wallpaper and a coat of paint under it like this. It was a real dive—"

"So there's something going on here that's objectively bizarre," Mariposa interrupted, "something that doesn't add up regardless of what we might think of Winston and what he's saying."

John was silent.

"Anyway," Mariposa continued, "I'm not sure his story is all that crazy either."

"No?"

"Well, lots of ancient peoples have legends about the past and future merging into one—I know several old stories—"

"From your Basque father?" John asked.

Mariposa nodded. "He told me a story one time…" Her eyes glazed, so that John was just a shadow. "I was a little girl, but I remember—"

John turned away, a thin silhouette suddenly speeding in his own train of thought at the very edges of Mariposa's vision. "Computer, typewriter, handwriting on paper, writing on the wall," he said. "Each new chapter older than the last, in forms of communication older and older. What's next? What form of communication is older than markings on a wall?"

"—the power of the spoken word," Mariposa said, "my father told me about the power of the word. The legends, the stories, passed down from our people since the beginning of our history—from our *Jatorri*—this has been our way …"

Mariposa was lying back in a chair now, tasting something more and less than consciousness with the tip of her mind...

Images that her father's father had witnessed flashed around her brain—horrible things, pain to her people, the Generalissimo airplanes assaulting her land with death from the sky.

And there was more—people and pictures from further back—they lit up the inside of her skull like a movie screen. Cruel men on horseback, trampling crops and torching villages, swinging their blades with wild delirium, screaming in a bastard tongue that her people should change their ways. But her people hung on...

"Tell me about the story, Mariposa," John's voice asked from another time. She thought she heard him click on a cassette recorder, the one he always carried in his pocket, but the click was so feeble and far away... and her father's voice was so much closer...

"He called to me one morning ... '*Mitxeleta*,' he said. I will tell you a story of a man who came from the past ... and the future ... he solved two of the riddles of our people ...'"

"Tell me more ... Mitxeleta," John prompted.

She moaned and shifted in her chair. Sweat dripped down her forehead. She saw an ancient sun burning low in the sky. She heard ships arriving from all ports of call. She was near the beginning. "The man had *uste—on*—he was a hero—but he was afraid. He was obsessed that the world should know about his achievement—about his decoding of our language and his discovery of our path, our *ataka*, between the future and the past. He craved fame, prestige. So he came up with a plan. Leave a series of messages—tell a story—with each later part of the story in a medium that could be proven to have been created earlier. In this way, the world would have evidence that he could move back and forth through time—that he could jump back a few years to tell each new part of his story."

"How did it end?"

"He got stuck in the distant past—his pathway to the future became jumbled—and he told this last part of his story to the fathers of my father. He left instructions that each of us should pass it down—in secret, *aopean*—and reveal it to the world at just the right time."

"What time was that?" John asked.

"We would know the time when we heard the words." Mariposa's eyeballs darted furiously under her lids, scanning for the right words. "'No one ever said the scholarly life is easy,'" she finally said. "Those are the words."

"What happened to Winston DeVries, Mariposa?"

"He died. *Gorputz!*" Mariposa curled her lip and shook her head in a spastic motion. "Winston, no!" She opened her eyes wide and sat up straight in her chair.

John clicked off the tape recorder. "Quite a story you reeled out there. Do you remember any of it?"

Mariposa exhaled shakily. "All of it. And he died for nothing, John, nothing!"

"Why nothing?" John said. "We've got the documents in this apartment, we've got your story, we've got it on cassette—"

"Adds up to nothing," Mariposa insisted. "You dignify the scribble on the wall by calling it a document. But even if that were taken seriously, what would it mean? I'm the key part of Winston's story—without my account, what Winston's left us is inscrutable. You yourself said he was nuts. And why should anyone believe me? I could have made this whole thing up. I slept with him, I loved him, he disappeared. I created an absurd twisted story to suck away my pain. And what good is your tape recording—a fantasy recorded is no less a fantasy."

John put a consoling arm around her.

"He had too much faith in people," she continued. "He never understood the rigors of academic proof. He placed his trust in me—put the denouement of his story in my mouth through the mouths of my ancestors—but what kind of evidence is a story from my fathers? He should have gone for something more substantial. Everyone loses this way—I've lost Winston, and he's lost the credit, the fame that he so much wanted. No one but the two of us will ever believe in his discovery."

"Maybe there is another piece somewhere," John said. Mariposa could see that despite what he was saying he hadn't made his mind up yet about the "two of us."

"Where?" she said with tears in her voice. Ragged fatigue pulled at her.

The doorbell rang.

Mariposa and John nearly tripped over each other running to the viewscreen. But it was a kid in a plaid jacket, no more than twenty, who looked up at them. "Ah, sorry to disturb you, but I've got a paper for Dr. Devries. I've been out of class for the last few weeks, and he said on the first day that if we ever had any late papers we could always bring them over…"

Mariposa buzzed him up, nearly ripped the paper from his hands, and shooed him out.

"I left a postcard with a stamp for my final grade …," the student stammered through the closing door.

Mariposa read through the paper and threw it on the floor. John picked it up.

"Don't bother," she said. "It has nothing to do with Winston or me or Basque. It's a description of similarities between online emoticons and Yiddish." She knew she'd never know anyone as foolish as Winston, nor anyone who'd know that special part of her so well. People who knew her well had always been in short supply—maybe because most of them were already millennia dead. But now that she knew that, where could she turn?

John took her in his arms and slowly rocked her. "I'm coming to see that the origins of Basque are pretty fascinating too, you know," he said, and kissed her on the temple.

I: Near Altamira

Dear Mariposa,

This will be my last letter —

I've placed my evidence carefully. I have the utmost confidence in the Basque oral connection—I know you and your love for your people, and I'm certain that you'll be able to tell your part of the story at the right time. You're a gifted scholar, and you'll be able to read the clues of my disappearance. But will you be believed? Nothing is certain.

So I've decided to leave this postscript—this extra message—because redundancy in communication can't hurt. I discovered that Basque is a future language, that its speakers also developed a mode of time travel, and came back to this Cro-Magnon age to really start the human ball rolling.

I know the caves near the ceiling with the inscriptions in Altamira have been thoroughly explored in the 20th century, with no sign of this message. That makes sense, because of course I'm first writing this now, but I can't take the chance that somehow this writing will be destroyed long before the 20th century.

So that's why I'm writing this in a little cave a bit off the beaten track here. I'm using English, so there'll be no doubt of who I am and what I've done when someone who understands English reads this. I can only hope that this cave survives into the 20th century, and some boy, some farmer, some oddball linguist with a penchant for the incredible stumbles upon it.

Mariposa, my Mitxeleta, I hope you understand. I think on some level you do. I wanted so much to tell you, when we were together, but I could not. I guess I'm better with history than with real people.

The eyes of your great-great-great who knows how many times back grandmother through the ages are just like yours—amazing the way that a thread of genes can carry a trait unchanged over thousands of years. The instant I saw the hot restless eyes of my Basque wife here at the start of human history I knew those eyes were yours. And being with her was like loving you twice at the same time—a *menage a trois* with the past and the future—like consummating our relationship over the full stretch of the human species end to end. That feeling has eased the pain of losing you. I hope some of that feeling can ripple through to you.

You carry a part of me, not only in your intellect, not only in you culture, but in the story in your DNA, in the script of molecules and motion that charged you into being. And as for the future beyond us, Mariposa—well, I hope we created something special for that as well. Redundancy in communication is good, you see. Not only in culture and language, but in transmission of DNA, the language of life. I'm just sorry I'll never know if we conceived a child. Only tomorrow knows.

Love, Winston

Critical View

He worked quickly—his eyes teared from the smoke, his throat was dry from the uneven heat—but he worked quickly. He had to. Soon the days would shrink and get icy cold, and he would have to leave this place. So he worked quickly on the sides of this cave—quickly in the on—again/off—again light of the fire, because he wanted to leave something behind.

He loved his children. He knew so much—he was not modest—and he wanted to leave some of his knowledge to guide them. He was old now, and weak, and would not be around here or anywhere in this world much longer. Truth is, he was never very strong even in his prime. He was a listener, a thinker, and he got his knowledge of the hunt from others. This is what he wanted to leave for his children.

He worked quickly on the wall. It was a communal wall, and many others had left their knowledge here. But he had something new to add, something he knew was very new. He was adding motion. To the static symbols of hunter and hunted, the knowledge of image and proportion swollen in time, he was adding connection—relationship, story. For his figures moved. In the flicker of the firelight, they joined in his vision, and came to life. His wall was more than a group of pictures—it was a wall of life, a motion picture.

He worked quickly on the wall of the cave near a place that would someday be called Lascaux. And his tears flowed, not only from the smoke, but because he knew he was capturing the essence of being and becoming on this wall.

Or at least he thought so. For who really knew what was real in its own sense, independent of us, and what only seemed to be real to us because our vision, our imagination, saw it somewhere, painted it on the world? Maybe motion itself was in the eye of the beholder.

He knew that those who understood this would have an advantage over those who did not.

But so few did.

And the reason was that to see the world in motion was almost always to assume that that was the way it came, of its own will not ours.

But what of those who lacked this second sight, this sight not only of things but of things in flight?

Would these special sightless know what he knew?

Perhaps. But only if they survived.

For a man who was blind to motion would have a hard time getting out of the way of a raging beast or a speeding spear, and might well die before he had children.

Or might well die before he had time to teach them.

Guillaume and Henri strolled through the chapterhouse of their monastery near Lascaux. Intricate tapestries hung on one wall of a narrow passage. Tapestries in a style that would one day be called Bayeux—frames of animation in the 13th century AD.

Light leaked in from small windows, holes in the wall, on the other side of the hallway. A large oak grew outside, casting intermittent shadows when the wind blew and its leaves grew fat in the summer.

The wind was blowing this amethyst August afternoon.

"Tell me, brother, what do you see in those tapestries?" Guillaume asked.

"Why, the story of Alexander, of course."

"Yes. And does Alexander move?" Guillaume asked.

Henri looked quizzically at the tapestry. He thought carefully before answering, not wanting to say the wrong thing to the older man. "Well, yes, the tapestry is the story of Alexander riding into the conquered city of Tyre. Of course he is in motion there. How could a rider not be?"

"Yes, yes," Guillaume said. "Obviously the story told in the pic-

Critical View 135

tures is one of Alexander in motion. But what I mean is: do the pictures themselves seem to move to you?"

"Forgive me. The lack of understanding is mine," Henri said in a tremulous voice. "But how could anything that isn't alive—possessed of neither animal nor human nor divine spirit—how could it actually move?"

"Is not that tapestry a reflection?" Guillaume prodded.

"Yes..."

"And haven't you seen reflections of others, of yourself, in motion in a pool?" Guillaume continued.

"Well, yes, but..."

"Well, then, why do you deny the possibility that these images on the wall, images outside of ourselves, can move?"

Henri considered. "It's not that I deny the possibility," he finally said. "I grant you it's possible. But I don't see motion, other than *portrayed* motion, in that tapestry."

"So it doesn't actually move for you," Guillaume said.

Henri looked again at the tapestry, at the light going on and off each piece of it, as the wind moved the leaves off and onto the sun outside. "No," he said again. "I see no motion there. Only frozen images, tickled by the light and shadows." For a frightening moment, Henri wondered if this were some kind of test of faith—of faith that Alexander was actually moving there.

But Guillaume didn't seem agitated, now that he had his answer. "Hmm," he said, "very few left with your kind of vision."

Henri started to ask Guillaume what he meant, but—

"Come," Guillaume said, "enough of this rambling." He put his arm on the younger man's shoulder. "Time, I should think, for a light repast."

"He goddamn didn't see it! I saw him sitting in the screening room, and the movie was on the screen, but he didn't see the damn movie! My movie's not the movie he wrote about!" Sam threw the whole Arts and Leisure section overboard and spat.

The paper stood up to the water for a second, then collapsed in a yellowish dripping mess and slid under.

"It doesn't matter," Janice said and leaned over in a tight one piece bathing suit that usually would have taken his mind off the review. "Nobody pays attention to what Seeley says anymore anyway."

Sam exhaled in disgust and looked out over the water in Barnstable Harbor. He had to admit it was beautiful. "I pay attention to what he says when it's about my movie," he said with a bit less steam. "I know I shouldn't, but I can't help myself."

Janice offered him a glass half filled with dry white wine. "What did he say exactly?" She sat down next to Sam, thinking the sooner she helped him get this out of his system the sooner they could get back to enjoying this splendid afternoon.

Sam shrugged. "He, I don't know, the same thing he always says about my work. Camera angles, lighting, red dresses, lipstick—but nothing about the movement, the relationships, the *flow* of images that tell my *story*. It's always components with this guy—a scene here, a cut there—and never a word about what they add up to."

"He doesn't care about your story. He cares about *his* story, how his words will come across to his readers."

"I put some incredible things in this one." Sam sipped the wine and stared at the water, barely hearing Janice. "I put my heart in this one. But it's lost on him. Lost on him!" Sam smashed the glass on the side of the boat. A curse not a christening.

Janice sighed. She could see this was more serious than usual. "It doesn't matter," she said softly and pulled Sam close to her, so he could feel what was under her bathing suit. "The box office will prove him wrong. The people will see what you put in there. *They'll* have the final say as to what's really in your movie—not even you, certainly not Seeley."

George Seeley jabbed at the button and looked at his watch.

Critical View

Fifteen minutes in a stalled crosstown bus, and now this ancient, quaking elevator. At times like this he almost wished he could drive—right up into the screening room. But driving was utterly beyond him. The flow was all wrong. He'd known this since the first day of his driver ed class, when he was 16, and had rear-ended three cars in his first three right turns. He was driving all right, but in a world different from everyone else's.

Images and time—these had always been the main players in his life. But they never seemed to play fair with him. Too many images, too little time. Here he was, the *New York Views* film critic, reprinted in the *Times* of London, New York, LA, and a hundred other *Times* and *Heralds* and prestigious whatnots around the world, and his feet were no further from the rasping fire than when he'd started out a dozen years ago. Success, he had found, only increased his sense of peril.

"George, glad you made it!" Len Rothstein shoved a limp, damp hand into his, and slapped him on the back with the other. He hates me, George thought, and I don't blame him. Rothstein's eyes held the same pathetic message these sleazy producers always had for him: Please, love my little movie, don't hurt me. Did it ever occur to them that having to sit in a room and watch their pictures hurt *him*? Likely never—they were too mesmerized by their images, too far gone in the joy of seeing their own reflections on the screen. It never occurred to them that what they were seeing on the screen was not what they had put there, but the infinitely more facile—and to them, beautiful—display of what they had merely wanted to put there, and usually hadn't. Everyone has dreams; the rarity is managing to embody these in creations.

"George!" Now Sasha was up from her seat, come to take him by the arm to his. Her eyes were quite the opposite of Rothstein's—luminous and questing, with something behind that he found intensely pleasurable. She was a student intern from the New School, doing some sort of dissertation on dyslexia and the arts, and he knew that if he let himself go he could become quite a slob over her. But that sort of tangle was the last thing he needed.

They sat down. Sasha briefed him quickly on the background of this film. He nodded and looked at the opening credits, which hung like stale hunks of cheese on the screen. He sighed and made an effort to get into this, absently shuffling the mail he had picked up an hour ago but had not yet opened. It wasn't until well past the middle of the film, when he needed some escape from the droning soundtrack and incomprehensible scenes, that he began looking at the mail. An ivory laid envelope caught his attention in the dim fluttering movie-light.

It was from the Editor of *New York Views*. He was utterly unready and kicked in the stomach by what the letter said. It said please call me and come to my office so we can talk about your contract. He knew the Editor well enough to know that this meant come to my office so we can talk about your termination.

Some primitive survival mechanism that he had noticed before—like a maintenance of minimal life functions in an ice water drowning—clicked in and allowed him to sit through the rest of the movie, colder than usual to what was up on the screen.

"Sit down, George." Richard Karlin offered him a seat in his rotundo radio voice. He was gay, but that was ok. George was more tolerant of people than movies, and that ironically was precisely his problem right now.

Karlin was shaking his grey head. "George, George, we've been over this ground a dozen times in the past few years. Your reviews are too damned negative. And worse."

"What's worse than negative?" He laughed and coughed, a weak little cough. He knew exactly what Karlin was getting at.

"Worse than negative? How 'bout This guy didn't see the movie he panned. He was there at the theater alright, but must've been sleeping with his goddamn eyes open.' That's a nice version of what Sam Waterman screamed on the phone to me last week. And you know something? He's right."

"About what, Richard? That I was sleeping during the screening?"

"No, but that you write reviews like you were sleeping. You talk about actors and scenes and imagery—you write like an angel—but somehow you always miss the point of the film—"

"Most of the time there isn't a point."

Karlin ignored the interruption. "I've noticed this for years. You write splendid essays, but they're not movie reviews, not critiques of *cinema*. And in the end, with all of your metaphors and turns of phrases and flights of language, no one knows what the hell you're talking about."

"You mean the big newspapers are dropping their syndication of my review column. Let's cut to the quick here, Richard."

Karlin's cheeks turned an ugly reddish purple. "We've been very generous with you, George. You know that. But maybe it *is* time that you try your hand at a book or something, or maybe some interpretative essays for the *Southern Review*—"

"Thanks for the advice, but no one reads those things."

"And the people who read your current stuff can't understand what you're saying, so what's the point?" Karlin took a deep breath and held up his hands. "I'm sorry, George, I don't want to get petty over this. You've been part of our team for years, and I don't want us to degenerate into stupid, oh-so-sophisticated, nouveau sniping. But I'm not the only one who makes decisions here ..."

"Go on." Here it was, and George felt no inclination to make this any easier for his Editor.

"We'd like to pay you for the next six months, and all we'd like from you is one last goodbye column. You'd be free to write elsewhere immediately and—"

"Take your money and your column and shove it all up your ass," George said, and stalked out of the office.

He stepped out into the evening street and carefully hailed a cab. As always, this was a moment of tension for him, for he was powerfully drawn to the slow ballet of traffic and color that hovered around him. He wanted to run with the cars, flick away the headlights with his fingers, leisurely lie on his back in the street and bat around the buses like beachballs. He knew he could do this—he could feel the pavement massaging his back, the high orange steetlamps above him like sun ... If he couldn't see this world, he could at least be part of it, exercise a kinaesthetic option in lieu of the visual one, the blind man caressing, validating the world with his cane, except George Seeley's cane was his body...

With great effort he directed himself to open the door of the cab that zoomed up beside him. He leveraged himself into the back seat, and instructed the driver to take him home.

He was getting worse. He could feel it. The discrepancy between what he knew the world to be, thought it to be, and what he saw in the world grew wider every day. What the hell then was he writing about when he looked at a film?

The only thing objectively wrong with Karlin's assessment of his career as a film critic was the implication that he had always been an incomprehensible writer. The truth was that when he started writing about films, his condition had given him an edge—a special way of seeing images that uncovered surprising things in the films. Now that edge had grown so long and jagged, it shredded his capacity to uncover anything.

Or maybe, just maybe, he had discovered a deeper truth, a deeper meaning—that truth being that there was nothing more to uncover in the world other than its form, its material. Maybe motion was just a spice, a ketchup, that everyone else childishly took for the main course itself...

Sasha was waiting for him on the stoop of his Eastside brownstone. She had two white boxes held by cheap metal wires in her hands. Chinese food, George realized as he paid his fare. Thank God, an adult food—no french fries, no ketchup. He wondered for an instant how similar Sasha's and his tastes truly were.

In any case, he knew almost for sure what was coming after the food, and wasn't inclined to fight it anymore.

"You ok?" she asked. "You practically ran out at the end of the screening."

"A fitting finale to my career," George said. "I won't be writing for *New York Views* any more."

"Why not?"

"Because I see in stone…" George answered, because I detest the flutter of wings and the shuffle of feet and grubby fingers shoving french fries in and out of the ketchup and all things that everyone else in this world says move, he thought … and his attention flared and contracted onto a crystal teardrop earring that danced in the wind at the end of Sasha's soft pink lobe. He stared at it, wide-eyed, fixated. He saw other pale pinks… "Let's go upstairs," he said.

And the crystal dangled in his face as Sasha talked at him over dinner. White bright flashes of light punctuated the freeze frames of her lips as they sucked in a shrimp, curved in a smile, quivered with pale pink invitation for him … Soon his index finger was upon them, and he and Sasha were down on the carpet, and Sasha was murmuring, "I know you … I can help…"

Did she? Did she know that these were the only times that the flow slowed down, or sped up, enough to seem right to him? And for a moment impossible to hold or extend, the world and its disjointed unconnected spasms fell into a tempo that was sane. He kept his eyes open, and sighed with satisfaction at what he saw.

And then it was gone. Though he strained with all his might to hold it together, the images before his eyes inexorably separated and moved apart like shards of glass in slow motion. He looked at Sasha as she rolled an inch away from him, Duchamp's Nude

Descending a Staircase in bed beside him, and his eyes winced from the staccato pain. He closed his eyes, and wondered if she was dreaming, and wondered when he would be dreaming, though he never had the vaguest recollection of what if anything he actually saw in his dreams, which was probably just as well, considering what he saw when he was awake.

And he wondered if the rest of the world was also in ecstasy when they saw what they thought was normal motion, which for him was extraordinary, and he realized of course they could not be, because to be in ecstasy all the time was never to be in ecstasy at all.

Morning singed his eyelids. He looked over at Sasha, and for a second in the stillness he couldn't tell whether she was asleep or dead. Then she moaned—the difference between sleep and death was a moan, yes, that was one way of looking at it, though, no, there was more to it than that, for the perceiver could moan upon seeing someone dead, so one had to be specific that the difference between sleep and death was a moan from the unconscious body...

He eased himself out of bed and into the shower.

He could feel the continuous movement of water on his skin, but his eyes reported a series of snapshots all around him—like the water was perceiving him, rather than vice versa—splashes of wet transparency that dissolved into liquid as soon as they touched him. He had no sense of time within this shimmering curtain—or rather, everything that had happened earlier in his life, making love to Sasha, Karlin giving him the ax, rear-ending those three cars when he was a kid, all were equi-distant from this place—and that was a relief. They had equally invalid—as in wrong, and as in sick—claims on reality. Or, who knows, maybe they were all right.

Karlin wasn't such a stupid man. He saw something in movies that George didn't see. So did the people who made the movies, and the people who saw them on screens of all sizes. Who was to say that George was right and they were all wrong? Or that any one of their views was better—more primal, more privileged—than the others?

Ah, but one could have the luxury of such relativism in art. For art was really minor league compared to life—a re-creation, a recreation. "We do everything as well as possible, we have no art," the Balinese say. Plato knew this, saw that human reenactments inevitably distorted the deeper state of being.

But whose vision was right about that deeper state? Whatever it was, the world was no one's movie. It was its own.

And so George stood there immobile for what felt like a very long time, soaking in and enjoying the discrepancy between his skin and his eyes, between the part of him that was irreducibly a piece of the world as it was, a bit part in its movie, and the part of him that insisted on seeing the world differently, as his avant-garde film, or, better, as non-film.

Sasha was non-Sasha, gone, when he walked back in his room.

"Meet me at the Cafe Loupe later. Twelve-thirty for lunch, ok? I know what's wrong. I can help you," her scribbled note said.

He laughed. She knew what was wrong. A lot easier task than knowing what was right.

The old regulator clock on the wall began to chime. He counted twelve of them, to his amazement. Jeez, had he been standing like a statue in the shower for four hours? His sense of time was further gone then he had realized. He fumbled for the phone and called a cab. He dared not hazard the subway or a street hail in his condition. He'd barely have time to make the appointment with Sasha.

The Cafe Loupe looked good this chilly November afternoon. A real fire crackled and spat shadows on the wrought iron, red brick wall-shadows that flickered and moved and told a story of quick cuts and freeze frames. This is the way it all must have begun, George thought. A cave somewhere in the past. A Cro-Magnon painter sweating and squinting in the stinking smoky light of an unsteady fat lamp. And the images appeared on his walls. Stories of the hunt and the gods that came to life whenever someone paid for a ticket with a piece of meat or a basket of wildberries. The first matinee. The Brooklyn Fox in its primal den. The start of George's problem.

Sasha waved him over from across the room. The same crystal teardrop hung motionless in midair from her ear, and George strained not to look at it. But he could not avoid her eyes, and they were even more commanding now than the earring.

"I know why you were fired," she said when he was seated.

"Oh? And is this the help you're supposed to be giving me?" He picked up a menu and clutched it tightly in the hope that it would stop his hands from trembling.

"It's better that we talk about it than you keep it inside," she said.

"Go on," George said.

"Motion pictures are actually an illusion," Sasha said, "a series of still photos presented so quickly that the mind blurs them into a single continuing image. You know that. And you know that you lack this ability—you have no persistence of vision. For you, each image ends when it's over—there's no carryover between them. You see the world too clearly—exactly as it is."

George sucked in the water from his glass; it gave him a few seconds more to slow down his racing thoughts to the point where he could grab them and speak. That Sasha knew about his condition was jolting enough—he was sure no one else in his carefully shielded life had ever realized what was wrong with him. But she was also implying that somehow his vision was *better* than the human standard... "I've got a very severe handicap," he finally managed.

"Well, for a film critic, yes," Sasha said, "though you used it to good advantage in your early years. Your analysis of the components of film—how the individual notes blended together to make the melody—was exceptional. I'm surely not the first to tell you that. But now you've got to move on to other things."

"How do you know so much—so much about me?" George asked.

"We spotted you early on, from your film reviews, though we couldn't be sure," Sasha said. "Lots of critics trying to be cool mimic your style. But I knew for sure after spending last night with you."

Her eyes were soft, but George was angry anyway. "And what the hell are you? Some sort of government agent?" he asked.

Sasha smiled. "No. We've been around since long before there were governments—we go back to a time when the ultimate authorities were animals painted on the ceilings of caves. We've always lived along the peripheries of the human race, in the margins of history—"

"McLuhan says the electronic world has centers everywhere and margins nowhere, or margins everywhere and centers nowhere…"

"Well, we've had some pretty shrewd people in recent years. Leonardo da Vinci was one of us, probably Einstein. We see the world as it really is. Persistence of vision is the handicap—continuity the illusion. Surely you already know this."

George said nothing.

"Motion gets in the way of the deepest science," Sasha continued. "It makes things stick together, appear to be in a relationship, when they aren't. That's why quantum mechanics is so confusing—it preaches relationship almost to the annihilation of matter. Some of our kind have tried to tell that to the rest of the world over the years, but the world never really gets it. Maybe it's better that way."

"Great, a cult of the film—blind—motion deficiencies anonymous," George said.

"Well, no, I wouldn't put it that way. Look, most people are prone to view differences as deficiencies, disabilities. Someone who's color-blind, who sees fewer net colors than anyone else—ok, that person has a difference which is a disability. Assuming, of course, that she in some way doesn't see the colors she sees with greater accuracy, intensity. But let's say we find someone who doesn't see all the colors we do, but sees others that we don't—say, along the infra-red or ultra-violet spectrums. Now, clearly, this person is different, but this difference in perception clearly contains an advantage. Now we—"

George spotted a waiter approaching them out of the corner of his vision. He walked as if in a light show-five or six freeze frames to their table. "Can I take your order now?" the waiter inquired with robotic courtesy.

"I don't think so." George pushed his chair back and slowly stood up. "I don't like being cast as a new version of a Tourette's syndrome civil rightist. I'm not wild about Oliver Sacks. Whatever I may be—whatever capacities I may have—I don't relish being a part of an *organization* about it. So I thank you for your time and concern but I'm going now." He turned towards the door, noticing it had a deep blue stained glass inlay on top through which sun flickered, as if in a medieval monastery...

"George, please, be careful," she called after him. "I know this is a lot to adjust to..."

George heard but walked through the door.

The daylight was bright and complete. The car patterns were quite beautiful. One row, right next to the sidewalk, was utterly stationary. The rows in the street moved in slinking syncopated strings—almost like a game of chess, but with multi-colored pieces. And on the far side of the street, against the other sidewalk, the cars were all stationary. Like an artery, maybe, or a vein in a plant. The two stationary rows were the walls of the vessel, and the cars that flowed in the middle were the nutrients within. A stream of light and life, and George wanted in. He was tired of going against the flow, affronted that his only alternative was the conspiracy-theory of that girl inside.

He stepped off the curb. If he could reach out and touch one of these red blood cells, one of these gels of chlorophyl, he could be part of the system, be part of its life. It looked so easy—each cell stopping and starting—he could have his pick. Just step in front of the cell and take it in his arms.

He took another step forward and focused on a big shiny yellow cell that approached down the green-black vein in measured paces. This was better than any dead movie he had been obliged to sit through. This was reality. This was life as it was—not some director's cut. And he was about to be part of it.

Sharp acrid gusts assaulted his face, and he thought he heard obscenities whizzing by his ears—yes, some of the smaller cells had heads sticking out of them and were screaming at him. A nightmare—he forced himself to pay no attention to it. The important thing was the big yellow cell. It was coming towards him.

A hand touched his shoulder. A hand that didn't belong here—was outside of the flow. "George," a voice said.

Maybe it was Sasha. He pushed it off and walked another step.

The big yellow cell was right in front of him now, a gleaming amoeba with bright white eyes. He was so tired of walking, so tired of being always on the outside looking in. Let me be carried along like everything else...

"George!"

The voice again, more insistent. A hand on his shoulder, pulling him back. "George, look at me!" The hand moved down to his hand, took him by the hand, pulled him off the street and onto the curb.

Sasha guided him back into the Cafe, back through the stained glinting glass to the crackling fire and shadows on the wall. She sat him down at a table, and they looked at the wall. Like the millions of couples who had gone to the movies in this age of movies, George thought, except that this wasn't a movie house, not even a movie, at least not for him. But the breath of the flames felt good on his face. Better than the acrid air outside.

"Sometimes you have to be outside of a process to understand it best," Sasha said. "That's the great advantage of people like us."

"I know," George said, "like McLuhan's point that the fish is the last creature to fully understand the properties and boundaries of water. But sometimes it's fun to be a fish—sometimes the easiest thing is to just be carried along."

"You were on the verge of being a dead fish out there on the street," Sasha said. "That couldn't be much fun."

"I might have jumped back at the last minute, if you hadn't pulled me."

"Might have."

George sighed. "I was a fraud as a film critic. No amount of proselytizing about the truth we really see can change that. Yes, a frog may be a more astute critic of water than a fish because it can see the water from outside in as well as inside out. But I was a goddamn reptile in the desert when it came to the medium I presumed to critique—I had no experience in that water at all!"

"No? What about last night?"

"Well..."

"Ok, so even say you're a fraud as a film critic—maybe," Sasha said. "But not as an observer of the world, of the cosmos beyond. That's what I was starting to tell you before. In that realm, you can be extremely valuable. You see the world as a series of snapshots, not as a motion picture. You see separate still images where everyone else sees unclear motion. Why do you think consciousness has evaded satisfactory explanation by psychologists and cognitive scientists? Why do physicists have such problems at the big and little ends of existence? It's because such fundamental processes are more clearly seen as a series of still cuts—of discrete bodies and particles, of idea webs and networks on an eternal screen—not as the self-spiralling motion that leads to paradox at every turn. The secret that so few seem to realize is that ultimate truth is not four or five or ten dimensional. Not three-dimensional. But two-dimensional. Either/or. On or off."

"Hah!" George said. "So you're proposing what? That I suddenly take on a new career as a quantum physicist in mid life? Become a Plato in search of permanent ideal forms? I'm no philosopher—I'd have more fun hugging that amoebic bus out in the street."

"Don't get hung up on a word," Sasha said. "You don't have to study Wittgenstein to be a philosopher. And you don't need to be a philosopher to take on another career. Leonardo was an artist and a scientist. Jefferson was an inventor as well as political theorist."

"What, was Jefferson film-blind too?"

"Our guess is a lot of people were—many more than history acknowledges," Sasha said. "But who really knows, because obviously there was no film, no major public attempt to capture and replay motion—that would draw people out like you and me. Plato certainly writes like he was. I don't know about Jefferson. But multiple perspectives, renaissance pursuits, are another consequence of our peculiar condition. To see in motion is to usually see one line going from past to future. To see in still frames is to see many things horizontally at once—you can go sideways, to alternate universes, rather than just back and forth in the same. McLuhan called this acoustic space. Everything at once. It's in a sense what cyberspace is too. Centers everywhere, margins nowhere, as you said."

The waiter approached their table again—a parody of deconstructed abstract art in sliced diced motion. George burst out laughing. So did Sasha.

"Are you ready to order now, Sir?"

"Yeah, I think maybe we are," George said, and looked at Sasha. "Not the world, not by a long shot, but maybe our food, yeah."

It felt good to at last be sitting across a table from someone who saw the world the same way as he.

The Harmony

The old IRT train lurched out of the elevated station on the corner of Allerton Avenue and White Plains Road in the Bronx. Window panes on the Hebrew National deli rattled like a drum-roll fade-away intro to the three-way harmony we were weaving. Our singing was all encompassing, our voices our only instruments, absorbing the dust and the shudders of the train station and everything else on that late April street corner like some vortex out in space, like the hole in the center of a 45 record spinning round and around on a black turntable...

It was 1966—JFK was dead less than three years—and Lenny, Dave, and I sucked in and breathed out the new world through our music. We were remnants of a last-gasp doo-wap group from the early 60s, much the rage at Bronx House and the Y's on the Concourse a few years earlier. But now we had taken up Peter, Paul, and Mary for the Five Satins. We even dared a Dylan or Phil Ochs song once in a while.

This evening, though, we labored on a old folk standard—"The Banks of the Ohio"—and Len and I were close to despairing that Dave, our second tenor, would ever get his part right. Still we pressed on, train station shaking and rattling and rolling, until a voice stopped us cold.

"Is that a folk song you're singing, or what?"

We turned around to see a cop. He had crept up to us on some kind of silent shoes.

"Uhm, that's right," I answered, ready for the inevitable time to break it up and take-it-home-boys lecture.

"Good harmony parts there," the cop commented. "But you were a little off on that suspended fifth." He looked at Dave.

I was too flabbergasted to speak.

"Yeah," Lenny chimed in. "We picked it up from the Mamas

and Papas."

The cop shrugged. "Never heard of them. But if you like that kind of barber shop, I can show you some good parts."

"Sure," I said, by no means ready to give up my distrust of cops—hell, I'm not too hot about them even now—but by no means ready to say no to such an offer either. "Officer, ah ..."

"Jimmy, just call me Jimmy." He extended a big hand, and I shook it. He had jet black rock 'n' roll hair and Newcastle coal in his eyes.

Harmony is like no other progression in this world. Two voices are night and day in comparison to one, and three can do things utterly unattainable by two—chords become possible for the first time with three—but the returns diminish sharply with the addition of the fourth voice and beyond. Still, the fourth voice makes all manner of sixth and seventh chords possible—the crystal cool icings on the cakes of chords—and Officer Jimmy was exquisite at them all.

I have no idea how long we were actually singing there on that corner. It felt like years. We lit the street with our music. And we must have been quite a sight as well. Three kids and a cop—decent name for a group, in some eras—and we attracted all manner of onlookers, more than a few truly pleased.

"Good to hear those old sounds again, right Pop?" Jimmy said to an old guy, seventy at least, who watched with rapt admiration as we finished an inspired rendition of "Pennies from Heaven." Dave never sang so well in his life, and Lenny and I were flying.

"You betcha," the gent said, "like the boyez on Simpson Street." He sounded just like my Great Uncle Abe.

Jimmy smiled oddly. "Long time since I've been by Simpson Street. You think these boys are ready?" He gestured expansively to us.

Uncle Abe shook his head. "Simpson Street's quite a responsibility. Not a decision you should make lightly."

"You're right, Pop. You know the bass on Down by the Old Mill Stream?' We could use a little help on the low end."

Abe gave a sharp wave of his hand. "Nah—I'm too old for the street corner now. You just sing and I'll give a listen, and then I'm gone. I've stayed too long here already."

And when we finished, he was indeed gone, maybe up the downtown side of the train station to Simpson Street, though how a man his age could have climbed those stairs so quickly I couldn't say.

I was about to ask Jimmy about Simpson Street when a cop car pulled up to the sidewalk. "Excuse me," Jimmy said, with a degree of embarrassment and irritation that surprised me. "My buddies are probably wondering what happened to me."

Jimmy's buddies got out of their car on both sides, slamming their doors shut with a flourish, swaggering on to the sidewalk. One talked volumes into Jimmy's ear and the other glared at us. Jimmy eventually came back to us, looking even more embarrassed than before.

"I've got to go back to the station now," he said. "Look, I had a great time with you guys."

"Did singing with us get you in trouble?" I asked with real concern.

Jimmy looked at the cop car and frowned. "I can take care of myself, don't worry." He pulled out his ticket pad, and scribbled something down. "Here." He handed a thin yellow piece of paper to me. "It's the address of the place on Simpson Street. But they don't keep regular hours there—they're only open after midnight, a couple of times a month. If you go, tell them Jimmy the cop sent you—otherwise they may not let you in." He paused a second. I started to ask how he knew that my brain was already veering to Simpson Street, but I stopped—it somehow felt right that his mind would be so in tune with mine, maybe it came with the harmony. "And you *should* go," he continued. "They've got the best harmony you'll ever hear, and you've got real talent." He said this to all three of us, but I knew he meant it for me.

I saw a door of the cop car open out of the corner of my eye. Jimmy saw it too. "All right, I've got to get out of here now. Thanks for the singing—it was grand."

Jimmy and the cop car were gone a few seconds later.

"What time is it?" I asked Dave. He was the only one of us who carried a watch—stuffed deep in his pocket for some reason, along with used tissues and who knows what else.

Dave fished for the watch and took a look. "It says 9:30, but that's impossible. We've been singing here for hours."

"The snot on your tissues finally got to the mechanism," Lenny laughed.

I laughed too. But my guess was that if anything had stopped Dave's watch it was the incredible harmony we had been singing with Jimmy.

Ten parts girls—or the imagined pursuit of—and one part homework kept us from getting together again for most of the month. And when we did, our harmony wasn't so great.

"You think we should go down to Simpson Street and see what's going on there?" I asked.

"Not tonight," Lenny and Dave said, and heaped a wilted salad of excuses on me. I realized that my days with these guys were ending, and I'd have to go down to Simpson Street on my own.

Not that I was thrilled to go any place in the South Bronx myself after midnight. I mean, 1966 wasn't as bad as in later years, but even then the city was none too safe at night.

Still, I took a typically urine-tainted train down to Simpson Street a few nights later. I had no idea how to process Jimmy's remark that the place was open only a few nights a month, but I showed up at 12:45 at the address Jimmy had written on the yellow paper. It was a ground floor apartment in a building that was worse than seedy but still standing.

A nondescript guy answered the door. The fact that he was nondescript somehow made him weirder to me than if he had been outrightly peculiar.

"Uh, Jimmy the cop—a police officer my group and I were singing with a few weeks ago—gave me this address," I said.

"Group?" Mr. Nondescript said and peered over my shoulder. "I don't see no group."

"Right," I said, "I came here alone. Jimmy said you've got some great harmony going on here this time of night." Much as I strained, I couldn't hear any sounds within.

"Been a long time since Jimmy been here," he mumbled.

"Look, if this is the wrong time, I can come back again," I said.

"Nope, if it's right for you, then it's right for us," he said, and gestured me into the apartment.

As soon as I entered, I was blinded by the voices I heard. Not deafened—because, whew! could I still hear—but blinded, because the sounds packed my mind so full there was no room left for vision.

People gradually came into focus. The room was some sort of huge hall, and the people were clustered in every sort of singing group imaginable—some, like rap groups, that I couldn't even imagine in 1966. There were doo-waps, barber-shops, madrigal harmonies, modern jazz, British rock sounds—if I said I felt like a kid in a candy shop I'd be lying, 'cause I never cared that much for candy.

I was next to some black guys singing Drifters songs. I joined right in with a falsetto part. They liked it and we sang on.

"Sound good, don't it," the guy next to me said—a baritone with a voice like hot roasted peanuts whose name was Elias. "You oughta stay here with us—what we got too good to throw away."

I smiled at the compliment—pretty much standard courtesy but still nice to hear. "How often do you guys practice?"

Elias shook his head. "We never practice—got no need to. We're here all the time."

I nodded. I understood well the addictive tug of fine harmony—that feeling of being close to the cosmos when a chord from your voices sounds just right. Most people who sang like this would gladly trade the flat clack of everyday life for the music of the spheres, but few us ever got the chance. We talked about it, though—incessantly—as if our words could somehow do the bidding of our music. But in fact the real world is ruled by other things, and we turned out to be lawyers and doctors—far worse, if we weren't lucky—the music fading even as we assured ourselves that we were ever holding on to it.

But the music was strong that night on Simpson Street, and I sang till I was hoarse, and when I left I hardly noticed that it was still pitch black outside, because I was too tired and happy to care.

I came back night after night.

"I thought this only goes on a few nights a month," I asked the deadpan man at the door one night. This must've been well into the second or third week of my visits. I was so involved with the music that I had trouble telling minutes and months apart, let alone days and weeks.

"That's right for the first time," he said. "But for you, we're here all the time now. If that's what you want."

I couldn't say I understood what he was talking about, but it didn't matter—only the singing did.

Harmony, you understand, by its very nature breaks the rules, providing a much greater thrill than three or four or five voices singing together should in all logic deliver. I had long been aware of this—knew about it from the time I was a kid who first just listened and then joined in on the street corners for hours and hours. My parents and non-singing friends had all wondered what had come over me then...

So I was accustomed to strange glistening things, whenever and wherever harmony was involved. But the room on Simpson Street was stranger than I realized, because despite the night after night I spent there, no one on the outside world seemed to miss me. Not because I was wrong about how much they cared about me—always a possibility in my case—but because, well, I wasn't really gone too long by their reckoning. In fact, I came to realize that I was barely gone at all—just the time that it took those swaying clanking trains to get from my place near Allerton Avenue down to Simpson Street.

I asked Mr. Nondescript about this one night. "Just a little gift we give you—a gift of time—don't worry, it won't last forever," was all he said in reply.

I asked Elias about it, too.

"Well, that's why I told you should stay with us," he said. "Now you know what I was talking about."

But I didn't, and Elias was too busy blowing harmony to tell me more. That's the way it was with everyone.

I kept coming back—the singing was too good not to—but I was bothered by this thing about Simpson Street that made no sense, and everyone there was either unwilling or unable to explain to me. I mean, I understood that harmony takes you out of this world, but the logical part of me just couldn't swallow being taken out so literally.

A few nights later, I ran into Officer Jimmy as I was about to climb the two flights of the Allerton Avenue station.

"You're going to Simpson Street," he said.

I nodded.

"Without your buddies?" he asked.

"Nah, we don't sing together anymore," I said. "We tried one or two times, but there's just no comparison to—"

"I know," Jimmy said with an intense, almost envious gleam in his eyes. "Nothing in this world compares to Simpson Street.

Your partner Lenny told me the same thing last week."

"Lenny's been down to Simpson Street?" I was shocked. "I've never seen him there." Why the hell hadn't he told me? Well, I guess I hadn't exactly been in frequent touch with him either in the past few weeks.

Jimmy grimaced. "What can I tell you—it's a big room, easy to get lost in there."

I suddenly had a bright idea. "When do you get off-duty? "Why don't you come with me tonight?"

"I—" an uptown express roared by and blocked out Jimmy's words. "I don't get off-duty till morning," he began again. "And besides, I can't go back there ever again. I guess you've got a right to know that."

"I don't understand," I said.

"Come on, don't play dumb with me." For the first time I noticed a little anger in Jimmy, too. "Look," he said more softly, "don't tell me you haven't noticed some of the peculiarities of the place."

"Yeah, I have," I said, "but I'm not too clear on what they add up to." I could hear my train approaching the station. So could Jimmy.

"The joys in this life aren't always free," Jimmy said. "One of these nights they'll tell you the price."

"Which is?"

"Look, you and I are really strangers, except for the harmony," Jimmy said. "I met you and your partners on a street corner. I saw you had talent, so I gave you the address. The rest is up to you now. You'll find out soon enough. I made my decision, and you'll have to make yours." Jimmy squeezed my shoulder in a good luck, older brother sort of way, and walked off.

I knew there was no point going after him. I hustled up the stairs, shoved my token in the slot, and dove into the train.

The nonentity at the door had a little smile on his face this time. I guess that made him a nonentity no longer, and that in itself was disturbing. "Make sure you come see me before you leave tonight," he said with a cloying relish, and strode away.

I kept away from the Drifters this evening until the end—saving the best for last. I sang with two modern harmony groups, a Beatles-type group, a folk group, and even a spectacular Shirelles-type group. I kept my ears and eyes tuned for Lenny—a waste of time—and then I ambled over to the guys who sounded better than the Drifters. We did "Up on the Roof," "Under the Boardwalk," "On Broadway," and a rendition of "Save the Last Dance for Me" that pulled my mind so wide open that our five part harmony is still bouncing around inside somewhere…

"You stay with us." Elias put his arm around my shoulder. "Like I told you the very first time you came here, this kind of sound is too good to throw away. You remember that when you talk with the man at the door."

The man at the door was positively leering at me now. He beckoned me over with his index finger.

"You've had a good time here the past few weeks?" he asked.

"The time of my life," I said, and thought that the weeks felt like years at least.

"The boys have a high opinion of you." He looked over in Elias' direction. "Everyone here does. They want you to stay."

I didn't care for the way he seemed to separate himself from the others and their good opinion of me, but I had a more serious concern at the moment. "Why all the sudden talk about staying?" I realized as soon as the words were out of my mouth that the talk wasn't all that sudden.

"You'd like to leave, take our gift of time, and come back tomorrow—no fuss, no bother, just like you've been doing so far, right?"

"Right," I said. "Is that some sort of problem?"

"I'm afraid so. You have a little decision facing you. You can leave now, and come back whenever you please. But you may want to think about coming back here, because if you do, if you show up here even one more time, you'll be obliged to stay forever. Your free pass is over tonight."

"What are you talking about? What the hell kind of choice is that?" I asked.

He laughed. Have you ever seen a nondescript person laugh? It can be frightening. What he said was even worse. "You can curse as much as you like, but it won't change the facts. I'll give you Elias' full name, and the names of everyone here you've sang with. Check them out for yourself. You'll find that they have all been long or short dead on the outside. That's the price you pay for staying with us—that's the price of this magic." He shoved a piece a paper in my hand.

"You call what you're talking about magic?" I asked. I put the paper in my pocket without thinking, right next to the paper Jimmy had given me. I always carried it with me.

"You know exactly what I mean," he said. "You feel the harmony—you know what it does to you. A blind man could see how it affects you. You won't have a feeling like that again the rest of your life. Sure, you'll have your successes and satisfactions. You'll have the big ones like a wife and kids and a good profession. You'll have the little ones like getting the last copy of a hot movie in the video store. But you'll never have a feeling like this."

I hadn't the vaguest idea what a video store was, but I knew what he meant anyway. I was amazed at how articulate the guy had suddenly become—like this speech he was giving me was his command performance, his reason for being here. "You're not the only harmony parlor around," I finally managed, "I can always find other people to sing with."

Again, that laugh. "Come, come, you know and I know that you'll never find another session like this."

"We'll see about that." I stalked out of the door.

"Remember," he called after me. "Think hard before you come

here again—because next time is for keeps."

The sky, which an instant before was black-as-your-hat, suddenly burst into full daylight. And along with the light came a ragged chorus of car horns and midday noises. "The sound of reality ...," I heard him say. But when I turned around and looked in his direction, the door he had just opened was long since shut and bolted.

Well, I checked out the names on the list, Elias' and every single one of them. And it was just as he said. They were all dead. Elias had drowned three years before in some stunt off the Hudson River—his body had never been recovered. It was the same with the rest. By the time I was finished, I knew more about the heartbreak of families than I ever needed to know.

Or maybe I did need to know; maybe Mr. Nondescript wanted me to know so I could make an informed decision.

And if that was the case, I guess it worked. My parents got on my nerves plenty in those days, but the thought of their going through what Elias' family had suffered was way too awful for me to pursue. I couldn't do that to my folks. Besides, I've always been a bit of a coward at heart, avoiding risks most of the time. I doubt I would've taken a chance on actually ending my nonharmony life in any case. As much as I loved the harmony. I was only seventeen.

But yeah, I went down there more than once after that last night—never had the courage to even knock on the door, though. I just stared from across the street. Sometimes I'd stare for hours. And those times, the hours counted. One time I saw two girls knock on the door, and the nonentity let them in. I stared hard inside before the door closed and I thought I saw someone who looked like Uncle Abe inside.

I saw Lenny on campus a few times after that, too. At first he denied that he'd ever been to Simpson Street, and then that there was anything unusual about the place. Why? I don't know—I guess he felt uncomfortable talking about his encounter with perfection. I guess most people would. But then one night he opened up. He told me how he'd sang with a lot of great groups in the Simpson Street apartment—many the same as mine—but how he found one group that was extraordinary beyond belief, a combination of the Skyliners, Four Seasons, and the Beach Boys. When he added his part to those singers, Lenny said, he felt complete in a way he had never experienced before. Interesting that I never heard anyone at Simpson Street that sounded the way Lenny described. But I knew just what he meant, because I felt the same way about Elias' group. One man's Seasons is another man's Drifters.

"I wonder why there aren't any famous dead rock 'n' roll stars in there," I asked Lenny, "like Ritchie Valens or Johnny Ace."

"That's not what the place is about," Lenny answered. "The stars went a different way—Simpson Street's about beauty not fame." And I realized his understanding of the place was clearer than mine.

I never saw Lenny after that. The Spring term was over and he was off with his folks to his aunt's house near the Hamptons. He loved the ocean—said it made him feel like an East Coast beachboy. He must have walked on those sands alone at night, hearing the waves crashing like the trains moving out of the station, longing with a terrible hunger for those high tenor riffs on Simpson Street.

I can't say I was really surprised when I heard what happened—a part of me was crushed and confused, cut up in a texture of harsh pain and a keen reed of insane jealousy—but I wasn't really surprised. I knew the depth of Lenny's need. Dave said Len went out in a little boat one late afternoon, and must've caught the tide at the wrong time. It carried him too far out. He never returned. Dave had no idea what had really happened, but I knew.

I called Lenny's parents and tried to tell them, but my throat was stuck. So I stifled my tears and told them I'd never forget Lenny and that was all I said. But I knew where he was. I went down to Simpson Street one more time and kept a vigil through the night. Five maybe six times I walked towards that door. Each time I found that I couldn't move; each time the paralysis set in sooner.

Finally, I knew there was no point in coming back.

I love you Lenny, I sure hope you're happy in there, I sure hope you think of me once in a while when you break into falsetto. I'm sorry I wasn't a better friend to you when I had the chance.

My life has had—as that damned doorman predicted—its successes and satisfactions. I've had much happiness: Debra and the kids have brought me a fulfillment in a dimension that's in many ways far beyond music. And I've found ways of channeling my creative juices. Even made a few recordings at the end of the 60s, though nothing of that singing holds even a flicker of a candle to the harmony I helped make on Simpson Street.

Oh yeah, I even ran into Jimmy again a few years ago up at the Cross County Shopping Center just north of the city line. His black hair was shot through with grey, and he had been retired from the force for a few years. He told me his wife had died of cancer, they had no kids, and he was thinking of going down to Simpson Street for the big plunge.

"Is that building even still in existence?" I asked.

"Sure," he said, "of course it is. I know it is. It's always there for you if want it. That's part of the deal."

If we'd had a third voice—hell, I'd have even settled for Dave, whatever he became—we'd have sung some harmony right there at the mall. But seeing as there were only two of us, and you can't really do much with two, we let it pass. We wished each other well.

I still carry the address on the yellow piece of paper Jimmy gave me in my wallet. Now it's yellow not only because that was its original color, but because of its age.

I take the paper out every once in a while, look at that address, and think about it.

But I harmonize with the radio not real people these days. It's safer that way.

I stopped by Blockbuster Video at the mall last night. The Drifters were playing on the speakers, and I added my usual harmony part under my breath. A bunch of kids were standing around outside—I could see them through the window—and I knew, without hearing a sound, just what they were doing. I could tell by their stance. First group of singers I'd seen on the street in twenty years. Maybe that kind of singing is starting up again. The mall's not as good as a street corner under a train, but it has its appeal.

I paid for my tape and walked outside. The kids weren't bad. They saw me listening. I smiled at them.

"That's pretty good harmony," I moved closer and said after they'd polished off a song with a sparkling major sixth.

"Thanks," said a tall guy with a baseball cap pulled backwards.

I could feel how easy it would be to do my part now. To do Jimmy's old routine. I knew the whole arrangement—my lines and their lines—from start to almost finish.

"You look like you sing sometimes yourself," a girl with a voice of murmuring woodwind said, "why don't you join us on our next song?"

Sure, sing with them, impress them with some clever chords, give them a prelude of what could be ... I had to resist this, because I knew exactly where it would lead.

"I'd really like to," I looked at my watch, "but I'm late already."

I reached in my pocket for the car keys.

But I came up with the yellow piece of paper.

The Essays

On Behalf Of Humanity: the Technological Edge

A rational examination of technology needs to begin with a recognition of its role in the living world. We find that long before humans arose on this planet, its life forms manipulated their environments in all manner of ways that we still see very much in evidence today, in beaver dams and spider webs and bird nests. Indeed, we find that technology is a fundamental strategy of life itself—the cutting edge of an evolutionary process that not only responds to external environments but reshapes them on behalf of the organisms it serves.

Not surprisingly, the infusion of human mentality into the ancient biological process of technology—its animation with our penchants for dream and design—has lifted it into something that has literally transformed our entire planet perhaps more than all living processes before it. And with this human impulse writ large, and its capacity for destruction as well as construction, aggression as well as affection, has come all kinds of amplified perils. A gun is more dangerous than a fist or a claw, and an atomic bomb trumps them all in threat to ourselves and our planet.

Reasonable people thus find themselves not only appreciative of technology's benefits, but concerned about its dangers—concerned, to be more specific, about avenues for the human misuse of technology. But as often happens in matters so fundamental to human existence, what begins as a reasonable concern can quickly escalate into critiques and denunciations which lose sight of the underlying realities. This has happened in the view of

Jacques Ellul (*The Technological Society*, 1954) and others who claim that technology is essentially autonomous and out of human control; that it is in intrinsic and profound opposition to the natural world; that it is thus the leading source of danger to human beings and Planet Earth.

Such views not only miss the natural evolutionary situation of technology indicated above. They overlook the fact that by far the worse threats to humanity are and always have been non-technological in origin, in disease, drought, earthquake, and all manner of natural calamities that befall us. And they overlook the only effective response we can mount to these dangers—they overlook and/or misrepresent, in other words, the essential role of technology in dissemination and organization of information, in the growth of knowledge, medicine, agriculture, and the myriad of activities we daily perform on behalf of ourselves and our world.

In this essay, I propose to help rectify the above by (a) clarifying the great extent to which technology is indeed under our control, (b) demonstrating that two problems commonly laid at technology's doorstep—information overload and over-specialization—are the consequence of too little not too much technology, and (c) putting in sharper context the ways that technology has improved our lives on this planet.

Guns, Knives, and Pillows

Common sense, as the British philosopher G. E. Moore aptly counseled at the turn of the last century, is a good place to begin any serious investigation. The common-sense view of technology on the question of its good and evil consequences is that it most like a knife—which can easily be used for good, as in cutting food, or bad, as in cutting people. The knife, and the technology in general, are thus in this view thought to be thoroughly under human control.

But let's explore this a little further. Can we think of technologies which are intrinsically biased—to use the phrase introduced by Harold Innis (*The Bias of Communication*, 1951)—towards good or bad purposes? Well, surely a gun seems weighted towards doing people harm; and a pillow seems oppositely positioned on the scale to function as an innocuously beneficial convenience.

But upon further inspection we can see that, notwithstanding these technological biases towards bad and good, human direction can still direct that the technology be used for an opposite purpose: A gun serves a good end when it is used by a starving hunter to procure food; and a pillow can be no less an instrument of murder than the gun when the cause of death is deliberate suffocation.

So it seems that guns and pillows are but special kinds of knives: they may be intrinsically weighted towards evil and good, respectively, but ultimately they can be made to perform (or not perform) in whatever ways humans intend.

Let's raise the stakes a little more. Are there any technologies at all that we can specify as being so unremittingly bad, or good, that they defy any and all human intention in the opposite direction? Can we think, in other words, of any technologies that would qualify as "super-guns" or "super-pillows"—guns that would resist any attempt to bend them towards human benefit, pillows that would stand up to any plan to subvert them to evil?

Nuclear weapons are the obvious choice for the super-gun. They certainly cannot work as a direct provider of food. They perhaps can defend a just society from attack by an unjust; but, when actually used, they entail an horrendous cost to both innocent people and the Earth as a whole. Nonetheless: nuclear energy, of which nuclear weapons are a subset, has uses in medicine, and perhaps in provision of energy via fusion (safer than fission) reactors. Furthermore, as Freeman Dyson once suggested, nuclear weapons themselves could be hauled off of the Earth—once we further develop our shuttle-craft technology—

and assembled in orbit to power of our first starship to Alpha Centauri. This strategy would at once remove these weapons from our planet, and further our exploration of the cosmos. Certainly by these real medical and hypothetical space-exploration lights, nuclear weapons and its associated technologies are significantly less than 100-percent, unremittingly inapplicable to good purposes.

What about the other side of the street: Can we specific a technology that is 100-percent, unswervingly good in its consequences? Vaccines would seem a clear example of that: even technology's severest critiques are prone to see nothing at all amiss in the eradication of smallpox. But, alas, we also know that disease-fighting technology can easily be turned into disease-causing technology, and become the vehicle of germ warfare. What this in turn tells us is that, just as no technology, including nuclear weapons, can be so out of human control as to be unremittingly bad, so is no technology so out of our control as to be undilutedly good. Human direction, whether for good or evil, is decisive in all things technological.

All technologies, then, are one form or another of knives in our hands. This is good news, in that it shows the fallacy of the view that technology is autonomous or intrinsically out of our control. But, of course, it also confers upon us a continuing responsibility to use technology for positive purposes—and to do what we can to remedy a technology that may have negative effects.

In the next section, we consider a low-profile but highly instructive case in point of our capacity to exercise this responsibility: the window and its sundry coverings.

The Parable of the Window Shade

Once upon a time, people were obliged to suffer wind and rain in their faces if they wanted a glimpse of the outside world from within their abodes on a nasty day: they had to look through

On Behalf of Humanity: The Technological Edge   169

small holes in their walls. The window was a wonderful remedy for these circumstances, in that it allowed people to see the outside, but through a pane of glass that protected them from the elements.

As often happens in technological evolution, the window created a new problem even as it solved the old one: for the capacity to easily look out also confers a capacity for other people to easily look in. The window and its safe permeability to the outside, in other words, also brought into being the Peeping Tom.

Here we have a classic case of a technological benefit engendering a disadvantage—in this case, an unexpected loss of privacy.

The human response to this new problem is instructive: we invented curtains, Venetian blinds, window shades, and the like. Rather than passively suffering the Peeping Tom, we created new technologies that both preserved all the benefits of the original window, *and* eliminated the new problems it had brought into being.

Indeed, the development of what I call "remedial media" is a very fundamental pattern in technological development, and has played a role in many threads of its evolution. Television, to take another kind of window as an example, was criticized in its first 25 years for being an extremely ephemeral medium—providing no sense of past or future, just the present, to its viewers. Lewis Mumford, in his *Pentagon of Power* (1970), went so far as to say that such unremitting immediacy was akin to a brain damaged state for humans. But, as we have already seen above, nothing in technology is utterly unremitting. And thus, even as Mumford was making this criticism, videotaping devices were being developed which would soon give television a memory—and a sense of future as well—as people could record programs for re-viewing, and/or set their VCRs to tape a future program, etc. The VCR thus is television's window shade: it allows viewers the benefits of TV, while reducing the powerlessness that formerly characterized its viewing. It turned the television, at least on the question of viewer control, into something more like the book.

So remedial media give substance to the logical claim made above that humans have continuing control over our technologies. But some critics contend that the very prevalence of technology in our world is the problem—so that the introduction of any new technology, even a remedial one, is ipso facto not to our benefit. Two technological effects that are often cited in such concerns are information overload, or the view that we are drowning in the options our technology offers, and technological elitism and over-specialization, or the concern that each new technology, rather than solving problems for humanity as a whole, serves to set up a limited group of people as a special, privileged class, separated from other classes and the rest of the world.

In the next two sections, we'll see how each of these concerns is based on profound misunderstandings of the technological process—and how, in fact, the introduction of new technologies serves to help the two very problems that critics claim are engendered by technology.

Overload as Underload

Information is undeniably essential to life, and therein and even more so to human life. Are critics right that we can have too much of a good thing?

It is useful to point out in such a context that, socially, tragedies commonly arise from misunderstandings based on too little not too much information. The Battle of New Orleans, to use one of many examples than can be plucked from history, was fought *after* the treaty ending the War of 1812 between the United States and England had been signed in Paris. Why did this needless, bloody battle take place? It was because news of the treaty's signature was making its way to the New World by speed of sailing boats. The Battle of New Orleans was thus a direct effect of insufficient, or in this case, simply missing, information: the invention of the telegraph some 20 years later would have prevented this battle from ever occurring.

But what of the claim that the sum total of information has increased so greatly in the past two centuries that the balance has shifted from too little to too much? Here we need to look a little more closely at how human cognition processes information—for to say that we have too much information is to be saying, in effect, that our brains have limitations on how much information they can handle, and these limitations have already been reached.

We can begin by recognizing that our brains are not mere passive buckets, into which the experience of the world is deposited, until it reaches a certain "full" point beyond which, like water in a pail, it overflows. As philosophers and psychologists from Kant to Dewey to Piaget have recognized, our cognition is very much to the contrary a highly active digesting agent—rather than merely absorbing information, we process it as it comes in to us, changing it in the processing, categorizing it, shaping it, linking it to other information at all steps so that the end result is both more complex and unified than the raw ingredients with which this activity of understanding began. While there may not be any reason to assume this processing is somehow ultimately immune from all possible overflow, neither can this Kantian active view of the mind support a model that has our mentality simply overwhelmed by too great a *quantity* of information. The mind just doesn't work that way.

Indeed, contrary to popular impressions of our society as being overwhelmed with information, the actual evidence suggests that our mentalities are dealing quite well with the big, booming, buzzing world of confusion identified by William James more than a century ago as the proper pool from which our consciousness selects candidates for its attention. We daily walk into bookstores and libraries, stocked by packets of information—books—

on a magnitude thousands of times more than we can possibly read. And although we may well feel a little pressured or momentarily baffled as we would in any large, crowded environment, we rarely feel the kind of acute, overwhelming anxiety associated with overload that paralyzes or disrupts our ability to respond or act. We instead usually make our selections from the huge array quite effectively and comfortably in the end.

Why would bookstores and libraries not be loci of information overload, in presumed contrast to computers and their output which are the usual suspects in current overload castigations? A closer scrutiny reveals that we have, not surprisingly, developed navigational techniques for processing the high informational invitation of bookstores and libraries. Every child learns in school that books can be meaningfully organized according to subject and author. Special cases are accorded special, rationally coherent treatment. Biographies, for example, are usually shelved in alphabetical order of neither the title nor author, but the subject's last name. Paperbacks may be put in special sections regardless of their subject, and so forth. The result is a complex system—a remedial medium for the bookstore and library, to use the parlance introduced above—which is internalized by most literate people well before attainment of adulthood.

And this in turn suggests that what may be vexing about current computer networks—the Web, the Internet, and the enormous access to information they provide—is not that we that they give us too much information, but that we have too little information, *navigational* information to be more exact, with which to adequately process these new possible sources of knowledge. Indeed, when we consider that we have had more than 500 years of the printing press and its output to devise effective navigational strategies for its output, and little more than 5 years of a burgeoning world-wide Internet to devise strategies for *its* effective navigation, our feeling of being overwhelmed its quite understandable.

But it is, on the basis of the above development of navigational procedures for other media, quite transitory. Characteristically, critics of technology who have simply attacked the problem as access to too much information, with the implicit or explicit call for a reduction of technology, have made the problem only worse. For if this information overload is really underload—a problem that arises from too little, not too much, informational technology—then the call for a reduction of technology cuts precisely in the wrong direction. What is needed is more not less technology. The problem in the case of information overload is not enough technology—not enough social and technical structure to support our cognitive capacities in this new realm.

Indeed, new technologies that are daily becoming more available are already providing some of the wherewithal to deal with the huge amounts of information they offer. And this wherewithal goes well beyond search engines. Active processing of of information by the mind is the natural antidote to overload, as we have seen, and personal computers connected to online systems via telephone lines turn out to be opening not only enormous gateways for receipt and sorting of information, but easy means for insertion of information by users back into the system—allowing for *contribution* of information, which is the most active type of information—processing of all. Indeed, unlike television and books and all mass media before it, online communication allows for a dialogue in which readers become authors. And the process of reading a text of which you are in part an author, in which some part of what you read is a response to your words, instantly gives you an inside understanding of the information, puts you on top of rather than underneath the mass of data it may engender.

Of course, new technology—even education—costs money and resources. Thus, while some critics of technology might even be prone to agree with the above, they could still argue that the newest computers—the newest systems with the most sophisticated techniques for connecting to online realms and processing information—are the most expensive, which puts at least that prong of remedial media beyond the reach of the common person. And this in turn poses the danger of technological elites, or small groups of people isolated from others by virtue of their expensive communication devices, and consequently communicating only with each other, inside of their groups.

A world of arcane, self-insulating specialists is not a healthy prospect. Can it really be that technologies designed to increase communication have actually had the perverse effect of fragmenting our social structure?

We look now at this question of technological elitism.

Computers and Self-Eliminating Elites

An examination of the evolution of media discloses that new media have tended to "dissociate" one group of people from another almost from the very beginning. Critiques of the written word itself, ranging the Socratic condemnation of writing in the *Phaedrus* to McLuhan's concern about the "flattening" effect of alphabet in *The Gutenberg Galaxy* (1962), have noted that literacy creates new sets of people and perceptions, breakpoints with earlier people and perceptions based on oral and aural rather than alphabetic modes of discourse. Socrates, in particular, worried that reliance on the written word would cause our memories to atrophy, and would work against the ideals of dialogue in which an "author" could always be immediately questioned; McLuhan was concerned that the re-presentation of full-bodied experience via a series of abstract squiggles on a page robbed the human experience of certain crucial dimensions. The Socratic critique is not without some merit, but has essentially been proven wrong—our memories may have indeed atrophied since Homer's time, but our dialogues have flourished across immensely greater reaches of time and space when conducted in the durable encasement of letters. McLuhan's assessment of the alphabet may be well taken, yet whatever its immediate psychological effects the alphabet has also undeniably provided an informational foundation for development of a civilization that has brought people vastly greater amounts of full-sensory experiences in terms of just transportation than any pre-literate culture.

What we can therefore learn from our historical experience with the written word, and its separation of people and cultures and historical epochs into literate and illiterate, is that yes, new media divide, but in the long run such divisions tend to be levelled and equalized. What specifically happens over time to lead to this diminishment of division? Unsurprisingly, new media—remedial media, from the perspective of the problem of fragmentation—are developed and deployed to continue the benefits of the earlier media in a way that does not divide the culture.

In the case of writing, the deployment of the printing press in the West served this purpose admirably: Luther's advice that people should read the Bible for themselves rather than rely on Roman Catholic teaching became practical for the first time with the new availability of printed rather than hand-copied Bibles; the difference between lay and clergy was henceforth reduced. Scientists could test each other's findings and theories more easily when these were disseminated through the press; the resultant scientific revolution made the pursuit of knowledge a public endeavor rather than a matter of the occult. And all of these new texts—religious, scientific, political—created a crucial need to learn how to read: a need that led to the rise of public education, whose primary function is still, quite appropriately, giving children the keys to our culture via literacy, comprehensive library cards for the current ideational world. By the early modern age, there likely was not a person alive who took the Socratic critique of writing seriously.

And where do we stand today? The books, magazines, and newspapers that still pour from the press—indeed more than ever before in terms of sheer circulation—are taken to be the de facto rules of engagement for literacy. Motion pictures, television, and now computers have each been taken to be threats to the literate order (see Neil Postman's *Technopoly*, 1992, for his critique of computers in this regard). Computers, the most recent medium in the hot seat, are especially criticized because not all of our culture has them—under 50 percent of American households do, and the figures are less than half of that in most other parts of the world. The wonderful conversations on Usenet and other groups on the Internet can thus be portrayed as whisperings among the privileged that take place in the middle of the night, while the rest of humanity sits not even on the sidelines, but away from the action completely, rendered less than second-class citizens to this Great Dialog.

Such a picture, however, misses entirely the evolutionary progression of technology and media discussed above, in which each new medium both solves problems of earlier media, and creates new ones of its own. Viewed in that evolutionary perspective, the medium of print turns out not only to have greatly equalized the dissociation of the alphabet, but to have created some polarization of its own. The physical reality of books, for example, means that bookstores and libraries have limitations on what they can stock and offer to readers: no bookstore or library can have anything more than a sample of the total number of texts available. Newspapers enjoy more widespread dissemination than books, but are not easily stored outside of libraries—with the result that, unless one lives near a major library, access to any newspaper other than today's or yesterday's or last week's may be extremely difficult to attain.

The online communication of text speaks eminently to just such deficiencies. Once word-processed on a personal computer with access to the Internet, a text is in principle instantly accessible to anyone any place else in the world with a personal computer and a Web connection; moreover, the text can be read instantly by an unlimited number of people; and it will be there in perfect condition not only tomorrow, but a year, a decade, and likely a century from tomorrow as well. Online communication is, in other words, even more equalizing than the printing press: it makes geographic distance irrelevant, for when speed of light is the mode of transport, all places on the Earth are the same.

But if access to this new system costs money—more money than some people have—then what good is this equalizing access? If I can communicate with anyone in the world, instantly, but lack the funds to do so, then the technology would hardly seem to be equalizing.

There is no doubt that the average book still costs far less than the average computer. But the differences are not as great today as they were 10 and 20 years ago. Indeed, perfectly serviceable computers for the dissemination of text can be purchased today from $50 to $200—the cost of second-hand 386-class machines—and even older, more primitive computers can work fine for these purposes. Further, the cost of online communication has been steadily dropping: universities have long offered it for free to their students and faculty, and the public can in an increasing number of areas have unlimited Internet access for less than $20 per month. While this is no doubt still more than some people can afford, neither is it in the province only of the very rich.

Indeed, the history of media and technology also shows that the cost of new media quickly plummets to levels affordable by most people. The home VCR sold for $2,000 when introduced in the mid 1970s; now VCRs are readily available for a few hundred dollars. The book itself cost an average working-person's monthly salary in the year 1800; books are obviously far less costly now.

When we combine the likely continued reduction in computer prices, and the diminishing cost of accessing online networks, with the intrinsically egalitarian capacity of online communication—accessible to anyone in the world, anywhere, at any time—we can see that the elites brought into being by the computer revolution are temporary and indeed self-eliminating.

Further, online communication, as is also the way with most new media, seems poised to eliminate elites and fragmentations of interests that are not of the computer's making, and were firmly in place before its advent. The first three quarters of the 20th century brought us scientists and scholars in fragmented disciplines who talked mostly only to their closest colleagues at special conferences and or in departments at universities located far from each other in disparate locations around the world. In contrast, any scientist now online has instant access in principle to any other scientist online—and for that matter, members of the public—regardless of the specialized discipline or far-flung geographic situation. The traditional patterns of specialization and dissociation are deeply ingrained, and will no doubt take decades to dissolve. But the point is that, far from further fragmenting our culture, digital communication is providing unprecedented prospects for its weaving together.

A Tale of Two Earthquaked Cities

Ultimately, though information and life are essentially intertwined, life is the more important measure of value: we can be alive, with a paucity of information, and live to remedy that paucity; but lacking life, we have neither life nor information.

The most significant test of technology and its value then, resides not in the realm of media and information, but in the larger realm of human life itself. We have already noted that the gravest threats to our existence come from traditionally natural rather than technological precincts: as much as 3/5ths of the population was wiped out by the Black Plague on some continents; as horrible as war in the 20th century has been, it has thankfully approached nothing like that toll.

Most people are also well aware of the enormous saving and extension of human life via technological strides in medicine and agriculture.

But sometimes a pair of specific, pinpoint events can make the case for technology and its benefits even more dramatically.

In the 1980s, earthquakes of very similar proportion on the Richter scale occurred in two areas: Armenia and San Francisco. In the city of Yerevan, Armenia, hundreds of thousands of lives were lost or severely damaged; in San Francisco, the loss of life was less than 100. The difference between these areas was technological. Yerevan's construction, not designed with earthquakes in mind, collapsed like a house of cards under its quake; in contrast, San Francisco, having learned from its own devastating earthquake at the dawn of the 20th century, had buildings which were by and large able to sway rather than crumble in response to the quake (and indeed, those that crumbled were for whatever reason not in compliance with the earthquake-sensitive standards).

Earthquakes, of course, have plagued humanity through history. We have been subject to their literally pulling the ground out from under us in all manner of dwellings we created. This was the case until we at last devised technologies of architecture that allow us to live with some degree of safety.

Technology that can withstand earthquakes is powerfully symbolic of the role of technology in human existence as a whole. Other than our brains, we have little to commend us in the struggle for existence that is the lot of all life on this planet. But our brains on their own can only do so much: they can think and dream and imagine and plan, yes, but the implementation of these plans, the embodiments of these yearnings, requires technology.

That the resultant devices sometimes turn out not to perform as intended, to create unintended consequences, to perform *as* intended in the case of weapons, means that of course not all technological consequences are beneficial. We are, after all, only human, and can hardly expect perfection in what we create.

We can, however, expect and require improvement—in the availability of food and medicine to more people, in the dissemination of information to greater numbers, and the protection of ourselves and our planet as we know it from ravages that arise out of the natural condition.

And the single best vehicle of that improvement—indeed, the only one we have ever known—is technology, and its capacity to change the world in favor of our finest impulses and ideas.

Innovation in Media and the Decentralization of Authority: the View from Here, There, and Everywhere

Introduction

Harold Innis captured the relationship of information and state power very well, when he observed (1950, 1951) that those who control the means of communication quite naturally control therein the mechanisms of government. Innis further noticed that the more cumbersome, expensive, or otherwise difficult-to-utilize the medium, the more it tended to fall under the control of centralized powers that had the wherewithal to use it. Conversely, "lighter" or more easily disseminated media tended to encourage a decentralization of power—in political, religious, and economic arenas. The classic case in the modern world was the printing press, whose introduction of books and newspapers as mass media shattered the religious monopoly of the Roman Catholic Church, and facilitated such mutually-catalytic decentralizing trends as the Protestant Reformation, the rise of national states, the scientific revolution, capitalism, and, eventually, democracy.

But in such a recognizably modern decentralized age, state monopolies of power continued—and, indeed, in many respects reached their height in the 20th century. This was in part because media evolution also continued, endowing central forces with new modes of power. For example, as McLuhan pointed out (1964), radio was an enormously effective centralizing medium, allowing heads of state to talk to everyone in their nation at once, as a father talks around a table to members of his family. Not surprisingly, the radio age is typified by the four most powerful political leaders of this century—Churchill, Hitler, Roosevelt, and Stalin—each of whom was adept at the radio address (see Levinson, 1997, for details).

Radio, of course, has been replaced by television as the dominating medium in world culture, and now online communication via personal computers and the Internet is beginning to play a major role. For the first time in human history since the "invention" of speech itself, people are able to initiate conversations, on a world-wide individual basis, as easily as they can receive the communication of newspapers, radio, and television.

In this essay, I will explore some of these decentralizing effects—in particular, the way that online communication seems poised to undermine state monopolies of information, and therein other coercive concentrations of power, on an extraordinary and unprecedented basis. We can better understand the significance and impact of such a development by first looking at the role of media in fluctuating cycles of centralization and decentralization in the past five hundred years—our focus in the next several sections. Thumbnail View of the Modern Age Till the Eve of the 20th Century

The revolutionary decentralizing impact of the printing press in the 16th century and after provides a highly instructive prelude to our comprehension of what is happening with the decentralization of text via personal computer communications today.

Heresies had of course been commonplace throughout the history of Christendom, but none had anything like the effect of Luther's. Why? Well, the content of Luther's "protest"—people should read the Bible for themselves, and be ultimately responsible for their own relationship with the Deity, rather than be totally reliant on the Church as a medium—was certainly a provocative ideal. But more provocative still—and effective—was the implementation of that ideal in the actual Bibles that the printing press put into everyone's hands. The Church might well argue against such an ideal, and did; but its argument was lost with every Bible that came off the new presses (see Levinson, 1988, 1997). No ideology of centralization can survive a shift in information technology that pulls the rug out from under it—and turns it into a flying carpet more or less available to all.

But the power of underlying technology is not the whole story. Shifts towards decentralizing may temporarily put centralized authorities out of business, even inconvenience and disadvantage them in the long run, but the wellsprings in human psychology and sociology that engendered centralization in the first place will not disappear (Erich Fromm's *Escape from Freedom*, 1941, still provides the classic accounting of this). Indeed, they sooner or later find expression elsewhere—sometimes via the very media that led to the decentralization. Thus, although the press put teeth in Luther's protest that people should read the Bible for themselves, and although this permanently weakened the power of the Church with sundry consequences, including the rise of national states, these national states themselves soon began utilizing the new powers of the press to shore up their own centralized hegemonies. Monarchs in England, France, and elsewhere quickly established royal printers as a way of placing this new medium under central control; and the very words published, in national vernaculars rather than Latin, served to further crystallize the sense of national identity (see Innis, 1950, for more on the significance of printed national vernaculars).

The Age of Discovery added fuel to this secular centralization, and was itself made possible by the press. Voyages to the New World (much like heresies) had taken place before Columbus, certainly in the now-documented visits of the Norse to Greenland and the east coast of America. But word of these astonishing events was conveyed by word-of-mouth only, and the emphemerality of such communication, like northern winds whispering through the night, seemed more like legend than reality, and ultimately had little if any lasting impact on Europe. In contrast, Columbus's voyage to the New World occurred 50 years after Gutenberg, and word of that momentous event was indeed carried in the new press, which made it a momentous event with commensurate impact. Reading about a New World in black-and-white made it a new world worthy of strategic political and economic investment (see Levinson, 1988, 1997; see Jones, 1984, for Vikings in America; and Morrison, 1942, ch. 27, for dissemination of news of Columbus' voyage as early as 1493, in a pamphlet that became a bestseller').

Interestingly, the economic forces set loose by investment in the New World—first the mercantile revolution and then capitalism—tended to work against the concentration of political power that monarchs sought to wring from the press. In England especially, thirst for information about new markets led merchants to support non-royal presses supported by the new social invention of advertising; and the output of these presses, functioning now as agencies of voluntary rather than coercive order, soon conveyed ideas that could be critical of central authority. Thus were the seeds of a free press sewn, and with it the enduring backbone of democratic society (and, by extension, of libertarian society as well, which also is dependent upon maximum flow of unfiltered information). This process achieved its strongest effect in the United States, where Jefferson and his colleagues wrote a Bill of Rights that forbade any governmental interference whatsoever in matters of the press, and decisively squashed an early attempt by statists (the Alien and Sedition Act) to judge publications critical of the government as reason nonetheless (see Emery & Emery, 1992, and Levinson, 1997).

The 19th century saw democracy further strengthened in England, and in the general spread of constitutional (rather than absolute) monarchies throughout Europe. The press, for its part, became even more efficient, with new "linotype" devices in the second half of the century pouring forth vastly greater quantities of books, magazines, and newspapers than ever before.

But the twentieth century had some surprises in store, in the other direction.

The Centralized Tug of the Twentieth Century

The forces of centralization and decentralization, of coercive and voluntary social orders, as we have seen, each received support from the press through 19th century—though the net result was a world far more decentralized than before the press. In the 20th century, that trend would by and large be drastically reversed.

The "clear and present danger" decision of the US Supreme Court in 1919 was an early and ominous turn of events: the decision, contrary to the Bill of Rights ("Congress shall make no law ... abridging the freedom of speech, or of the press"), held that government had not only a right but an obligation to restrict certain modes of communication, including speech—namely, those communications whose implementations could threaten life, limb, and property. And since one person's distant drum could be another person's clear and present danger, thus was the legal door to any and all censorship flung wide open in the United States.

Meanwhile, a new media basis of centralization had already come into place, quite accidentally. Marconi had sought at the turn of the century to develop a telegraph/telephone that worked without wires; technological constraints, which made receipt of electro-magnetic carrier waves a lot less expensive than their transmission, conspired to make Marconi's "wireless" a one-way mass, simultaneous medium: the radio. Political leaders, as suggested above, were quick to seize this medium as something through everything from relaxed chats to emotional patriotic exhortations could effortlessly reach just about every person in the nation—instantly, and at the same time.

Of course, decentralizing forces were not completely overwhelmed. In the Third Reich, the "White Rose" used early photocopying devices to spread their underground critique of central policy (see Dumbach & Newborn, 1986). And samizdat video in the Soviet Union provided a continuing spring of counter-governmental information in the 1980s (see Levinson, 1992).

But until the last few years, the thrust of our most advanced communication environments was to put more power in central hands. This was because our dominant media seemed intractably one-way vehicles of communication: we can all effortlessly receive news and entertainment from radio and television, but few if any of us can contribute. From the perspective of a thriving democracy, this is clearly not a healthy situation: a citizenship informed only by its government can hardly be informed enough to offer well-grounded criticism of that government. In most cases—including England—this was precisely the case, with the modes of broadcasting being literally under the control of a governmental agency such as the BBC (see Levinson, 1995, for a case in point as to how such restrictions were implemented during the Falklands War in October, 1988). In the United States, the situation was a little better—but even here the news was in the grip of three oligarchic networks, themselves subject to government regulation, and hardly foundations for a widespread non-coercive order (see details on the Federal Communication Commission and its operation in the US, below).

And then, people began communicating online.

The Re-Assertion of Dialog

The limitations of one-way media, indeed, their freezing of dialog, was recognized long ago by Socrates, who worried in the Phaedrus (secs. 275-276) that the written word was capable of giving but one, unvarying answer to all questions put to it: namely, the answer it already had given before the questions. The unprecedented dissemination of information first by the written word, and much more so by the printing press, as we have seen, had enormously powerful decentralizing and democratizing effects anyway. But almost all media throughout history subsequent to speech—the sole exceptions were the telegraph and the telephone—also had within them, regardless of their disseminative and decentralizing powers, profound centralizing capacities by virtue of their foreclosure of dialogue. We have seen that, prior to the 20th century, the tendencies towards decentralization by and large held the upper hand; but we have also seen that, for most of the 20th century, one-way centralizing media shifted that balance in the other direction.

Few would have predicted that the computer, long regarded in the popular culture as a prime vehicle of totalitarian, mathematically organized society, would serve to decisively counteract this centralizing juggernaut. Vannevar Bush was one, perhaps the first, who in 1945 suggested the development of a "memex" device that would sit in everyone's office, and allow electronic transmission and storage of memos and data to everyone else in the world with a similar device (see Levinson, 1997, for details).

The keys to such a device—which were attained in personal computers and modems that began to be used by the general populace in the 1980s—consisted of (a) something that allowed for easy creation and storage of text, and (b) something that allowed for its equally easy dissemination. Instant, global receipt of information was already in place in most of the world via broadcast media. What was lacking, then, was a device or system that could both create and transmit data; and the online computer network—the Internet—is just such a system.

The online network became possible, not surprisingly, by "piggybacking" computer connectivity to an already world-wide and powerfully effective telephone system. The telephone was the lone tower of modern technology in undiluted service to interactivity: unlike even the telegraph, which required people to leave their homes to send messages, and became a marginal medium in the 20th century in any case, the telephone allowed people to communicate to anyone else in the world with a telephone, at any time, and all from the comfort of one's place of business or home. This was, and is, a powerfully decentralizing device indeed.

The only drawback about the telephone, from the standpoint of political impact, is that it is *too* personal-favoring just one-to-one communication—and of course deals only in spoken words. The consequence is a medium used for everything from personal chats to serious business conversation, but usually not for the building of social consensus required for reservoirs of voluntary political power, a consensus requiring groups of people able to consider (and contribute to) a body of information reliably in place and accessible over a period of time.

The plugging of text-producing devices—personal computers—into this phone system provided the necessary balance, for written text has the capacity to endure as long as needed to become a locus of group analysis and critique (see Levinson, 1995). The asynchronous interactivity this allows—in contrast to the synchronous interactivity of phone and in-person conversations—is powerfully conducive to rational discourse.

Let us look at the traditional in-person classroom as an example of what occurs in a situation of synchronous communication, at its best. Only one person can talk at any one time; thus, at any given moment in this environment, all people save one are unable to contribute. Partially as a necessary vehicle to keep order in such an environment, a strong leader is necessary—indeed, a leader who functions more as a dictator than a facilitator—the teacher, who strictly controls who speaks to whom, about what, and when. Further, once the class is over, so is the active dissemination and analysis of knowledge that occurred there. Yes, people can and do contemplate what they obtained (and in some limited degree, contributed to) in the classroom; but this is an after-the-fact act of retrospection. Once the group is adjourned, there is no opportunity to actively continue the discourse. (Of course, the class may meet again the following week, and a punctuated series of related discourses are possible, but this is not the same as a continuing discourse.)

Now consider the online class (or any online discussion) in contrast. Anyone can post a note to such a discussion, any time of day. Further, once posted, such contributions can be read and re-read at any time, as often as desired. Leaders are still necessary—and assume that position either by appointment or emergence—but their role becomes more of a moderator or guide than a dictator of discussion. Even the physical dynamics of online communities support this: people are judged solely by what their words convey on the screen, rather than the clothes they wear or their position at the table. Hierarchies are thus leveled; the coercive centralized authority of the teacher in a classroom dissolves into a more voluntary pedagogic order of active learners guided by the moderator of an online course.

A highly significant further advantage of online in comparison to in-person discourse obtains from the capacity of anyone, anywhere in the world, to in principle participate. The in-person meeting, after all, is only as valuable as the people who are able to be in physical attendance. But obstacles of all kinds—geographic, economic, even physical—can prevent people from attending such meetings, from being part of that intellectual process. In contrast, the online discussion is accessible to anyone with a personal computer and a telephone.

Much has been made by critics of the digital age about the de-facto economic restrictions of online communications that flow from the cost of computers, and, secondarily, of telephone connections. The first is warranted—but only in regard to the part of the population which cannot afford an expenditure of several hundred American dollars, the current cost (at least, in the United

States) of serviceable second-hand personal computer systems capable of Internet access. And while this is certainly more expensive that the cost of an in-person conversation, neither does it make the online world a plaything of just the rich. Likewise, the cost of phone connections, while certainly more than nothing, is little more than what people would pay for general phone service in their homes without online connections.

In any case, the number of people on the Internet is currently estimated as 75 million, and growing—large enough to attract the interest of governments anxious to keep a lid on these centrifugal forces. In the next section, we look at some of the first salvos of their counter-reformation.

Grounds for the Counter-Reformation in Media

The two time-honored occasions for government intervention in media that have come down to us through the 20th century are national security and public standards of decency.

National security was the driving force behind the above-mentioned "clear and present danger" decision, intended to give the government a means of stopping anti-draft campaigning during war time. It continued to surge as a rationale for government censorship in the US until the Supreme Court in 1971 refused to let Richard Nixon more than temporarily stop (for 15 days) the publication of the "Pentagon Papers" in *The New York Times* and *The Washington Post*. The restraint of the press for even 15 days was an abrogation of the First Amendment in the Bill of Rights, but the Supreme Court's decision not to continue that restraint, despite the pleadings of the Chief Executive, dramatically demonstrated that mere invocation of national security was not necessarily enough to sustain such abrogation, or even initiate it again in the future.

But concern about pornography had by then already moved up the ladder as the prime occasion for government control of broadcast media. The Federal Communications Commission had been created in 1934 to make sure that the scarce resource of broadcast airways—there was a low technical limit then as to how many stations could broadcast clearly on the bandwidths—was utilized "in the public interest." Whatever the intentions of the framers of the law that brought the FCC into being, in practice its mandate was at once interpreted as an obligation to make sure than nothing "offensive" was put out over the air. Further, as technology increased the number of stations that could broadcast in the given bandwidth, and all but eliminated the initial "scarce resource" concern, a new reason for government regulation of broadcasting was put forth: people have no prior knowledge of what might be broadcast over a given radio or television channel, so radio and television have an obligation to keep things "clean". The Supreme Court, in staking out this new reason, offered the following argument: whereas people make a specific purchase decision about likely content every time they buy a newspaper or a book, or see a movie, they make no such informed decision about content when they turn on a radio or television, which in principle can broadcast anything. So, in effect, a deal was struck between the ever-contending forces of decentralization and freedom of expression versus centralization and government control: newspapers and print media in general were entitled to protection from coercive government interference under the Bill of Rights (a position strengthened in the Pentagon Papers case), but radio and TV were to be held accountable to government-imposed standards.

Since broadcast media are inherently centralized in any case, in a sense the imposition of governmental control on radio and TV did little to further centralize those media: they were already unlikely to have any profound decentralizing effect, due to the one-way limitations of their technology.

It was into this situation that the extraordinarily decentralizing possibilities of online communication suddenly inserted themselves. What could the government do in response?

National security had already waned as an issue, especially so with the end of the Cold War. And besides, online communication in its first widespread public expression was much more rooted (and still is) in the realm of entertainment than politics.

Well, there was always pornography.

But wait: people who log on to online networks are making conscious decisions each time they do so. The online participant is thus much more like the purchaser of a newspaper than the person who turns on a radio in a car, or sits back half asleep as the programs change on a television screen. Further, cable television—which, unlike network television, must be specifically paid for—had already been ruled outside of the FCC's strict guidelines on indecent programming.

Nonetheless, the Communications Decency Act—which held people criminally guilty for what they write online—was signed into law in 1996. It was struck down by the Supreme Court a year later, essentially on the grounds that the Internet is more like a newspaper than a broadcast medium. But Congress is at work on a successor law.

Twilight for Monopolies of Knowledge

To be clear about the current state of online communications and its impact: the decentralizing effects suggested above are at this point mainly hypothetical, certainly in the political arena. No election or issue has been decided, certainly no government has been severely comprised or overthrown, due to anything that has occurred online.

The specific occasion for current public clamorings for some governmental regulation of online communication in the United States is the growth of pornography created by adults and directed to children on the Internet. Leaving aside the volatile child's rights' libertarian issue of whether children should be entitled' to receive such material, we can certainly think of ways other than censorship for keeping such material away from children—namely, better parental supervision of the children's time online. Typically, those who call for censorship are unimpressed by such decentralized strategies—which suggests that child pornography, if not a pretext for government intervention online, is certainly being seized upon as a propitious circumstance for such action.

A vivid explanation of any central authority's interest in controlling such widespread decentralization of information comes, again, from Harold Innis (1951), and his observation of how the difficult system of hieroglyphics in Ancient Egypt (even modern ideographic systems, such as Chinese, can take decades to fully master, with its thousands of different ideograms) concentrated enormous knowledge and thus political power in the handful of priests who could write and read it. So predominating were these priests and what Innis aptly termed their "monopoly of knowledge," that they managed to eradicate a rival monotheistic religion promulgated by none other than a supposedly all-powerful Pharaoh, Ikhnaton (Amenhotep IV), a few generations after his death. In contrast, the politically powerless Ancient Hebrews were able to set in motion a similar monotheism that eventually proselytized most of world—with only the alphabet, a vastly simpler (20+ letters) and thus highly decentralizing system, as their scepter. (See Levinson, 1997, for more: the alphabet also had the advantage of providing a highly efficient mode in its totally abstract system for communicating about a Deity that was omnipotent, omni-present, yet invisible.)

However, the alphabet—and all the grounds for the emergence of voluntary orders it afforded—was nonetheless a prisoner of the medium it was written upon. Thus, although it was liberating in comparison to hieroglyphic cultures, it came to be a favorable vehicle for new monopolies of knowledge held by new groups of priests who were all but the sole practitioners of literacy through the Dark and Middle Ages in Europe. Those monopolies were in turn shattered by the placement of letters upon the mass-produced pages of books that issued from the press—but the cycle continued with new centers of knowledge, in universities and national capitals, also constructed with printed books.

Cycles continue—the pendulum between coercive and voluntary orders swings on—as long as the underlying media structures permit a swing in one direction or another. The alphabet and other modes of human expression on the Internet offer unprecedented decentralizing opportunities—libraries, universities, publishers all become more or less the same on a world-wide system that instantly conveys one's written word anywhere in the world, to a number of people limited only by the number who have access to computers, with likely more permanency than books that can go out of print. Moreover, technologies are bringing the human voice, still and motion photography, and all manner of graphics, into this growing, universally participational arena.

No wonder, then, that governments are looking for any opportunity to put at least some of this under their control. But the technology has already outstripped them. The tendencies towards centralization have had enormous resilience throughout history, for they speak to some human needs, but they now seem likely to be stretched to their very limits as they try to rein in a medium that is transforming a world of speakers and authors into publishers.

References

Bush, Vannevar (1945) "As We May Think." *The Atlantic Monthly*, July, pp. 101-108.

Dumbach, Annette E & Jud Newborn (1986) *Shattering the German Night*. Boston: Little, Brown.

Emery, Michael & Edwin Emery (1992) *The Press and America*, 7th ed. Englewood Cliffs, NJ: Prentice Hall.

Fromm, Erich (1941) *Escape from Freedom*. New York: Rinehart.

Innis, Harold A. (1950) *Empire and Communications*. Toronto: University of Toronto Press.

Innis, Harold A. (1951) *The Bias of Communication*. Toronto: University of Toronto Press.

Jones, Gwyn (1984) *A History of the Vikings*. Oxford: Oxford University Press.

Levinson, Paul (1988) *Mind at Large: Knowing in the Technological Age*. Greenwich, CT: JAI Press.

Levinson, Paul (1992) *Electronic Chronicles: Columns of the Changes in our Time*. San Francisco, CA: Anamnesis Press.

Levinson, Paul (1995) *Learning Cyberspace: Essays on the Evolution of Media and the New Education*. San Francisco, CA: Anamnesis Press.

Levinson, Paul (1997) *The Soft Edge: A Natural History and Future of the Information Revolution*. New York and London: Routledge.

McLuhan, Marshall (1964) *Understanding Media*. New York: Mentor.

Morrison, Samuel E. (1942) *Admiral of the Ocean Sea*. Boston: Little, Brown.

Plato, *Phaedrus*.

Entering Cyberspace: What to Watch, What to Watch Out for

The instant, worldwide exchange of information via the Internet and its sundry computer nodes and pathways has created a learning cyberspace—new electronic fora accessible to people anywhere in the world with telephones and personal computers, and thus located everywhere but nowhere (or in no one physical place). As Marshall McLuhan aptly pointed out more than a quarter of a century ago (see McLuhan, 1960), the concept of a center and margins flows from a world in which ideas are expressed and disseminated on pages of fixed lines and four frozen edges. In contrast, words in electronic text move through ever-renewable venues of all centers and no fixed tops and bottoms and margins (or all margins and no centers, which amounts to the same equi-accessible situation). The cognitive and social dimensions of these new realms differ in many ways from the traditional in-person scholarly locales of universities, think-tanks, and libraries closed after midnight.

Patterns of information that work simultaneously in many places predate human beings, in the biological sense that genes provide similar directions for expression of traits within numerous members of a species located across great distances and times. Indeed, fractal similarities in organic and inorganic arrangements of matter (as in crystalline structures) show a cyberspace in form that encompasses not only the living world, but the realm of inert material from which life sprang.

Human cultures celebrate aspects of cyberspace in the notion of a deity that is omnipresent (located everywhere) yet invisible to normal perception (located nowhere). So transcendent of physical reality is this idea that it required a medium which itself had no connection to the physical world—the alphabet, which was indispensable to the Hebrew dissemination of monotheism (see Innis, 1950, and Levinson, 1988, 1997, for more). In contrast to pictographic writing and its hieroglyphic and ideographic offspring, in which a different symbol is needed for each representation, the non-mimetic alphabet and its 20-or-so letter code is tied only to vocalizations, and can thus easily represent anything and everything in the visual world, or nothing in the physical world at all. The importance of the alphabet as a platform and vehicle for cyberspatial monotheism prefigures the role of digital technology in enabling the cyberspace of today. Like the letters of the alphabet, the binary codes of computers have no physical resemblance to the events they describe.

The distribution of scientific and other texts across continents and centuries via printed books can be seen as an attempt not only to further cyberspatial ideas (like monotheism) but to create an actual cyberspace by mechanical means. The result was what I call "pocket cyberspaces"—separate informational communities that were more or less simultaneous within each community (as in geographically dispersed people reading a mass-produced book at the same time, or in a given university or class, where the informational and physical community coincided) but which had far less simultaneity between communities. Motion picture theaters are the high watermark of such pocket cyberspaces in the entertainment arena. One might say that, in the evolution of cyberspace, live theaters are to motion picture theaters are to television as in-person classrooms are to books are to online education and scholarship.

Electronic media quicken the flow of information, and therein bring cyberspace into more unified and fuller dimension. Television distributes the same images to an unlimited number of screens simultaneously, but in a way that at first did not allow interaction or response from the receivers (this was McLuhan's "global village," circa 1964). Computer networks add the crucial component of interactivity, and encourage creation and transmission as well as reception of text from all members of an online community.

McLuhan's notion of "acoustic space" (Carpenter & McLuhan, 1960) and Roxanne Hiltz's "virtual classroom" construct (DeLoughry, 1988) are early theoretical attempts to describe and analyze unified cyberspace environments, in first emergence. Ted Nelson's study of hypertext (1981/1990) and J. David Bolter's concept of "writing space" (1991) address text further along the reader-equals-writer axis (in an online computer network, readers and writers of text constantly switch back and forth). Various meditations on "e-fiction" (electronic text fiction) by observers like Sarah Smith (1993), Stuart Moulthrop (1994), and John McDaid (1994) embrace similar territory. But such studies focus primarily on the figure of text and not enough on the ground of online community that gives electronic text its distinctive life.

On the other hand, Howard Rheingold's vetting of "virtual community" (1993) makes text almost as invisible a constituent of the online community as the circulatory systems of the human beings who comprise it, and the domain of "virtual reality"—which, along with the Internet, was one of the two standard bearers of online activities in the first half of the 1990s—is thus far more a plaything of entertainment and demonstration than a vehicle of serious scholarship, though the two obviously have their points of connection.

The development of completely online university programs in the past few years has been accorded only footnote if any status in most of the above studies (the exception is Hiltz), yet the online course provides a nearly equally high-profile forum for text and online social dynamics, and thus may be the best place to seek clues to the path and constitution of worldwide cyberspatial intellectual communities now emerging. Online education—in which the book and the classroom, the library and the university, the faculty and the students, all converge into equally accessible exchanges of knowledge, that is, they all become the same online—thus teaches not only its participants, but the rest of the world about its future.

The limits of cyberspace stem from the DNA that both presaged it and, through the human brains it gave rise to, actually brought it into being. This DNA insists not only on the technological implementations of our dreams for instant, universal access, but in a myriad of interactions of in-person presence and the flesh. We may someday wish to change such needs, but until we do, and acquire the power to do so, cyberspace will still pale in key aspects of comparison to walking on a windy beach in September, dining in a fine restaurant, or being anywhere in touching distance with someone dear to us.

Moreover, this hardwired need for physical presence informs our formal knowledge acquisition processes. The thought of robots rather than people making first contact with the universe beyond our planet, of space probes flown from the ground via virtual reality cockpits, is distressing with good cause to some space advocates, who recognize the enormous advantages in subtlety and flexibility that our biological means of perception yet enjoy over any technologically extended or vicarious mode.

We consider each of these limitations of cyberspace in the next two sections.

The Limits of Cyberspace on Earth

My grandmother had a reputation as a fruit-squeezer among the bustling stalls off Pelham Parkway in the Bronx. "Mrs. Hoff," they'd see her coming, "we've got some great cantaloupes for you." And they'd hand her one, which she'd hold up to the light, divine in some indefinable way, and either accept or reject regardless of the hype from the fruit store. And she'd do the same for every carrot and head of lettuce she bought.

In-person presence—the full interplay of every relevant sense in the sensorium—was the only way of interacting with reality for my grandmother. At least insofar as fruit and vegetables were concerned. (She did read newspapers.)

As we've seen above, the 20th century can be regarded as an age of increasing surrogacy in our relations with the outside world. We started a hundred years ago with a shift from live theatrical performances to movies on the screen. Midway through the century more and more people started watching movies at home on little TV screens rather than going out to public theaters. Recently many Americans have acquired the option of ordering movies for the TV screen via pay-per-view—eliminating the quick trip to the video store—though some of us, grandmothers of the information age, still get a kick out of actually handling the video cantaloupes, hefting the boxes and reading the blurbs on the back in the store.

All this, of course, blanches in vicariousness to the precincts of cyberspace, where not only our interactions, but the very stuff of our choices—the very carrot or face on the screen—is an informational construct, a digital concoction through and through.

What residue of "in-personness," of fruit-handling, will be left in the 21st century? Is the yearning that most people alive today no doubt feel for in-person presence akin to the continuing preference of some recalcitrant nostalgists for typewriters and fountain pens?

Not likely—certainly not for some aspects of life which can only be experienced in the flesh. A dinner at a fine restaurant, with its rich mixture of tastes, smells, sights, and sounds—a walk on a moonlit beach, soft sand and salt air—these indeed simply have no online analogue. The hottest chats on the fastest iconic networks hold not a candle to the restaurant and the beach. Some parts of our lives, I think we can safely say, will always be conducted with best result offline.

In-person environments also still provide a dimension of choice missing in even the most global and diverse digital realms. Since the digital world is deliberately constructed, it is inevitably pre-packaged, and pre-packaging limits options in its early phases. Ultimately the reach of purely informational access will offer options undreamed of in the old-fashioned store—online bookstores are already giving us such glimpses—but at present I have a far greater selection of tapes in the video store than via pay-per-view. Just as my grandmother had far greater choice of cantaloupes in the fruit store than had she bought one from a mail order catalogue. Indeed, in the fruit store she could forego the fruit altogether if it didn't pass her tactile muster.

But that still leaves a lot of room even in today's communities of representations. Most modes of education, which after all move on discussion and bouncing around of ideas, can be better conducted online. Yet even here there are significant exceptions: were I to need brain surgery (as some who oppose my championship of technology might well urge), I'd prefer a doctor who had been trained in the old-fashioned, hands-on way, thank you.

The best guide to the likely survival of modes of communication is media history: Sound-only radio flourishes in an age of sight-and-sound TV, whereas sight-only silent movies fell by the wayside once talkies came along. Why? Because hearing-without-seeing is a mode literally embedded into our specieshood: we have eyelids not earlids, the world grows dark every night but not necessarily silent, etc. For the same reasons, seeing-without-hearing is an awkward mode of perception (we can put our hands over our ears, yes, but this isn't very effective). Thus, radio, in tapping into an already-profound human mode of communication, survived; silent movies did not. The same analysis can be usefully applied to other media: still photography survived the advent of motion pictures because stillness is a fundamental part of human perception (most things far off in the distance look still); black-and-white photography, on the other hand, is no longer used except as a deliberate artistic statement, because we see in color. (See my "Human Replay," 1979, and *The Soft Edge*, 1997, for more on the survival of the most humanly fit media.)

In activities in which surrogacy satisfies the already-present patterns of our species, it will likely not only survive but supplant some in-person modes. As Donald T. Campbell (1974) pointed out, the lowly amoeba has no capacity for vicarious perception or interaction—all it knows of its world is what it physically bumps into—and thus dies the instant it comes to "know" something noxious. Evolution has given more complex organisms better buffers to help them navigate the world-perception in animals, ideas and technologies in humans—and these allow us the safety, the dignity in some cases, of knowing things without the risk of our physical commitment. The vicariousness of our newest media thus has a deep-rooted evolutionary imprimatur.

But in human activities in which only the real thing will do, in which the call of the amoeba is still eminently felt, we can expect the spirit of my grandmother to prevail into the 21st century and well beyond. Hefting the cantaloupe still has its appeal.

But what about spaceships designed to heft our species off of this planet? Here we encounter some who feel the risk of sending humans is too great—that space is therefore best explored by cyberspace.

But here we also encounter some, myself included, who think that complete substitution of cyberspace for outer space would be a miscarriage of cyberspace, a failure to achieve our best cosmic potential.

The Limits of Cyberspace Beyond

Cyberspace (the digital "intraverse") and outer space (the analogue universe) coincide insofar as relativity says that as mass approaches the speed of light it grows to infinite proportions—thereby being everywhere at once, just like cyberspace. But Einstein's theory could be wrong, metaphors can deceive, and besides, issues of speed-of-light transport are as yet far away in the human exploration of space.

Here is a blurb on where we stand —or fly—today:

Successful test launches of the Delta Clipper X in the early 1990s—capped off with the rocket vertically landing on its haunches in the classic science fiction style—rekindled enthusiasm in some quarters for human penetration of the cosmos. The repair of the Hubble telescope and its corroboration of black holes, its discovery of planets around distant stars, and like extensions of our vision to further reaches of the universe added fuel to the new ferment about space. We scanned the moons of Jupiter, and also returned to our own Moon and Mars in the 1990s. Extraordinary robotic sojourns on the surface of the Red Planet beamed pictures right into our living rooms.

But therein resides the problem. Although humans still venture into space via shuttles, and space stations and trips with humans to Mars are on tap for early in the 21st century, our communion with the cosmos in the 1990s was almost entirely vicarious. The high watermark for direct human exploration of worlds beyond Earth in the second millennium, in the 20th century, was attained three decades prior to the end of the century, when we walked upon the Moon.

Why is this a problem? What does it matter if humans see worlds beyond on screens, through the eyes of robots, rather than our own?

Although vicarious exploration is vastly safer, we pay a price for this safety. No planet on a screen can convey the sensation of actually being there. And with our inability to sense all there is to sense of a new world on a screen, to directly do things there, comes a restriction on our capacity to deeply learn more of the unknown. For as John Dewey (e.g., 1925) pointed out early in the 20th century, our most profound knowledge often comes from doing rather than seeing—from being on and in, rather than looking at and listening to, something.

This loss of the full interactive experience in realms which we do not otherwise know is ultimately the only danger of cyberspace. We need not worry that people will live here on Earth through their computer screens, because in-person contact with people in physical proximity will ever be too sweet and easy to forego. But we need be on guard that the only windows through which we see the cosmos at large are computer and TV screens—digital transmissions—when real vision, and all that it may hold, awaits us.

Conclusion

We started as a species whose brain power greatly exceeded its technological expression, and thus we quite naturally devised all manner of social structures for exchange of information that seemed to require physical presence. That many of these activities do not intrinsically require in-person presence to the degree we supposed (if at all) points to the many areas in which cyberspace will replace or complement in-person exchanges in the future. Indeed, the main task for people who understand cyberspace will for some time continue to be to alert the rest of the world to its value.

But to the extent that some of our social structures—not only personal but scientific—seem likely to defy replacement by information and representation, because they have value incapable of supply in cyberspace, we can say that the enduring value of cyberspace is the way it makes us better equipped to physically navigate and ingest the real, offline, world.

References

Bolter, J. D. (1991) *Writing Space: The Computer, Hypertext, and the History of Writing*. Hillsdale, NJ: Erlbaum.

Campbell, D. T. (1974) "Evolutionary Epistemology," in Schilpp, P. A., ed. *The Philosophy of Karl Popper*. La Salle, IL: Open Court, pp. 413-463.

DeLoughry, T. (1988) "Remote Instruction Using Computers Found as Effective as Classroom Sessions." *Chronicle of Higher Education*, 20 April, p. A15.

Dewey, J. (1925) *Experience and Nature*. Chicago, IL: Open Court.

Innis, H. (1950) *Empire and Communications*. Toronto: University of Toronto.

Levinson, P. (1979) "Human Replay: A Theory of the Evolution of Media." Ph.D. diss., New York University.

Levinson, P. (1988) *Mind at Large: Knowing in the Technological Age*. Greenwich, CT: JAI Press.

Levinson, P. (1997) *The Soft Edge: A Natural History and Future of the Information Revolution*. New York and London: Routledge.

McDaid, J. (1994) "Luddism, SF, and the Aesthetics of Electronic Fiction." *The New York Review of Science Fiction*, 69, May, pp. 1 ff.

McLuhan, M. (1960) "The Effect of the Printed Book on Language in the 16th Century," in Carpenter, E. & McLuhan, M. eds. *Explorations in Communication*. Boston: Beacon Press, pp. 125-135.

McLuhan, M. (1964) *Understanding Media*. New York: Mentor.

Moulthrop, S. (1994) "Electronic Fictions and The Lost Game of Self.'" *The New York Review of Science Fiction*, 66, February, pp. 1 ff.

Nelson, T. H. (1981/1990) *Literary Machines*. Sausalito, CA: Mindful Press.

Rheingold, H. (1993) *The Virtual Community*. Reading, MA: Addison-Wesley.

Smith, S. (1993) "Electronic Fictions: The State of the Art." *The New York Review of Science Fiction*, 63, November, pp. 1 ff.

Learning Unbound: Online Education and the Mind's Academy

Like most activities as old as humanity, the underlying structures of education seem so obvious as to be taken for granted. Formal learning requires a teacher, a student, a subject to teach, and a place to teach it—whether in the personal tutor and small academies of the ancient world or the clusters of buildings teeming with classrooms in the present day. The advent and evolution of writing, culminating in mass-produced books, changed the equation a little, bringing into play the notion of wisdom that could be at first engaged and acquired outside of the classroom. But even in education mediated by books, the nub of the process—the essence of the education—takes place in the physical classroom, the place to which students bring back the lessons they've acquired in books, for confirmation, clarification, and elaboration.

When environments are as deeply ingrained in our culture as the classroom, their limitations are difficult to see. Thus, most of us accept without much objection the fact that once the physical classroom is vacated, the active dialogue of the class is put on hold until the next class meeting. If obstacles of time and/or geography prevent us from attending a specific class, or taking a particular course, or, for that matter, attending a university that's too far away, we tend to accept that also as something that just flows from the very nature of education—much as we understand (though may not like) that a book we want to read may be out of the library, or that we need to stay silent when someone else is talking in a class because of course two people cannot talk at the same time.

But imagine a classroom equally available to anyone, anywhere in the world—or, that matter, off of the world—with a personal computer and connection to a phone system. Think of a classroom whose discussions, proceeding asynchronously, went on continuously, 24-hours a day, with no limitation on how many people could participate at any one time. And picture yourself with access to a library comprised of papers that could be read by thousands of people, all at once, and yet these texts would still be there for you whenever you wished.

Such conditions are not only not imaginary, they are not even near-future. These are, in fact, the basic structures of online education—a radically new mode of learning that has been quietly underway nearly two decades

A Thumbnail History of OnLine Communication and Education

The advantages of a computer as a communications tool—as distinct from a programming instrument, data manager, or word processor—were first developed in various government and corporate sites (such as Xerox's "PARC" in California) in the 1960s and 70s. In those days, people used "dumb" terminals that could do nothing other than connect to a central mainframe computer, on which people could word process, send and receive messages, and therein engage in all manner of discussion, trivial and profound.

By the early 1980s, the introduction of relatively inexpensive personal computers and modems had given this process a dramatic boost: people could now log on any time they pleased, from their homes or places of business, provided only that they had access to a telephone, which of course almost everyone did. Commercial online networks like CompuServe and the Source (later purchased by CompuServe) began flourishing. The Western Behavioral Sciences Institute in 1982 began offering a two-year program of non-credit "executive strategy" seminars offered completely online to busy CEOs and government officials, at a cost of $25,000. Two years later, the New York Institute of Technology began offering a few courses for undergraduate credit online at a more reasonable tuition. And in the Fall of 1985, Connected Education (the organization I founded and still operate with my wife, Tina Vozick) began offering a series of online graduate-level courses for credit granted by the New School for Social Research in New York City. By 1988, our program had developed into a full-fledged Master of Arts curriculum, with a specialization in Technology and Society—offered entirely online. More than 2,000 students from 40 states in the U.S. and 15 countries around the world including China, Japan, Singapore, Senegal, The United Arab Emirates, Colombia, and most countries in Europe have taken courses in our program—all without having to leave their families or means of employment.

Though transmission speeds have increased a more than a hundred fold since the mid-1980s—from 300 to 56,000 bps—the features of online education have remained pretty much the same since its inception. In that sense, online education, especially its general dependence on text rather than images, icons, and graphic interfaces, serves as a middle- or even low-tech oasis in an otherwise galloping, high-tech computer world. This, as we'll see in more detail below, allows people to participate with equipment costing hundreds rather than thousands of dollars, and is also consonant with the traditional image of the scholar in an environment somewhat removed from the hustle-and-bustle of the beaten commercial track.

Of course, advanced personal computer equipment is always "downwardly compatible" with text modes, meaning that those who have more expensive systems can take full advantage of online education, and indeed retrieve its written lessons via icon command, and read and write them via fancy fonts and windows, or via speech synthesizer in some cases, and interspersed with all manner of images and sounds if appropriate. In some specialized courses—say, a course on the poetics of relativity, where an equation or two might be useful—such specialized graphics might even be recommended. But even in these courses, the heart of online education is the text.

On the Inside of an OnLine Course

The actual process of online education works much like e-mail, except rather than one person communicating to another or a group of people, we have many people communicating to many, with the central computer system playing the crucial role of keeping track of who in the group has read who else's messages. Here's how it works:

I taught an online Masters level course called "Artificial Intelligence and Real Life." The course carried three graduate-level credits (in this case, awarded by the New School for Social Research), and took place over a two-month period of time online. This time frame contrasts sharply with that of an equivalent "in-person" course, which at the New School and most other "place-based" universities would usually extend three-and-half months—almost twice as long as the online course. Why is this? The answer lies in the intensity of learning that takes place in a course continuously in session online—a course in which students can constantly log on with their thoughts, comments, and questions, and read not only what the faculty member has to say, but, in some ways even more valuable, what all the other students have to say as well.

Prior to the start of an online course, I prepare an "Opener" (the equivalent of a first day's lecture in an in-person class), and a course outline. The Opener not only sketches out what the course will be about, but invites students to jump in immediately with questions about the course and brief descriptions of who they are. In an online course, participation in the form of entering messages into the course is essential. Unlike the in-person class, in which the teacher can have a sense of how well the class is following the curriculum just by looking at the expressions on the faces of students, the online class requires actual writing by students if they are to have an online identity and role in the course. Thus, a highly significant subsidiary benefit of taking any online course is that it sharpens the student's writing ability.

My course outline, which is posted along with my Opener on the first day of the online course, shows that this course will proceed very differently in each of its two months. The first month will entail students reading and discussing, with my input and guidance, basic texts in the field, including non-fiction works such as Bolter's *Turing's Man* and relevant fiction like Asimov's robot series. This part of the course will be most like an in-person course, although the dynamics of the in-person classroom and out-of-class readings will be fused together and transformed into a much more fluid, steadily progressing dialogue online. The second part of the course will take advantage of the online environment in a more unique and unprecedented way: students will play roles in a mock trial, in which a space captain is accused a murdering a beautiful female android.

In a classic "Twilight Zone" episode starring Jack Warden and Jean Marsh ("The Lonely," written by Rod Serling and first broadcast November 13, 1959), an innocent man (Warden) is found guilty of a heinous crime he didn't commit, and is sentenced to solitary life imprisonment on a barren asteroid. A Captain takes pity on him, believes in his innocence, and brings a beautiful android (Marsh) along on one on his stops, to serve as company for the prisoner. The prisoner at first rejects her, then falls in love in with her. The Captain returns the next year with good news: the prisoner's innocence has been established, and he can come home. But there's no room on the ship for the android, and the Captain eventually has to blow her head off, leaving her wires rudely dangling, to make his point. Here the "Twilight Zone" episode ends.

Our online trial begins several years later, back on Earth, when the freed prisoner brings the Captain up on charges of murder. I play the freed prisoner, and the students play all other roles—the Captain, Defense and Prosecuting Attorneys, Expert Witnesses of various sorts, and the Jury. In a class of 8-10 students, this works out perfectly.

Since 1985, when I first began conducting this trial online, it's worked well with as few as five and as many as fifteen students. And these numbers are pretty much the limits for any successful online course taught by one teacher—fewer leave an online discussion without sufficient critical mass, greater numbers can overwhelm any instructor's capacity to respond well to each of the students.

Thus, on the first day of this online course, I post my Opener and outline. I live in New York, but that hardly matters—I have on occasion started and conducted courses from places in England and numerous cities around the U.S. But let's say on this occasion I "upload" my opener and outline to the central course topic at 10 AM, EST, from New York. As soon as those messages have been entered, all registered students are admitted to the course topic. All students have access to our online campus and its campus-wide areas like the Connect Ed Library and the Connect Ed Cafe, but only students registered for a particular course have access to its Opener and outline. At 11:05 AM EST—actually 4:05 PM London time—John logs on from London, and "downloads" my message. Downloading means he has a copy of it now on his personal computer; he could also have printed it out at the time, or he may wish to print it later. He logged on using a local Internet provider he already had in England, but he could have just as easily used his CompuServe account to reach our system, or used a local public dialup number that also connects to our system through Sprintnet. Next, Laurie, an early riser out in San Francisco, logs on to our system at 11:20 AM EST, 8:20 Pacific time via a SprintNet node that's a local call for her, and similarly downloads my Opener and outline. But she has a few minutes, and is in a contemplative mood, so after logging off she writes (on her favorite word processor) a few paragraphs about who she is and why she's taking the course. And she also asks a question: What exactly is the difference between an android and a robot? She re-connects to our online campus, and uploads this text to our course topic at 8:55 AM her time, 11:55 AM New York time. Message 1 in the course is my Opener; Message 2 is my outline; Message 3 is Laurie's first note. Now Joichi logs on from Tokyo and reads these first three messages. He decides to enter a few lines about himself while still online, and also to answer Laurie's question. He types, "My understanding is that an android is a robot that looks like a human—either has flesh and blood, or seems to." That's Message 4. Two hours later, John logs back on from London, and enters about six paragraphs of text explaining who he is—he's a student completing his doctorate in evolutionary biology at Cambridge with a term off right now—and why he's taking this course.

I log back on now at 4:00 PM, NY time, and am delighted to find this multi-national dialogue already under way. Five more students located in various cities in the US and Canada have yet to log on, but I can see already that the course is off to a good start. Three students have already logged on. Further, one has posed a good question, and another has answered it. Students teaching each other is one of the prime dividends of online education. At the end of the month, when each student submits a midterm essay to me online, I will make them available to all other students in our course who have submitted essays. Students thus get the benefit not only of my comments on their essays, but the comments of their colleagues. By the time our online trial begins in the second month, a powerful online learning community will have coalesced in our course, with students who have never met each in person developing strong intellectual and often personal attachments—as friends, and, on occasion, even more. And these will be strengthened further in the give-

and-take of our online trial, as the adrenalin of role-playing leads students to log on four or five times a day to grapple with such issues as what constitutes life, intelligence, intelligent life?

But for now, I give a big welcome to Laurie, Joichi, and John; express real pleasure at Laurie's question; compliment Joichi for an excellent answer; and go on to provide a little more context and background of my own—going into a little detail on Capek's introduction of the word robot in *RUR*, etc. Our online course is well underway.

Advantages of OnLine Education

Edmund Carpenter (1973), a colleague of Marshall McLuhan, observed that "Electricity makes angels of us all—not angels in the Sunday school sense of being good or having wings, but spirit freed from flesh, capable of instant transportation anywhere." The online student—and teacher—certainly partakes of intellect freed from the restraints of flesh, in a milieu in which obstacles of distance, time, and many other sorts are either completely eliminated or significantly reduced.

We can make a list of these obstacles, and how online education overcomes them:

Obstacles of Geography: This is the most obvious impediment removed by online education. With information travelling to and from the central computer in seconds and minutes, even with slower modems, the online student who lives across the street from the central computer is no closer to the online course than the student who lives across the world. Indeed, with speed of light being the only ultimate underlying limitation on speed of online communication, students could easily take online courses from a space station or even a Mars environment with faculty back on Earth, and vice versa.

Obstacles of Time: One of the basic constraints of in-person education is not only that classes must meet at given places, but at given times. But at any particular time, either faculty or students might be ill, or plagued by subtler problems which make that time not the best for learning to take place. The problem rarely if ever arises in an online course, in which people are by and large able to log on at times of their own choosing. (The limit here would be that even an online course has a beginning and end, and a time for assignments to be completed and evaluated.) The result of such choice over when one participates in the online course means that all parties—faculty and students—tend to participate at their best, when they are likely to derive the most benefit from the experience. Further, the important thought that occurs to you after a vigorous in-person class session concludes is usually lost to that class; in contrast, in the online course, you can log on the next morning, or even in the middle of the night if that's when the thought occurs to you, and contribute it to the online discussion that is literally ongoing throughout the extent of the course.

Obstacles of Retention: As every student knows, taking notes in an in-person class is a highly inefficient method of storing information—the act of taking the note usually renders you incapable of hearing what else is being said at that time. In contrast, everything that goes on in an online course is automatically and continuingly available. This intellectual safety net for ideas makes for a richer, more informed, educational experience.

Obstacles of Economics: This is closely related to the geography and time limitations of in-person education. For many people, the need to work for a living puts them in a place too far away to take a course; or perhaps renders them too fatigued to take a course during the evening when they are off work. Online education overcomes both such problems—and greatly increases the number of people who can take part in what Comenius called the Great Dialogue. And this is why, to return to a point I made earlier, online education must be careful not to introduce economic restrictions of another kind, in the form requiring expensive equipment to participate, which would undo its natural democratizing tendencies.

Obstacles of Teacher Domination: Students learning from students is a basic dynamic of online education. This does not mean that online faculty abdicate their responsibility to teach; but it does mean that, rather then attempting to inject or spoonfeed information into passive student minds, the best online teacher is rather someone who attempts to elicit active student learning, in the tradition of such educational theorists as Montessori, Dewey, and Piaget (see Perkinson, 1982, for more on the active learner).

Obstacles of Physical Disability: In spite of recent strides made in facilitating access of physically disabled students and faculty to in-person classrooms, such access is by no means easy or comprehensive. Access ramps at urban universities provide no help in getting wheelchairs through traffic—clogged streets that lead to the university. Further, impairments of hearing and seeing can make the in-person classroom a difficult place in which to learn, regardless of how easily one might be able to get there. The online class eliminates most of these impediments. One of Connect Ed's first students, in the mid-1980s, was someone who had been deaf since birth. I met him in one of my in-person undergraduate courses at Fairleigh Dickinson University, where he struggled to keep up with the proceedings by tape recording my lectures and discussions with the students, and having them transcribed for later reading. His capacity to contribute to the class via this second-hand participation was of course severely limited. But within days after he registered for his first online course, he was playing a leading role in online discussions: in an educational environment in which intellect was already freed from the flesh, his intellect was able to roam and create with the same verve as anyone else's online. One of our most dynamic online teachers, Tzipporah BenAvraham, conducted her "Technology and the Disabled" course from her wheelchair. She is legally blind. But voice synthesizers convey all the words on the screen to her. Just as lack of hearing was irrelevant to my online student, so lack of vision is irrelevant to Dr. BenAvraham when she teaches online. Or rather: lack of external vision is irrelevant, just as lack of the outer voice was to my student. What counts online is the inner voice and the inner vision.

In view of the above advantages, we may wonder why online education has not taken the academic world by storm. Though many schools offer courses with some online adjunct, or a course or two offered entirely online, only a few schools—such as The New School for Social Research (New York), University of Phoenix (San Francisco), Nova University (Orlando, Florida),—have ever offered anything approaching a full-scale online program. The reasons are two-fold. The first, and far less significant, has to do with some of the intrinsic limitations of online education. The second has to do with the resistance of the educational establishment.

Drawbacks to OnLine Education: Intrinsic and Imposed

The first and foremost limitation of online education that must be acknowledged is that it is not a panacea: if a person, for reasons having nothing to do with geographic location, time constraints, and the like, does not want to take part in a graduate level course and its requirements in terms of reading and writing, then no amount of flexibility in terms of time and place of access can give this person a successful online experience. Further, success in online education—for faculty as well as students—obviously presupposes a facility, even a pleasure, in the written mode. My colleagues know me to be equally garrulous in speech and writing; but many faculty are more comfortable with the spoken than the written word, and the same is true of some students. Of course, participation in an online course can elicit and sharpen a student's written skills—some of our most successful students have been dyslexic—but there has to be an underlying joy in text as a mode of expression even in that case, waiting to be tapped.

And not all subjects can be taught with equal facility online. Certainly the liberal arts and humanities, the theoretical aspects of the sciences, and professions like the law are very well suited for the online curriculum. But other areas—ranging from horticulture to ceramic science to surgery—seem inextricably in need of hands-on tutoring. New imaging techniques available on the most sophisticated online systems can convey many kinaesthetic facets, but the personal touch seems an irreducible prerequisite, especially in schools whose graduates are graded in life and death.

So the intrinsic limitations to online education are substantial. Yet they by and large do not account for the very slow growth of this new mode, especially surprising in the academic fields for which it is so well suited. No: that discrepancy is more likely due to the resistance of many faculty and administrators in the academic world.

As an example, consider the views of Neil Postman, a leading professor of communications at New York University, who as recently as 1994 opined that computers in general, and online education in particular, were just glorified forms of television, with the same inconsequential or even actively destructive impact for literacy and education. The swipe against television aside (which is unfair in its own right), Postman overlooks completely the extent to which the computer functions not like a television, but a book, and an interactive book at that. Computers undeniably do traffic in screens—and, with the advent of the Web and Windows—with all manner of colorful pictures, graphics, and icons on those screens. But the essential currency of all serious online communication, whether on public commercial services like America Online, or in online courses such as Connected Education's, remains the written word, the text, and all its power for communicating highly complex and abstract ideas. When we add to this power the capacity of online participants to question the written words, to shape them in dialogue, we obtain a medium having almost nothing in common with television and its one-way communication of pictures and sounds. Socrates' yearning for an "intelligent writing"—one which responded to questions put to it, as in a dialogue, rather than preserving a "solemn silence"—is fulfilled online.

The Warm Option

The above rejoinder to unfounded criticisms and distrust of online education is logical; but the distrust is more deeply rooted, and flows from the plain comfort people have with the media that brought them to the positions of power that they occupy. All of us, and educators are no exception, tend to gravitate towards that which we know best.

We of course know best our in-person environments—from our family lives, the classrooms we attend as a children, the people most of us work with on a daily basis. From such a vantage point, the prospect of an online community—of people getting to know each other online, learning from each other, even caring about each other—may seem far-fetched. The computer, after all, for much of its still brief tenure in our popular culture, has been assigned the role of a cold, impersonal, programming instrument.

But the reality of online communities and online education is different. Students in online courses become good friends, visit each other in diverse cities years after their online courses are over. Online education, while not satisfying every educational or human need, is in fact an intensely warm and humanly interactive option.

There are obviously some human things that cannot be done well or at all in cyberspace—walking hand-in-hand on a windswept beach, dining in a fine restaurant with wine and candlelight...

But education, the realm of human activity that deals with the life of the mind par excellence, is not one of them. My expectation is that we will a find an increasing number of peaks of that kind of experience online in the new millennium.

References

Carpenter, Edmund. (1973) *Oh, What a Blow the Phantom Gave Me!* New York: Bantam.

Perkinson, Henry (1982) "Education and Learning from our Mistakes" in Paul Levinson, ed. *In Pursuit of Truth: Essays on the Philosophy of Karl Popper.* Atlantic Highlands, NJ: Humanities Press.

Plato, *Phaedrus*, secs. 275-276.

Postman, Neil (1994) "The John Culkin Memorial Lecture," delivered at The New School for Social Research, New York City, 16 February.

The Book on the Book: a Prognosis for the Page in the Digital Age

The book enjoys a position of unique authority in our world. Judges routinely "throw the book" at the worst criminals; professionals ranging from police to scientists conduct investigations "by the book"; when we receive the established wisdom on any subject, we get "the book" on that; and, of course, for the religiously inclined, we have the ultimate authority in the Good Book.

None of this is surprising, or unearned. As a portable yet permanent packet of highly abstract, precisely presented information, the book has been unequalled throughout most of its history. Its introduction in Europe as a mass product of the printing press made possible the Protestant Reformation: what impact would Luther's urgings that people should read the Bible for themselves have had without Bibles in everyone's hands? The book defeated early attempts to stifle the Scientific Revolution: Galileo's recantation in the court of Rome meant nothing with his words already in the hands and minds of the growing body of Europe's readers, courtesy of the book. The Age of Discovery was ignited via books—best sellers in their day—with reports of Columbus's voyage, reports in black-and-white which people could see again and again, and take seriously, unlike the Norse oral sagas of their voyages to the New World 500 years earlier, no more substantive than rumors whispered in the midnight winds. National identities were crystallized in books that allowed people to easily read—not just talk—in vernaculars. Public education emerged, capitalism was kindled...the list goes on and on.

The process was mutually catalytic. The Roman Catholic Church, weakened by the Protestant Reformation, was a less effective opponent of the Scientific Revolution. The new availability of books in all areas created more pressure for effective public education, whose prime task was soon seen as teaching children how to read. Each increase in readership intensified the effect on all levels. The result was our modern world.

But books were never without their limitations as vehicles of knowledge. How many books can be stored in a given library? What hours is this library open? How many books can one carry home from the library? What happens when the book you desperately need is being read by someone else? Bookstores may have more than one copy of a given book available for sale, but their selection is far smaller than the library's, and their books usually stay on the shelves a far shorter time.

Fortunately, the science and culture that the book engendered have created a technology that addresses just such limitations: Text digitally encoded, stored online, can be accessed 24 hours a day from any place in the world. One person reading an electronic text precludes no one else reading that very same text. Although online storage capacity certainly is not infinite, it is in effect limitless in comparison to the confines of physical bookstores and libraries.

In this essay, we consider the future prospects of the venerable book in this new electronic milieu, a source of both competition and support for the book's position at the pinnacle of intellectual media. We will examine some principles of media evolution that I have developed over the years, and we will use them to disentangle the extent to which our attachment to books is based on real advantages in performance versus rosy nostalgia. We begin with some of the defects of books, and the physical properties from which they arise.

Drawbacks of the Tome

Information itself—as distinct from its conduits and containers—has no physical properties. Like a restless spirit, it adopts the features of what it inhabits. Its physical characteristics reside in the means of its conveyance. Words spoken in the air move at the speed of sound; those same words electronically encoded and broadcast on electromagnetic carrier waves travel at the speed of light. When they are written on paper, published in newspapers, magazines, and books, they move at a pace far slower: the speed of everyday transportation. The roads of ancient Rome were thus as much a communications network as a transport system.

The irony is that the book in its day traveled faster and further than any other medium. Unlike carvings on walls and monuments, the book could be moved; unlike papyrus and parchment, books made of paper pages could be moved great distances without fear of disintegration. But compared to the lightness and speed of electricity, even the thinnest piece of paper seems a cumbersome thing.

The quickness of electricity engenders not only speed of transport, but unprecedented ease of copying. That is why a text electronically encoded can be read by one or a million people at the same time, assuming they have appropriate computer equipment: a new copy is generated at the source, perhaps on a central computer half a world away, each time a reader receives a document on his or her screen. In contrast, the poor book must be printed anew for each copy. And much as computers have streamlined the paper printing process, in the end the speed of book production is hostage to its slowest link. Books take time—not only to write, which is at the author's discretion, not only to read, which is part of the pleasure they convey, and in the reader's control—but to be moved and to be produced, which pleases no one.

And yet, for all of these drawbacks of the book in our electronic age, people retain a great affection for them, as well as their cousins the magazine and the newspaper. Some of you may be reading this on a computer screen; some of you in a book. I would wager that very few if any of you currently reading this essay in a book would prefer it scrolling on your computer screen. Part of that is due to the content of this essay—nothing in it is so urgent that you would have gained much from its instant delivery a week, a month, or a year ago. Part of this also flows from real functional advantages of books and print on paper, regardless of what its words say. And part of our affection for books may also stem from a nostalgic attachment we retain for products of the press—whatever their content, and their functional advantages.

In the next sections, we attempt to sort out some of these intertwining factors.

Lessons in the Pen and the Watch

When I was a kid growing up in the 1950s, the instruments of personal penmanship were a subject of some debate in my house. My father, an attorney, was a firm believer in the fountain pen, for all but the most trivial writing. He gave me a fountain pen for my tenth birthday. But I was already a subscriber to the upstart ballpoint, which I saw as superior to the fountain pen on nearly all fronts: ballpoints didn't smear, rarely bled in your shirt pocket, and were much easier to "refill". On the fountain pen's behalf, it perhaps permitted more personality, more flair, in its inscriptions. But my father's passion for the fountain pen was for the most part a brief for the medium he had grown up with—comfort with the device he had known and relied upon all of his life, rather than the result of a logical analysis of its benefits and shortcomings (which was otherwise his strong suit). Today, the fountain pen of course yet has its devotees, but they are few in comparison to the legion users of ballpoints and its progeny, persuaded by the undeniable convenience of the fountain pen's successors. As we embark into a new century, the fountain pen thrives mainly in the realms of nostalgia and deliberate attempts to be different from the pack. A slowly dwindling attachment to traditional, less efficient instruments of writing is apparently nothing new. Beckmann observed in his *History of Inventions*, 1846, p. 411, that "Notwithstanding the great advantage which quills have over reeds for writing, the latter however seem to have continued long in use even with the former."

Several decades after the advent of the ballpoint, another medium of the hand—or, more precisely, the wrist—made its debut. This one was digital, not in the manual sense of the pen, but in the mathematical sense in which the word has come to typify so much that pertains to computers, including the subtitle of this very essay. (Actually, both uses of "digital" stem from the same hand: the earliest form of mathematics was counting on one's fingers.) The digital watch displayed the time in numbers that were immediately comprehensible to even young children, in contrast to the positions of the hands of the analog timepiece, whose meaning had to be learned. Why contend with big hands, little hands, second hands, when the time could be instantly and exactly known with a glance at the numbers on a watch face?

And yet ... unlike the ballpoint's triumph over the fountain pen, the digital watch has failed to vanquish the analog. Indeed, to the contrary, the analog watch is more popular than ever: an informal survey of my undergraduate class at Hofstra University in Hempstead, New York, just a week before I wrote this essay, revealed more than 90 percent of the students sporting analog watches. What is responsible for this turn of events?

The answer is that the analog watch does things that the digital watch cannot—and, moreover, does things that are of significant interest and value to people. The analog watch tells us not just the present time, but where it came from and where it is going. Unlike the flat display of numbers on the digital watch, the hands on the analog face give us a sense of past and future—

not just a snapshot of the present, but a gestalt of the process of time, of where we were and where we may be. If, as cognitive anthropologist Alexander Marshack observes, humans are a narrative species, then the analog watch speaks to our specieshood in this quiet way that the digital watch does not.

Here we encounter a most fundamental principle of media evolution: a medium will survive to the extent that it performs a task (i) important to humans (ii) that no other media can perform, or perform as well. In the Darwinian evolution of media, humans are both the generators of new "organisms," and their external "selecting" environment. I first noticed and detailed this human "natural" selection of media in my doctoral dissertation, "Human Replay: A Theory of the Evolution of Media" (New York University, 1979), and develop it further in my most recent book, *The Soft Edge: A Natural History and Future of the Information Revolution* (Routledge, 1997). Silent movies, a sight-only medium, were eradicated by sight-and-sound "talkies" even more quickly than the fountain pen was replaced by the ballpoint; in contrast, radio, a sound-only medium, not only survived the massive competition of sight-and-sound television, but is today the most profitable medium in America, dollar spent for dollar earned.

Why did uni-sensory radio do so well in the face of its multi-sensory competition, whereas uni-sensory silent movies did not? The answer resides in the nature of the sense each medium played to, and the role of that sense in human life. The world grows dark every night but never really silent, we can easily close our eyes to block out sight but we have no earlids: hearing without seeing is a fundamental mode of human communication, one which keeps us in touch with the world in the dark, whereas seeing without hearing anything is alien to our biological being. Radio thrives in a television age because it inadvertently fulfills an eavesdropping niche, a human mode of communication, in residence long before the invention of either medium-hardwired, in fact, into our very sensory apparatus.

We can now put our question about the future of books in the digital age more precisely: will they go the way of silent movies and the fountain pen, relegated to the realm of deliberate artistic statement and nostalgia, or emerge from the information revolution proud, unbending, resplendent, like the analog watch and radio?

As we will see below, the answer will likely be a little of both.

Fleeting Phases

In gauging the survival prospects of any technology, including books, we also need to distinguish between features that are inherent and irreducible in the medium, and features that are transitory. The first kind of characteristic is so fundamental to the device that, were it changed, we would have by any reasonable designation a new device. The second could be changed, or we could imagine changing, without any injury to the underlying device itself. A horse-drawn vehicle with new kinds of wheels, even a horse bred for greater speed and/or strength, is a still a horse-and-carriage; a horseless carriage, powered by a combustible engine, is no longer a horse-and-carriage at all—it is an automobile. Clearly, any worthwhile assessment of a medium's survivability in terms of how well it performs human functions must relate to its intrinsic, defining characteristics.

But sometimes, in the heat of the present, these are not so easy to see. An objection often made against the ultimate success of books on screens is that you can't cuddle up with a computer—can't read it in the bathtub. Aside from the the fact that books, magazines, and newspapers are no particular joy to read in the bathtub either—if you are reading this in a book, would you think it might benefit from a good soapy soak?—the objection misses the point that there is nothing inherent in the screen that makes it "uncuddleable". Surely, if we value the warmth of cloth and paper, we could devise computer screens mounted in cloth and paper, that felt the same against our skin and laps as the well-worn book. That we do not have these right now is merely an indication that the medium of the electronic book is still in its infancy, in a caterpillar stage that yet reflects its clumsy cathode-ray tube origins.

And the same applies to the traditional book—not every aspect of its current configuration and delivery system is intrinsic and essential to its continued existence as we now know and love it. "On-demand" instant production facilities have long been proposed, and are already in operation in some sites, where texts are transmitted electronically from a central computer storage source and immediately printed and bound. (For all I know, if you are reading this in a book now, it may have to come to you that way.) In theory, there could come a time when everyone has such an immediate book-making facility in their home—much as many of us now have fax machines hooked up to our computers and phones. Such a facility would allow the book to compete on an equal footing with text on the screen as far as immediate access is concerned: one copy of the text, on a central computer source, could be transmitted to the same unlimited number of people as an electronic text, and at the same speed of light.

With the delivery thus equalized, what enduring advantages would remain for electronic over paper text, and vice versa?

The Enduring Difference of Hypertext

A prime principle of technologies and their impact is that their most profound consequences are often unintended. Bell invented the telephone in pursuit of a hearing aid for his wife; Edison's first thoughts about the phonograph were that it would quickly become a universal telephone answering machine; and Marconi's notion of the "wireless" was a telegraph or telephone without wires, an interpersonal two-way mode of communication rather than the simultaneous mass medium of radio that his invention brought into being. Online computer networks were first developed by the US military in the 1960s as a way of more efficiently moving words—as a way of keeping people in better contact. An unintended consequence was that words electronically encoded could not only be moved quickly, but could be linked to other words, instantly, provided they too were encoded on a connected electronic network. This unintended consequence is, of course, known as hypertext. And it may be the one advantage of electronic text that cannot be provided by books, however quickly they may be disseminated and assembled on the spot. "Clicking" on a word printed on a piece of paper, after all, goes nowhere.

Actually, although the hypertext consequence was unintended by the Internet's first funders, it was not unforeseen by everybody. Hypertext had been predicted by Vannevar Bush in his famous "As We May Think" article about a "memex" device published in *The Atlantic Monthly* back in 1945, and extensively mapped out as a hypothetical possibility by Theodor Nelson in the 1960s in his "Xanadu" work. Indeed, the rudiments of hypertext can be found in the references that adorn most scholarly texts printed on paper, including this one. If you were moved, after reading the first sentence in this paragraph, to seek out and read Vannevar Bush's 1945 article for yourself, you would be engaging in a manual, offline kind of hypertext—except rather than your fingers doing the walking (to invoke that old but still apt line from advertisements for the telephone "Yellow Pages"), you would be literally doing the walking, or driving, likely to your closest library, unless you had access to the Web. Other examples of hypertext ahead of its time would be Talmudic commentaries in the margins of written documents, which invite readers to follow diverging threads of argument (these could be considered a species of footnote), or Isaac Asimov's *Foundation* series, the novels of which can be read in order either of their publication, or in which the events take place in the stories. In each of these cases, readers rather than authors are determining the proximate sequences of texts—whether to proceed from the end of paragraph A to paragraph B, or to a new paragraph in a new book altogether—and therein sowing the seeds of hypertext.

Thus, although the Web and its hypertext connections and its first readily usable browsers like Mosaic took nearly three decades to emerge after the origins of the Internet for different purposes in the 1960s, the roots of hypertext—the human yearning for connections that exceed the page at hand—have long been with us. But the electronic connection made all the difference in fulfillment of this need. Nothing short of a complete electronic milieu can work effectively for hypertext—not even the hybrid technology of texts electronically conveyed yet produced as books right on the spot. Yes, we could "click" on Vannevar Bush's article and have it rapidly printed for us on paper. But what happens when we wish to further study people and books referenced in *that* article—these include Leibnitz, Charles Babbage, Matthew Brady, and the *Encyclopedia Britannica*—and then pursue references in those subsequent books, and so forth? Even were our immediate book—production technology up to such a task, we would soon be drowning in paper. We could slow the rising tide by producing just those pages in the books that seemed most likely to slake our interest. But such a strategy would reduce the possibility of discovering information in an unexpected place—which is one of the glories of hypertext. And, besides, we would eventually drown in single sheets of paper just as surely as in complete books.

The utter intangibility of electrons behind a screen changes all of that. A screen, unless and until it breaks or fails, can be "refreshed" to display as many texts as wanted. There are of course limits to how many hypertext links any computer can hold in its memory, and the speed with which any text can be delivered electronically is modulated by the quality of phone or cable lines, capacity of modems and like devices, and all sorts of external factors. But these, again, are examples of transitory limitations: modems in most homes today operate at 28 and 56 thousand bits-per-second speed, in contrast to the 300 bits-per-second speed of the early 1980s. And new ISDN and cable-phone technologies are already sending data at better than 100,000 bits-per-second. In the world of instant connectivity, in realms in which the association of one text to another is the goal, online communication is the undisputed king. Even electricity, of course, cannot compare to the speed of our internal, imaginative, mental connection of one thought to another. But electrons and light do a lot better than their rivals. When it comes to hypertext, books just can't compete. Paper can't compute.

But if the prognosis for books and paper as hypertext conduits is stark—if we can expect them to sink like stones in the multiply—connected data streams of the 21st century—does this mean that they have no enduring role as vehicles of information at all?

In our concluding section, we will see that the enduring role of books in the digital age may be just that: as repositories for information that we most want to endure.

Books as Centers

Giordano Bruno, as is well known, was burned at the stake in 1600 for his heresy that the Earth was not the center of the Universe; whereas Galileo was simply threatened about his. Aside from Bruno's refusal to recant, and the fact that as a monk his betrayal of Church teaching was all the more provocative, his heresy was also far more profound than Galileo's. To support the Copernican theory that the Sun rather than the Earth was the center of the Solar System, as Galileo did, was vexing enough. But Bruno held that even the Sun was the center of nothing—that the Universe, in fact, had no centers at all.

McLuhan, picking up on this radical notion three and a half centuries after Bruno's execution, observed that electronic media create a world whose centers are nowhere and margins are everywhere. If a radio signal is broadcast in a 300-mile radius, everyone within that range is equidistant from that broadcast—the radio receiver 10 miles from the "center" is no closer, effectively, to the origin of that broadcast than the receiver situated 100 miles away. And if that same radio or television signal is relayed by "booster" transmitters all over the country, or via satellites all over the world, then the "centerless" circle grows even larger.

Text electronically conveyed in a hypertext Web environment completes this decentralization process. Broadcasts may be without centers in terms of who receives them, but they nonetheless have discernible and economically significant points of origin in terms of who produces them. Indeed, they are classic examples of mass media, or technologies that deliver one message to many people. In contrast, the Web permits many people to distribute many messages to many people. A reader in pursuit of a hypertext trail—a trail in large part of the reader's own making, as the reader decides whether to click on McLuhan, Bruno, or Galileo in a text such as this, if it's in hypertext—will encounter so many points of origin as to render the whole notion of origin, as well as center, somewhat moot. It is more than poetic conceit to muse that the constellation of ideas in an online hypertext world bears a great resemblance to the stars ashine in Bruno's centerless Universe.

But is there no remaining human hunger for a place to call home, a reliable location for our favorite ideas to reside? We can agree that the Church was wrong to kill Bruno, but does that mean it was wrong in its recognition of the human craving for a center, preferably one that could be counted on, and was close at hand?

What the Church of that time missed is that humans could have their centers—spiritual as well as physical—even in a centerless Universe. Books might well continue to serve this purpose for ideas and information in a hypertext world. The very speed with which new operating systems, formatting codes, computer programs of all sorts are evolving threatens at any instant to render an older code unreadable on a current machine. I still use an ancient 286 computer with an external 5 and 1/4 inch drive and an old program called "Uniform" when I need to read one of the thousands of files I saved in CP/M in the early 1980s—yes, I know, I should have transferred them to DOS a long time ago, but who has the time?—and who knows how much longer this jerrybuilt system will work for me. In contrast, my books are as reliably readable as the sunrise—indeed, as an additional benefit, they require no source of energy other than sunlight, or electric lighting already ubiquitous in our culture. Books thus come in a "format" as endurable as the human intellect itself, and with batteries always included. One day we may have computers with as stable and universal a code, and which operate on sunshine. In this sense, the current advantage of books as "off the shelf" reading machines may be transitory. But the transition may well take some time—and seems unlikely to touch an even deeper sense in which books give us a sense of center.

For although computers can certainly be counted upon, and can be as close by as books, there is no doubt that once we are on the computer—once we are online—we quickly lose a sense of physical location, of "rootedness". This is, in part, why the Web "surfing" metaphor caught on so quickly. But the book, likely and precisely because its pages always display the same words, provides this sense of location, and the commensurate feelings of comfort and security—an unbeatable combination of logos and locus.

Does this mean the book will survive?

As a medium for the transmission of information, as a vehicle for the connection of one text to another, as a mode of transport across and throughout the intellectual landscape—likely not. Or, if the book does survive in this mode, it will be only in the manner of the silent movie and the fountain pen.

But as a place to pause, to return to, to be there for us whenever our minds wish to venture into just that area, the book and its paper relatives are far more effective than the computer screen and its ever-changing letters.

True, we could develop a computer screen of whatever size whose letters never changed.

But then it would just be another kind of book.

References

Beckmann, J. (1846) *A History of Inventions, Discoveries, and Origins*, trans. Johnson, W., 4th edition revised and enlarged by Francis, W. & Griffith, J. W., eds. London: Bohn.

Bush, V. (1945) "As We May Think." *The Atlantic Monthly*, July, pp. 101-108. Also available on the Web at: www.theatlantic.com/unbound/flashbks/computer/bushf.htm

Levinson, P. (1979) "Human Replay: A Theory of the Evolution of Media." PhD dissertation, New York University.

Levinson, P. (1997) *The Soft Edge: A Natural History and Future of the Information Revolution*. New York and London: Routledge.

Marshack, A. (1972) *The Roots of Civilization*. New York: McGraw-Hill. McLuhan, M. (1976) "The Brain and the Media." *Journal of Communication*, August, 54-60.

Nelson, T. H. (1980/1990) *Literary Machines*. Sausalito, CA: Mindful.

Author and Critic: Hazards and Consolations

Writers and critics work in a complex symbiotic relationship. Writers need to reach readers, and critics often play a crucial role in that process. Just as a recording usually has to be played on a radio station—or heard in a movie or a TV show—to reach its maximum audience of potential buyers, so the short story or novel is reliant on conduits beyond the work itself to attain its readers. Neither the record company nor the book (or magazine) publisher is quite enough. They can inject the work into the great outdoors, give it some circulation, but if the work is to have any chance of achieving lasting impact, of being more in the end than a sheaf of poetry stuck away in some closet, then something more is needed: the spin imparted by one or more reviews.

The situation is less acute for magazines, whose individual issues after all have a circulation at any given time nearly regardless of reviews of those issues. But the authors whose stories comprise science fiction (and fantasy) magazines are indeed significantly affected by reviews of their work. A positive review of a short story can presumably boost a novel's circulation by the same author, bring the story to the attention of an anthology editor, put it in the running for some award. At very least, good reviews provide an always needed dose of moral support. Conversely, either a negative review—or, in many ways worse, no review at all—will undoubtedly have a demoralizing impact on any author. The only question is how much.

The possibility of a negative review makes the whole enterprise of reviewing and criticism part company from radio station airplay, where the only decision to be made regarding a record is whether to play it or not. In the case of reviews, we have—in addition to the review or not-review decision—a whole continuum ranging from pans to rave reviews and everything in between (including the review that is just a neutral description of the work, and the closest analog to radio airplay).

Meanwhile, on the other side of this uneasy partnership, we have the critic's absolute dependence on the author's work for something to review and/or critique. We can thus see the immediate imbalance in this relationship: whereas authors can produce work without any help from critics and reviewers (albeit work that will likely not be read as widely as the authors would like—especially, again, in the case of novels), critics and reviewers are plain and simply out of luck without the work of authors to review. This has led many a writer less than pleased by a review to characterize reviewers as parasites who live off writers. The characterization is not really apt, however, in view of the author's lesser but still highly significant dependence of the critic. All in all, the relationship seems better characterized as a symbiotic situation—although one in which the partnership is certainly nothing like equal.

But things get really dicey when a given author elects to also be a critic or reviewer, or vice versa. Here we get into a wild territory of conflicting vital interests—not only between two or more people, but within one person, the author/critic, him or herself.

Yet people do it. In the realm of science fiction, we have the classic examples of Damon Knight and James Blish, all the way to contemporary, less established cases ... including me.

Hazards of the Job

Let's look in a bit more detail at the obvious: why it seems like a bad idea for an author to be critic, and for a critic to be an author—a bad idea, that is, for both sides of the equation, detrimental to one's primary pursuit whether it be writing or reviewing.

The problem, in a nutshell, is that the dual identity only exacerbates and extends the conflicts that already exist between author and critic.

Consider, for example, the common case of an author aggrieved by a negative review. If the author publicly objects to the review, he/she runs the risk of looking like a crybaby. Worse still, if the objection has merit, and the reviewer is made to look bad as a result of it, then the author can bask in the sickly light of knowing that a career-long antagonism may have just been ignited. Even pointing out naked errors of fact in a review can do more harm than the good to the author: reviewers, like all human beings, don't like to be embarrassed. The bottom line: a negative review is usually a no-win situation for an author. Best mode of response is usually no response, and whatever quiet bitter-sweet pleasure can be taken from at least seeing one's name in print, however negative.

But what happens when this already painful situation is transformed into a case of two author/critics, each of whom negatively reviews the other's work? (Note that problems like this of course do not arise as much with positive reviews, though other critics may at some point denounce what look to them like mutual admiration societies.)

In general, the minute that any critic begins to work as an author, he/she is entering troubled waters the likes of which make the natural antagonisms between author and critic seem like Cape Cod Bay on a placid summer evening. The critic working as an author puts all works so authored in danger of being slammed, rightly or wrongly, by any other author working as a critic whose work as an author was earlier critiqued with any negativity by the first party.

The only chance that the critic working as author has to escape such circumstances is if the second critic has no history as an author—or, of course, if the authors negatively reviewed by the first critic lack the wherewithal to express their criticism, i.e., the targets of the first critic's pans are authors only, not critics.

Further, to make matters even more aggravating, the critic working as an author in the above dyad puts his or her subsequent criticism at risk, certainly as it may apply to the second critic/author in the relationship. Who can trust a pan meted out by the first party to the second party's work as an author, after the second party has attacked the fiction of the first? Thus, once the noxious coupling of critic/author negatively reviewed by critic/author occurs, the first critic/author is damaged both as author *and* critic.

And the second critic/author fares no better. Assuming, for the sake of discussion, that this critic/author began writing as an author, and subsequently did criticism, then this author/critic must take special care not to review the work of another author who, serving as a critic, offered a negative review of the author's work in the past. Failing that restraint, the second author/critic's negative review is instantly subject to charges of being a hatchet job. Thus, the author who ventures into critiquing the work of a critic performing as an author is engaging in criticism which ipso facto has at least one big strike against it; the author who thus critiques is critiquing with at least one hand tied behind his or her back.

The sensible solution to this almost impossible situation that almost requires numerical tagging to keep track of (author1/critic2 reviews critic1/author2's work) is to keep authoring and critical reviewing in strictly separate hands.

But writers enjoy flirting with the impossible—science fiction writers, especially—and exploring just those solutions that go a bit beyond the strictly sensible.

Besides, there are some benefits to the duality, after all.

Consolations

The single biggest practical benefit of co-mingling reviewing and writing—perhaps the only one—flows from the point of view that the worst publicity is no publicity. Or, as Mae West is supposed to have quipped—I don't care what you say about me, as long as you get my name right.

Publicity is no doubt synergistic, even exponential, in its impact—meaning that two pieces of publicity, two pieces with one's name in print, have far more impact than just the simple addition of one and one appearances of one's name in print. Indeed, the reader who sees an author's name in print for the second time may really just start paying attention to that name then; or, even more likely, the reader won't be pay much attention at all until the third or fourth time the name is seen.

And public relations experts tell us that simultaneity is an important, perhaps even crucial factor. If the time between the first and second sighting of a new name on the horizon is too long, the reader may have all but forgotten about the first sighting, thus depriving the second sighting of its impact. In contrast, seeing a name in print everywhere one turns is to have that name jump into instant recognizability.

Of course, the content and context of the name sightings are factors too. If you want to be known as a science fiction writer, then having your name in print as an author of science fiction stories and novels would seem to be the best way to go.

But unless you're Isaac Asimov, such full court presses are rarely possible. And, indeed, even Asimov's astonishing productivity was spread over non-fiction as well as fiction genres. This is not surprising: public relations specialists also tell us that people remember names more than the larger texts, or circumstances, that surround them. Name recognition, in other words, can be radically transferrable across contexts.

So, for the science fiction writer who wishes to further his or her name recognition, getting a byline printed as a critic or reviewer has its obvious advantages.

Of course, these are tempered not only by the dangers of critiquing an author who later works as a critic, as mentioned above, but by such perils as negatively reviewing a magazine or a book edited by someone to whom you as an author may want to submit a subsequent work. Here the critic enters yet another no-win quagmire, in which the alternatives of true negative criticism and false praise can each in their own way be packets of delayed poison for the critic's career as an author. Panning the work of a potential editor is obvious in its drawbacks; but falsely praising a work to win a potential editor's favor can make the critic seem, well, like a prostitute to everyone else.

In this case, the only escape valve may be an understanding that the only indisputable practical benefit for an author working as a critic is in publicity in the largest possible sense—getting your name out to as many readers as possible, as explained above. The author working as a critic may thus do best to just forget about any other possible ramifications of a positive or negative review, and just call the shots as they are.

Of course, when writers of the stature of Knight and Blish embark on criticism, they are presumably somewhat past the point of having to impress editors about their work as authors. And perhaps this is the reason indeed these two names still are in many respects the high watermarks of science fiction criticism.

But I suspect that Knight and Blish offered criticism not because it was safe to do so—but for a reason, a very impractical but likely the most pressing reason, that all authors who offer criticism do so.

The Enduring Motive

I suppose there are some writers, somewhere, who are in it solely, mainly, mostly for the money.

I've never met one. Certainly not in the realm of science fiction.

What I've met—and what I'm a part of—is an amorphous group of people who for whatever reasons love stretching the boundaries in some way—love talking about it, in-person, on the phone, online, love writing about it, love writing *it*.

Review and criticism, however second-order and distinct from primary writing it might be, is still after all a form of writing. It may not be one's favorite kind of writing (it isn't mine; fiction and primary scholarly and popular writing are), but that still does not make it any less satisfying in its own right, when it's about something that satisfies so much as science fiction.

And to the extent that reviews and criticism satisfy a part of the science fiction compulsion, I suspect that none of the pitfalls examined above make a bit of real difference.

Given the chance to write about something that we'd no doubt talk about if given the chance, and certainly think about, who's going to worry about what possible negative impact that might have on our career as authors?

And ultimately, one's impact as an author is based not on whom one might offend or please as a critic, but on the impact of one's stories on, first, editors, and then readers.

With that in mind, my advice to all varieties of author/critics and critic/authors, including me, is: Take every opportunity that you can to write, including reviewing. When you're reviewing, don't worry about pleasing anyone or any interest save what you feel is right, true, and beautiful. Don't hesitate to slash a story that doesn't measure up to those standards, or to praise one that does. Don't worry about who may say what about how your criticism was motivated. Let your text speak for itself, stand or fall on its own examples and reasons.

Good writing, whether fiction or criticism, in the end transcends criticism.

Digital Amish

Most people consider the Amish an interesting oddity of throwbacks who have rejected all modern technology and have turned their back on the modern world. On a recent trip to Lancaster, Pennsylvania with my wife and kids, I found this popular stereotype even more mistaken than these images usually are. Beneath the pastel shirts and black trousers and horse and buggies portrayed so vividly in *Witness*, behind the cornfields and customs that sway layer upon layer back to seventeenth-century Swiss/high-German roots, the Amish have not so much said "no" to the high-tech world as developed an ingenious strategy for getting the most out of it.

To begin with, the Amish are not one, but a variety of subtly and in some cases drastically different groups, with a wide range of attitudes towards modern devices. Most importantly, no Amish group has rejected technology outright—rather, they struggle with the appeal of technologies, usually accepting a new machine at first, agonizing over its real and projected social consequences, and then deciding whether and to what extent it can be used. They come the closest I have seen to a living embodiment and conscious everyday application of a philosophy for technology.

In most cases, the Amish in fact accept new technology, while straining the limits of their ingenuity to keep it from disrupting their social order. Electricity from central power companies is forbidden—sockets in the wall make the home and place of business an appendage of an uncontrollable, huge external political-economic power structure—but electricity from 12-volt self-sufficient batteries is all right. Phones are frowned upon (not absolutely forbidden) in the homes of most Amish, but since the 1930s, phone "shanties" on the edges of property have been permitted. These are seen as affording most of the advantages of the phone, while strengthening communal use which the Amish see as crucial to a healthy life. As McLuhan pointed out, the phone line in the home is a snake that makes our private castle more public than a walk outside.

The Amish proscription on centrally supplied electricity dovetails nicely with their religious-ethical dislike of the content of mass media like television, which usually doesn't run on batteries. But now a new device has crept into some Amish homes and businesses: a clever little "inverter," which transforms 12-volt battery current into a reasonable likeness of the 110-volt power that comes from the socket. Bishop Beiler's 1919 ruling that anything that flows from a 12-volt battery is acceptable, and anything that uses 110-volt power is not, was once quite precise. How exquisite the irony, then, when television and ... yes, even computers ... are now connected by a few custom-abiding Amish into inversion 110-volt power.

Pocket calculators that run on batteries and sun are already in very widespread use. A toy-maker cheerfully rung up the little wooden pigs we bought for our children on a Sharp solar power model. As far as I could see, laptop and notebook computers are not, but the profound decentralizing effect of these media—creating a world whose centers are nowhere and whose margins are everywhere—makes them natural allies of the Amish.

Leapfrogging is a well-known feature of technological evolution—the French bounded in less than a decade in the 1980s from a phone system in which "half of France is waiting for a telephone, the other half is waiting for a dialtone" (in the words of a National Assemblyman) to the online sophistication of the Minitel. Remedial media also play their role—rather than boarding up the window to avoid its invitation to the Peeping Tom, we invent and deploy a window shade. The key insight here is that what's usually wrong with technology is that there's not enough it. Surprisingly, many Amish seem to understand this better than we "English" of the larger world.

How intriguing to think that the Amish, and their deep sense of privacy and independence, could be a source or even a spearhead for enlightened digital technology that empowers the individual and the pioneering community in the next century.

The Rights of Robots

Historically, the ethics of hypothetical attempts to create humanlike intelligences in our robots, neural nets, distributed networks, artificial life programs, and the like have usually amounted to concern about what dangers such newly minted beings might pose for us, their makers. Will our artificial progeny turn on us, in the tradition of the Golem, Frankenstein's monster, and *Rossum's Universal Robots*, and repay their creation with our death or even extinction as a species? Will they lead to our undoing in subtler ways, with the very help they render weakening our ability to cope with life, in scenarios such as those described by Jack Williamson? Or will our slaves, despite our best Asimovian programming to make them follow our orders, nonetheless behave in ways that run counter to some fundamental human interests?

But there is another side to this problem: given that we triumph in creating an artificial entity genuinely able to think for itself, what right do we have to expect it to mindlessly do our bidding like a slave? If we create artificially intelligent life, are we right to treat it like a machine-readable program? In other words, what ethics would we owe these creations, if we succeed?

Welcome to the world of the (un)natural rights of robots...

Between Protein Chauvinism and Artificial Idiocy

Of course for some overly-literal humanists, such questions never come up. They confidently think that the quest for self-sustaining artificial intelligence is bound to fail. To the Turing Test question of by what criteria do we deny intelligence to an entity that in every way performs as a humanly intelligent being, these humanists reply: the machine is nonetheless not really intelligent—and why not?—well, obviously, because it isn't human. Thus, they beg the question.

On the other hand, let us not conclude that the blissful simplicity of such protein chauvinists—who think intelligence cannot exist in anything other than a DNA-base, since that is the base for all its known forms thus far—means that the creation of intelligences in non-DNA bases, such as silicon chips, is a foregone conclusion. To the contrary, we're still very far from such creations in most crucial respects. Our best AI expert systems are more like computer idiot savants, doing only one or two things extraordinarily well, and the rest of what we take for human mentality little or not at all. Our most sophisticated neural nets are currently not even a fraction as complex as a fly's. Nor should we be misguided by the marvelously subtle intelligence we see in Lt. Commander Data of *Star Trek*. He is an android, yes—but an android portrayed by a human. Our reaction to the android's "humanity" is inextricably a reaction to the human actor's. I call this the human—performance tautology—the error of judging a robot's humanity by the characteristics of its human star in a movie, theatrical production, or television series.

But what moral code would we follow if we someday did bring into being a System of Code such as Data?

A "Meno" Paradox for Robots

We begin to get an idea of the difficulties that beset our quest for a Bill of Rights for robots when we ask ourselves: what tasks do we want our artificial creations to perform? The answers would likely range from activities that we find too boring (replacement of toll collectors by automated "Eazy-Pass" systems can be considered a first step in this direction) to missions we find too dangerous—such as some of those we want done beyond our planet. The common denominator in all of these is that, whether to remove ourselves from tedium or risk, we want our robots to perform tasks we would rather not. The robot, then, is from the outset and intrinsically a vehicle for the accomplishment of jobs that are for whatever reason unacceptable to humans. Not a good springboard from which to launch an ethical code for treatment of robots, especially if such a code is to be based on a do-unto-others philosophy.

The problem does not arise for machines in which we see no degree of life or sentience. Who would raise an objection to a motorist who raised a discrete middle finger to an Eazy-Pass eye? The only limits we put on our use of cars, or computers, is that they do not hurt us, or other people. No one cares if we kick them, curse them, destroy them utterly—except insofar as some might think it not a good idea to wantonly destroy our own property. But even that concern arises from how such loss of property might adversely affect *us*—that is, what negative effect such loss might have on our own sentient life. Absent such sentience, ethics are just not part of the picture. Just as Plato's Meno Paradox recognizes that, in order to acquire knowledge, we must already have knowledge—for how else would we recognize the new knowledge as knowledge to be gained?—so we seem to want to reserve our best ethical treatment for entities already capable of ethical judgement themselves, that is, for entities that are sentient.

But what is sentience? Interestingly, we take free will, the possibility of making our own choices, as a key ingredient. To the extent that a computer program does just what it is programmed to do, nothing more nothing less (short of malfunction), we take that computer to be not sentient. It indeed may be programmed to mimic sentience, but such contrived sentience is no more sentient than painting by the numbers is art or a parrot speaking is linguistic. In fact, to the degree that a parrot — or any living organism—displays unpredictability in its behavior that we might be pleased interpret as initiative, we are prone to it give more respect than the programmed computer.

But what if we developed robots that were in some significant sense our equal—or greater than us—in intelligence? What if in a living equivalent of the Turing Test, such robots and their neural nets qualified not only as intelligent but alive?

For the Children of our Intellect

Aside from the likelihood that they might not behave in accordance with Asimov's "laws" of robots—never harming humans and always following our orders—and thus might well resent we humans risking their lives (even Asimov's robots don't always behave as expected, which is precisely what make his novels such good reading), what obligations for decent conduct and respect would we have to *them*?

Perhaps ancient Romans and ante-bellum southern Americans would have had no such problem had they developed robots—they after all were quite sanguine about their slaves—but one hopes that we are now well beyond those centuries in our sense of respect for other mentalities and modes of thinking, however little or great their differences may be from ours. At last we've begun to practice a live-and-let-live attitude for diverse cultures and lifestyles on our planet; we've even come to respect the capacity of children to choose for themselves in some cases; will we come in the future to abandon such hard-won tolerance when it comes to robots?

I propose a single, over-arching ethical principle to guide our conduct towards all robots and artificial life forms, a fundamental inalienable right for all such aliens: if the entity is sentient, or judged to be sentient by whatever cognitive criteria we use to make such assessments, then it is entitled to the best ethical treatment we accord humans—a golden rule of behaving towards others as we would want them to behave towards us seems a good rule of thumb. Indeed, in as much as such artificial entities are our very creations, they may be entitled to even more consideration than we usually give our comrade humans. When we behave unethically towards another person, we are hurting a member of our species that most of our species had no hand at all in creating; when we behave unethically towards an artificially intelligent, living entity, we throw dirt in the face of the thousands of years of thought and research and experiment and work that lead to its creation. Robots and androids are the offspring of a myriad of thinkers—from Mary Shelley to Charles Babbage to of course Turing, von Neumann, Asimov, and thousands upon thousands of more recent minds. Truly intelligent machines would be the progeny of our entire species, and thus entitled to an unconditional love and protection equivalent to what we owe our children.

In the meantime, however, go curse out your non-sentient computer, whenever you like.

The Extinction of Extinction

The conventional wisdom regarding technology is that it is enormously destructive to life on Earth. Edward O. Wilson, for example, holds that human intelligence is "a misfortune for the living world," and a chart accompanying his *New York Times Magazine* (May 30, 1993) article adds that "scientists fear that species are being eradicated at thousands of times the pace that new ones are created."

Whether or not this fear is justified, it misses the point. Technology is more than pollution and the cutting down of rain forests; it is also bio-engineering, and the possibility of actually reclaiming living organisms lost to the Earth long before the appearance of people and technology.

Michael Crichton's *Jurassic Park* explored this possibility, but from the mixed perspective of wondrous and vicious dinosaurs alike brought back to life from fossilized DNA. This negativity is not surprising—a lot of science fiction has by and large turned its back on the sunny side of the future. And much polemic writing about genetic engineering—such as Jeremy Rifkin's *Algeny*—has painted scenarios of killer bacteria emerging from profit-hungry gene labs to ravage an unsuspecting population.

But clearly the same genetic reconstruction that could bring back dangerous creatures could also retrieve the sweetest flower that blushed unseen and died eons ago—as long as enough of its DNA survived.

This means that extinction ain't what it used to be—in fact, extinction may be going the way of the dodo. Whereas once upon a time extinction meant gone for good, the possibility of DNA re-creation means that the complete loss of all physically living members of a species need not be irreversible. Digital theorists—both current and throughout the ages—have always understood this. The culture of the Sumerians is not entirely lost to us, as long as something comprehensible survives of their writing.

Of course, the translation of DNA code into a living species is much more complicated, and the recovery of an extinct species's DNA is much like the discovery of a computer disk from the ancient 1970s: Unless we have a working machine into which we can put the computer disk, its programming will go unimplemented. But the good news about the natural biological world—in contrast to the yet much more limited technological world of our own creation—is that it teems with many living things that run on DNA, many models into which the appropriate disks of ancient DNA might be successfully inserted. In the case of dinosaurs, the Jurassic Park model of extinct saurian DNA inserted into the living DNA of frogs is certainly plausible—though as yet we have not recovered nearly enough dinosaur DNA to turn a frog embryo into a Tyrannosaurus.

But limitations in current physical resources are often insignificant in science and technology, where opportunities in theory are sooner or later fulfilled. Snatching extinction from extinction through DNA reclamation points toward an achievement of immortality based not on individual survival, or even the physical survival of species, but rather on the survival of biological information on tap that can drive the programs and mechanisms of life.

Heaven may well be a huge directory of DNA codes.

And coming back from the dead—at least insofar as a species goes—may be as simple as finding the right place in which to insert that code.

About the Author

Paul Levinson's books include *Mind at Large: Knowing in the Technological Age* (1988), *Electronic Chronicles* (1992), *Learning Cyberspace* (1995), and *The Soft Edge: A Natural History and Future of the Information Revolution*, published worldwide by Routledge in 1997. *The Soft Edge* has received major acclaim—ranging from *Wired*'s March 1998 issue ("Remarkable in both scholarly sweep and lyricism...") and *The Financial Times* of London ("a book that is both full of insights and provocative") to Amazon.com's Cyberculture editor ("Levinson has a knack for making his reader feel intelligent and respected")—and the book is the subject of a 90-minute talk Dr. Levinson gave at Borders at New York City's World Trade Center, which aired on C-SPAN2's "About Books" in February 1998 (available at www.c-span.org via RealAudio). He has appeared on more than 75 radio and television programs in the U.S. and worldwide. His next book, *Digital McLuhan: A Guide to the Information Millennium*, will be published by Routledge in the Spring of 1999.

He edited *In Pursuit of Truth: Essays on the Philosophy of Karl Popper* (1982) and is Editor of the *Journal of Social and Evolutionary Systems*. He has published more than 100 scholarly articles on the history and philosophy of communication and technology. His essays on technology and the future have appeared in *Omni, Shift, The Industry Standard, The Village Voice*, and eight times in *Wired*.

He has published more than 20 science fiction stories, which have been nominated six times for the Hugo, Nebula, and Sturgeon Awards in the past two years. He was winner of CompuServe's HOMer Award for the best science fiction novelette in 1997. His stories have been reprinted in *Nebula Awards 32: The Best Science Fiction and Fantasy of the Year* (1998) and in *Year's Best Science Fiction #3* (1998). His first novel, *The Silk Code*, will be published by Tor Books in 1999.

Paul Levinson holds a Ph.D. in Media Theory from New York University. He is President and founder of Connected Education, Inc., an organization headquartered in White Plains, NY that has been offering courses for academic credit in cooperation with major universities on the Internet since 1985. He is President of the Science Fiction and Fantasy Writers of America, and is Visiting Professor of Communications at Fordham University in New York City.

Printed in the United States
107583LV00004B/375/A